THE HAMDUN CHRONICLES
BOOK ONE

THE MULTIVERSE OF
MAX TOVEY

The Hamdun Chronicles
Book One:
The Multiverse of Max Tovey

European Geeks Publishing, LLC
info@europeangeeks.com
www.europeangeeks.com

Ordering Information:
Quantity sales. Special discounts are available on quantity purchases by corporations, associations, and others. For details, contact the publisher at the address above.

Print ISBN: 978-1-943755-12-7
Second Edition, Printed 2015

Library of Congress Control Number:
2015945834

DEDICATION

For Julie, Fred and Ella, who always believed in me, and for Elisha, who made me believe in myself again.

THE HAMDUN CHRONICLES
BOOK ONE

THE MULTIVERSE OF MAX TOVEY

ALASTAIR SWINNERTON

EUROPEAN GEEKS PUBLISHING

AUTHOR'S NOTE

All characters and events in this book are fictitious and any resemblance to real persons, living or dead, is purely coincidental.

However, many of the locations are very much real, especially Ham Hill, the largest hill fort in the UK. The Prince of Wales Inn, where Max comes to live, is also a real pub, situated right in the middle of the hill fort. At the time of writing it is run by the wonderful Mike and Nicki, and I highly advise a visit, especially if you have a dog.

Tinkers Bubble, the eco-community in the woods at Ham Hill, is also a real and very wonderful place, although as far as I know none of its inhabitants are Time Travellers.

This book draws a great many of its influences from the ancient mythology of the British Isles. These myths and legends would originally have been handed down through the generations by word of mouth, stories told by parents to their children, or recounted by the travelling story-tellers, or bards. In the early Middle Ages, these stories began to be written down, principally by the scribes of Wales, Ireland and Scotland, and each race placed their versions of the ancient stories within their own lands, and attributed them to their own heroes. However, before the conquest of much of Britain by the Romans in the first century AD, these peoples were largely all one race, known as the Celts. They shared a common language, which these days is known as Common Brittonic, and would almost certainly have shared a common mythology, known just as well by the people of Somerset as by those in Wales, Ireland and Scotland.

However, with the exception of a few scattered inscriptions, a written Common Brittonic language has not survived. Modern scholars have attempted to reconstruct the language, but not to a level that allows a writer to use the words with any confidence. And so, where I have used names, or places, or figures from this ancient British mythology, or even occasionally made up new ones, I have used the Welsh words – after all, Somerset is only a few short miles over the River Severn from Wales. There is a glossary of the words I've used after this note, with rough pronunciation guides. If any Welsh readers are offended that I have 'stolen' their legends, please don't be - this was not my intention. My intention was merely to celebrate the wonderful ancient myths and legends of our isles, and bring them to a wider audience.

GLOSSARY
(With rough pronunciation guide)

Note: the Ll sound is notoriously difficult for non-Welsh speakers to pronounce. Imagine you're making the letter 'l', but hissing air out around your tongue at the same time. The nearest English equivalent is probably 'thl', as in Thlangoth-len (Llangollen).

Anhrefn (pron. Anhurefun) (pl. Anhrefnau, pron. Anhure-funey) – Demons, Chaos-Bringers.

Annwddwyl (pron. Annoothweel) – one of the three Gwragedd Annwn (Water Faeries) who take Max into An-nwn.

Annwn (pron. Annoon) – the Celtic Underworld, neither Heaven nor Hell, but merely the next world after the first death.

Ballistae (pron. Ballisteye) – a Roman siege weapon, much like a large wood and metal catapult.

Belgae (pron. Belgeye) – one of the tribes of pre-Roman Brit-ain, some of whose territory bordered that of the Durotriges (pron. Durotreegays), the tribe that controlled the area con-taining Ham Hill.

Blaiddud (pron. Bleyethud) – see Ancient British Kings, be-low.

Brutus Darian-glas - see Ancient British Kings, below.

Bryn Cwrdun (pron. Brin Cooerdun) – Cwrdun Hill, now Corton Hill near Corton Denham, Somerset.

Bwbach (pron. Boobach, the ch being soft as in 'loch') (pl. Bwbachod) – small brown Faeries, known in English folklore as Brownies.

Caer (pron. Keyer) Eggardun – Castle Eggardun, now Eggardon Hill Fort, near Bridport, Dorset.

Caer Fandwy (pron. Fandwee) – The Fortress of God's Peak in Annwn, equating to Ham Hill in Max's world.

Caer Glasdun – Glastonbury Castle (no longer remains, possibly situated on Glastonbury Tor).

Caer Maidun – Maiden Castle Hill Fort near Dorchester, Dorset.

Caer Ochren – The Fortress of Enclosedness in Annwn, equating to Dundon Castle, Compton Dundon, in Max's world.

Caer Pilsdun – Pilsden Pen Hill Fort, near Broadwindsor in Dorset.

Caer Sidi – The Fortress of the Mound in Annwn, home to Gwynn ap Llud, the Lord of Annwn, and the Tylwyth Teg, chief among the Faeries. Equates to Cadbury Castle in Max's world.

Caer Tanddwr (pron. Tanthooer) – the underwater castle of the Gwragedd Annwn.

Coblyn (pron. Koblin) (pl. Coblynnod) – small Gnome-like Faeries who live in the mines of Annwn.

Cwn (pron. Koon) Annwn – the giant hounds loyal to Gwynn

ap Llud (see below), the Lord of Annwn. See also 'Gurt Dogs'.

Dwrandwn (pron. Durandoon) – one of Fymbldwn's giant friends.

Efroc - see Ancient British Kings, below.

Ellylldan (pron. Ethlithdan) – tiny Fire Faeries.

Ellyll (pron. Ethlith) (pl. Ellyllon, pron. Ethlithlon) - tiny, almost transparent Faeries of the valleys and groves.

Fomori – Large, grey, water-dwelling Faeries who can shape-change into serpents.

Fymbldwn (pron. Fimbledoon) – a giant.

Garcharwyr (pron. Garcharooear, the ch being soft, as in 'loch') – small black demons that meld with a captive's mind and control it.

Grwmbldyn (pron. Grumbledin) – one of Fymbldwn's giant friends.

Gurt Dogs – another name for the Cwn Annwn, the giant hounds of Annwn, but also Guardians of the Nine Hills, and of Time. In the Somerset dialect, 'Gurt' means 'large'.

Gwaldredyr (pron. Gwaldredeer) – one of the three Gwragedd Annwn (Water Faeries) who take Max into Annwn.

Gwaredwr (pron. Gwaradooer) – Saviour.

Gwendoleu (pron. Gwendolay) - see Ancient British Kings, below.

Gwragedd Annwn (pron. Goorageth) – Water Faeries.

Gwyll (pron. Gooeeth) (pl. Gwyllon, pron. Gooeethlon) – Large black Mountain Faeries.

Gwynn ap Llud (pron. Gwin ap Thlud) – the Lord of Annwn.

Gythreuliaid (pron. Githraileeade) – the demon horde.
Joseph of Arimathea – Adoptive Grandfather to Myvi after he arrived in England. Supposedly the uncle of Jesus, and the man who took Jesus down from the cross. Also supposedly the builder of the first church at Glastonbury.

Lleon (pron. Thleon) - see Ancient British Kings, below.

Llyn Tanddwr (pron. Thlin Tanthooer) – the lake home of the Gwragedd Annwn (Water Faeries).

Locrin - see Ancient British Kings, below.

Lutgaresbury – Saxon name for the settlement on and around Ham Hill.

Madawg (pron. Madowg) - see Ancient British Kings, below.

Maesgeirchen (pron. Meyesgayerchun, soft ch, as in 'loch') – a modern town outside Bangor in Wales, where Max grew up.

Majyga (pron. Majigga) – the three objects that Roger Bacon and Max's grandfather turned into the Time Travelling objects.

Mynyr (pron. Mineer) - see Ancient British Kings, below.

Oddwrau (pron. Othureye) – a fruit that grows in Annwn, that smells, and tastes, of bananas and custard.

Onegars – another type of wood and metal Roman catapult.

Plant Annwn – the highest ranking of the Faeries of Annwn.

Rhun Baladr-Bras (pron. Chrun Balader Bras (short 'a', not brars), the ch being soft as in 'loch') - see Ancient British Kings, below.

Teithwyr (pron. Teyethooear) – the Time Travellers, known only in Annwn by legend.

Tylwyth Teg (pron. Tilooeeth Teg) – chief among the Faeries of Annwn.

The Ancient British Kings & Queens of the Brut Tyssilio (The Chronicle of the Kings of Britain)

The 'Brut Tyssilio' (Chronicle of Tyssilio) is an ancient history of the British People, supposedly written by the Welsh Bishop and Saint Tysillio (also Tysilio) in Saxon times. It is supposed to be the original ancient British book on which Geoffrey of Monmouth based his own Chronicle. The names of the Kings and Queens have many different spellings in the various versions of the book. Many now however believe the Brut Tyssilio is the Mediaeval copy and Monmouth's book is the original. Either way, the Kings and Queens are all of course purely legendary – until Max finds out differently!

Locrin, son of High King Brutus, first King of Ancient Britain, who according to legend arrived in the isles after the Trojan Wars. Locrin reigned 1050BC.

Gwendoleu, estranged wife of Locrin, reigned 1041BC. Her forces fought those of her ex-husband Locrin in battle at the River Stour in Dorset, at which he was killed.

Madawg, son of Locrin, reigned 1027BC.

Mynyr, son of Madawg, reigned 1000BC. Killed his brother Mael in order to rule alone.

Efroc, son of Mynyr, reigned 974BC. Founded the city of York.

Brutus Darian-Glas, son of Efroc, reigned 935BC.

Lleon, son of Brutus, reigned 923BC. Built the city of Chester.

Rhun Baladr-Bras, son of Lleon, reigned 898BC. Built the cities of Canterbury and Winchester, and the town of Shaftesbury.

Blaiddud, son of Rhun, reigned 859BC. Founded the city of Bath, and discovered the hot springs there. Legend has it that he was a necromancer, and brought magic to the country for the first time.

PART ONE

PROLOGUE

In the middle of the eleventh century, in the time of King Cnut, a giant flint cross was discovered on the top of St. Michael's Hill, near Stoke sub Hamdon in Somerset, then called Lutgaresbury. A local carpenter had had a dream of an angel, who had told him to go and dig for it. The carpenter went back to sleep, but the angel appeared to him again, and this time clasped his wrist so hard that the marks were still there when he awoke the next morning.

The carpenter told his story to the local priest, and soon all the people of the village were processing to the top of the hill. They began to dig, and to their amazement they did indeed find a great cross, as well as a small wooden cross, a bell, and a black book. The local landowner was called Tofig the Proud, the standard bearer to the King. On hearing the news, Tofig rushed to the hill, and, despite the protestations of the parishioners, put the great cross on the back of his wagon, and took it to his estate at Waltham in Essex, where he founded a great abbey. Many miracles were performed in years to come in sight of the cross.

Local legend has it that the people of Lutgaresbury were so angry that Tofig had taken their cross that they cursed him and his family, vowing that neither he nor his descendants would ever be at peace until the cross was returned. But it never was returned, and in the sixteenth century, the cross was taken from Waltham Abbey, and has never been seen since.

CHAPTER ONE

"The Demons are breaking through Max - get out of here!"

Max knew the Chieftain was right, but his feet wouldn't move, his gaze locked onto the near-apocalyptic scene playing out on the vast hill fort stretching out below him. Everything was on fire. A huge cloud of smoke and spitting sparks was blowing up into the moonless night sky as the Roman Second Legion and their barely-controlled Demons took violent possession of the ancient Somerset hill fort from its brave but vastly outnumbered defenders. And in the middle of it all, controlling everything, was Roger Bacon, thirteenth century Alchemist, Philosopher and Time Traveller, who had unleashed the forces of the Celtic Otherworld Annwn on this world, in order to rule it. Max's grandfather could have saved him, saved them all, but he was dead. Max had seen him die, at Bacon's hand. And now he was alone, a Time Traveller who couldn't get home.

A great screaming suddenly came from the high walls opposite as the last of the huge settlement's inner defences exploded into a cloud of flame and splintered wood, its guardians hurled through the air like shattered puppets. As Max watched helplessly from the opposite ramparts, the three gigantic Demons smashed their way through the last desperate resistance, spewing out the fire that pulsed around their deathly dark yet glowing bodies. Behind them came the Roman soldiers, spears and swords out, shields up. The villagers did what they could to try to stop them, but it was hopeless.

"But what will you do?!" said Max to the Chieftain as the old man drew his sword.

"Fight to the death of course! Max, you must go *now* – you cannot save us, but you can save yourself!"

The Demons crashed and burned their way towards Max, which was their only purpose. He knew they had come for

him, but still he couldn't move, transfixed by the pure horror of the sight of them.

*

Max woke in a panic, sitting bolt upright, breathing in and out heavily to try to stop his heart racing. Still half asleep, he stared around the room, recognising it with relief as his own, before collapsing back into his pillows and falling instantly back to sleep.

Outside his room, listening at the door, his parents also breathed out in relief as all went quiet on the other side of the door. They knew he was having The Dream again, and it always got noisy when he did.

"I just wish we could help him more," said Sarah in a whisper. "If we could just tell him we know what he's going through..."

"You know what Dr. Llewellyn said," said Owen. "He mustn't know that we know – as soon as he thinks we're taking his side he immediately thinks there's a hidden agenda and clams up. He just has to have time to work it out for himself."

Sarah shook her head gently. "But it's just so frustrating – it breaks my heart to watch him go through all this and not be able to do anything to help. If we could just tell him about...!"

"We're not those people any more love," said Owen, cutting her off with a little more force than maybe he intended. "We're finished with all that."

"Are we? We're going back to Ham Hill..."

"It'll be different – Da isn't in control any more, we are."

"You sure about that...?" said Sarah with a raised eyebrow.

"I know love, I know," said Owen, taking her hand. "But Dr. Llewellyn thinks this move will be good for him, and we have to trust him on this."

Sarah sighed, and gave Owen a look. "You know what's go-

20

ing to happen when we get there – it's either going to solve his problems or it's going to make them a million times worse."

Owen just shrugged, in a 'yes, but what can we do' kind of way.

"It's in the hands of the Gods now, love."

"I know," said Sarah. "Just hope none of the bad ones turn up."

*

Max was back in The Dream, at the hill fort, but this time outside it as it burned. He had escaped, and had taken others with him. But they weren't safe yet. The girl and the old man stood nearby, both looking at him in desperation. It was always them, but he could never quite see them clearly. All he knew was that he had to help them. The pressure was killing him, as it always did in The Dream. He just wanted to scream 'I'm only ten, don't do this to me!' But he never did. He always did his duty. He first had this dream four years ago now, and kept having it, night after night, until Dr. Llewellyn finally got his medication right a couple of years ago. But now it was back again, pills or no pills. The Dream never changed, no matter how much he tried.

"Come on Max!" said the girl. "Get us out of here – take us to *your* time!"

Max looked down at himself, but The Brooch wasn't pinned to his jumper, The Ring wasn't on his finger, and The Coin wasn't in his pocket.

"But I don't have the Majyga – how am I supposed to Travel without the Majyga?! Only Grandfather could Travel without them!"

"No, you can do it too Max," said the old man with authority. "You know this to be true."

"You are The One, Max," said the girl. "He told us so!"

Max just sighed. Too much pressure, but he had no choice

21

but to try. "Alright, but don't look – not till I tell you." Max held out his hands, and they took one each and closed their eyes. "And don't let go, whatever you do!"

Max took a deep breath, then let it out slowly and relaxed his body. He looked down at the charred and smoking ground, and then slowly looked up, not at where the Inn would be, but slightly to the left, at the winding shadowy hillside that led to what would later be called St. Michael's Hill. Concentrate, must concentrate.

Then, like heat haze on a summer road, something began to take form in the corner of his eye. Max controlled his breathing, and focussed his mind on nothing but the mental image of the Inn. Slowly it became more than a wafting mirage, solidifying, as history played out before him like a time-lapse movie. First the wooden chapel that Joseph of Arimathea had built when he had first come here, then the stone chapel that replaced it nine hundred years later, followed by the Norman Fayre House and then its mediaeval replacement, then the eighteenth century tin glove-making shacks that sprang up almost overnight and were removed just as quickly, and then the hamstone Inn that still stood where Max was trying to get to. Almost two thousand years of building, development, decay and rebirth washed in and out of his vision, until finally the disparate buildings coalesced into the greying hamstone walls, slate roof and outbuildings of his grandfather's Inn, complete with folded umbrellas, benches and recycling bins.

Now came the tricky part. It was now all very real, in his peripheral vision, but usually when he turned to look, the past disappeared, as he fully expected the future to do now. But now a great roaring and crashing from the fortress behind them told him that couldn't happen this time. Must believe!

"Hurry Max!" cried the girl. "The Demons are almost upon us!"

Max took one last deep breath, exhaled softly, and then very, very slowly turned his head to look at the Inn. It was

22

still there, its windows the only point of light in the deeply dark night. Max picked up a stone and threw it – it bounced off his grandfather's car.

"Come on – we're back!"

The girl opened her eyes and saw the Inn, then turned around rapidly and saw in horror the towering Demon stomping towards them, roaring and exuding fire like a bonfire with the wind behind it.

"It came with us! How did it come with us?!"

But the Demon didn't get any further, for now a massive white dog, as big as a small horse with glowing red eyes the size of plates, leapt out of nowhere and pinned the Demon to the ground before dispatching it with one bite from its massive jaws.

"It's the Gurt Dog!" exclaimed the girl with a gasp. "The Guardian of the Hill!"

"How many times must I save you Max Tovey?" said the Gurt Dog in a deep, thunderous voice, before to their astonishment transforming into a tall, dark-haired, strong-looking man who Max knew he knew, though he also knew he'd never seen him before.

*

Max woke in a panic again, but this time got out of bed before he could go back to sleep, and go back to The Dream again. He'd been having it for weeks now, ever since his father told him they were moving to Ham Hill to take over his Grandfather's Inn, and it never got any better. He peered out of the curtains, to see the winter dawn beginning to spread over Maesgeirchen, the small North Wales town they'd lived in for the last four years, and which, this afternoon, they were leaving. Max put on his duffle coat and slippers, and opened up his laptop. Someone somewhere would want a game, even at seven in the morning. Anything was better than The

Dream.

*

CHAPTER TWO

Max had always been able to see the past. It was constantly alive around him, out of the corner of his eye, like a ghostly overlay on the present. When he was very young he didn't realise there was anything wrong with this, until he discovered that no-one else saw it. That was when they started to call him *special,* and later, by the age of eight, diagnosed him as such, and put him on medication, both to control his 'condition', and to suppress the hallucinations.

The young nurse peered around the door into the waiting room until her gaze fell on the short, round-faced, red-haired teenager in the sensible shirt, jumper, trousers and shoes, and of course his beloved black duffle coat. She smiled a little sadly to herself. Most kids his age would be in an aggressively-designed hoodie and jeans starting where their underwear finished, but then she knew this one wasn't like most kids.

"Max? Dr. Llewellyn's ready for you."

Max rose, and followed the nurse through the door and along the corridor into the all too familiar room. It didn't look much like a psychiatrist's office, more like a sitting room, with old comfy armchairs, dark wooden furniture, an open fire and warm-toned paintings on the wall. It had been designed like that, to put patients at their ease, and to a certain extent it worked, for Max at least. Dr. Llewellyn completed the homely picture, with his old tweed jacket, checked shirt and worn corduroy trousers. He was only in his early fifties, but the slightly round, genial man had the comforting appearance of everyone's ideal grandfather.

"Hello Max – please, have a seat. So, today's the day, eh? I shall miss you, but Dr. Chant in Yeovil is fully briefed, and will look after you."

Max sat, but didn't answer for a long moment, instead staring down at the deep red on brown Victorian-style carpet pattern, trying to think of the right thing to say first.

"I've been having The Dream again."

"Oh? Which dream is that?"

"*The* Dream..."

"I see."

Dr. Llewellyn knew exactly which dream Max was talking about, but he tried to keep his tone light, so as not to make the troubled fourteen year old nervous. When Max was nervous he would barely get more than a few words out of him in the hour long sessions.+

"And is it the same?"

"It's *always* the same."

"So, the giant dogs, the Demons – your Grandfather...?"

"I told you, it's always the same."

Max raised his eyes to the Doctor's now.

"You said I wouldn't have it any more! What's the point of all the pills and therapy if they don't stop me having The Dream?!"

Max held the doctor's gaze accusingly. Dr. Llewellyn smiled gently, then looked down at his notes. It had been two years since the boy had had this dream, after another two years of trying every combination of drug and therapy he knew to stop him having it. But Llewellyn still couldn't find what had happened in what was referred to as the *incident*. Whatever had happened to the ten-year-old Max was now so deeply buried it was almost as if Max didn't believe it *had* happened, like someone had wiped it from his memory. Certainly no amount of hypnosis had managed to bring it out of him.

"You *are* taking the medication...?"

"Yes, for all the good it's doing!"

"Alright Max, come on, calm down, let's see if we can't get to the bottom of this. Are you having any other symptoms?"

"What do you mean?"

"You know what I mean, Max. Are you seeing anything?"

"No. There's nothing to see around here anyway."

It was the reason Max's parents had moved here four years

ago. A self-contained town with no history whatsoever, built on fields that had been there for thousands of years, with barely a stone of archaeology. No past for Max to see at all. But since Dr. Llewellyn had taken him off the medication prescribed by his previous doctor, and finally struck on the right therapy/pills combination, Max's visions had stopped. Of course, he very rarely even left his bedroom anyway, let alone his house. After the *incident,* his parents took him out of school and moved from the Victorian semi in the North Wales city of Bangor, that they'd lived in since Max was born, to Maesgeirchen, an estate built in the 1930s on the Bangor outskirts. If Max was honest with himself, it was helping, even the home-tutoring. Until now.

"How are your parents?"

"The usual. Walking on eggshells around me in case I break or something."

Dr. Llewellyn smiled to himself. Max was a conundrum. Extremely self-aware, and yet unable to control his condition. He saw himself as if through the eyes of the outside world, and yet he couldn't see, or refused to see, that the outside world didn't know how to deal with him. Especially his parents. They'd taken him to every specialist going from the age of six onwards, getting diagnoses of everything from autism to schizophrenia. It wasn't until they moved to Maes-G, as it was known locally, and found Dr. Llewellyn, that they finally discovered what was *wrong* with Max. His lack of social skills, bad handwriting, inability to concentrate or remember important things coupled with an infinite memory for things important to *him,* a very low boredom threshold and a tendency to say whatever was in his head without filtering it for weirdness, all pointed at mild ADHD and major Dyspraxia. Several of the other specialists had also worked this out, but the diagnosis didn't explain everything. It didn't explain the abnormally high anxiety levels, the panic attacks, the tendency to jump at the slightest unexpected noise and the emo-

tional numbness. These all pointed towards Post Traumatic Stress Disorder, more usually suffered by military casualties. It took Dr. Llewellyn a while to accept that this was what Max was suffering from – but no matter how deep he dug, the only trauma he could find was The Dream, of fighting Romans and Demons alongside his grandfather at Ham Hill. The trouble was, Max had never been to Ham Hill, and he'd never met his grandfather.

Of course none of the other specialists could explain the hallucinations, and more importantly, none of them had found out about The Dream. If he was honest, Dr. Llewellyn didn't know what they were either but he had, eventually, found a way to control them – and get Max to trust him.

Max, of course, didn't think there was anything wrong – he just saw the world differently to everyone else that was all; and most of the time, he just wanted it to leave him alone. But he was happy with Dr. Llewellyn, and accepted the diagnosis, and the therapy, if only to keep his parents off his back. But now he had a new theory.

"I'm going to stop taking the medication."

Dr. Llewellyn sat up at this, taken aback.

"I don't think that's wise, Max."

"I don't care – we're moving to Ham Hill, and my *problems* have something to do with that place, so if I'm going to sort them out, I have to do it straight."

Dr. Llewellyn drummed his fingers together. "Max, I think I know what's good for you, and – " But Max cut him off forcibly.

"If you knew what was good for me I wouldn't be having the dream again!" Max had got out of his chair and was inches away from Dr. Llewellyn's face now. "I'm doing it, and there's nothing you can do about it!"

Dr. Llewellyn attempted a calming smile, sitting back in his chair. "Very well, Max..." Now he sighed, and shrugged. He knew Max was right – there *was* nothing he could do about

it, except inform Max's new doctor, but he also knew Max would go his own way whatever anyone did or said. That, too, was part of his condition, and a large part of his problems. He was fourteen. Almost no fourteen year olds know their own minds, let alone one whose mind was so disturbed. But Max was almost psychopathically unable to be told. Dr. Llewellyn knew he had no choice.

"Well, good luck then Max..."

*

It was late when they got to Ham Hill, almost eleven. Max looked   up from his laptop and saw the Victorian Inn, oh-so-familiar from his dream, dimly silhouetted by the full moon as it tried to shine through the ink-black rain-clouds that were lumbering across the sky. And below it, the sharp drop that edged the huge hill fort to the east and led to the Under Warren, as the ancient terraced fields below are known, where once thousands of Englishmen died in the last battle of the Wessex rebellion against the Normans.

"We're here, darling," said his mother, turning and smiling at him wearily.

"Come on Max," said his father, equally wearily. "Let's get the bags inside."

They'd been arguing for the last half an hour or so. They obviously hadn't thought Max could hear them with his headphones on, but he'd heard parts of it. It was about him, of course. Something his mother wanted to tell him but his father didn't, but Max couldn't work out what it was. Max didn't dislike his parents – they weren't unkind to him or anything. They just didn't know how to deal with him, and apart from his looks he had absolutely nothing in common with them. He was very much a cross between the two of them physically, with his mother's big blue eyes and round face, and his father's red hair and thin, wiry frame. He got his

height from both of them, or lack of it, all three of them being around five foot four. They were definitely his parents, even though sometimes he fantasized that they weren't.

As they hurried with their bags into the bar out of the driving rain, the few remaining drinkers stopped their conversation and looked at them as one, and each one of them looking at Max very curiously, like they knew they knew him but not where from. A tall, young man in his mid-twenties with short dark hair and a small goatee beard came out from behind the bar and shook Max's father's hand, and then his mother's.

"Mr and Mrs Tovey, welcome, good to see you again. Can I get you anything?"

"No, thank you Nick," said Owen. "We'd really like to get to our rooms. It's been a long drive."

"Of course. I'll show you up. I saw your father earlier..."

Owen gave Nick a half smile. He knew they'd been close.

"How is he?"

Nick just gave Owen a look and a shake of the head that said 'not so good'. Owen nodded, and sighed.

Max wasn't really listening to any of this, but instead was gazing around the Inn in wonder. It looked *exactly* as it did in The Dream - the stone floor and walls, the roaring fire to the right of the thick wooden bar, the real ale barrels on shelves behind it. Every detail, from the jumble of assorted old furniture to the books and board games on the shelves next to the opposite fireplace was etched into his brain. He'd been here so many times, in The Dream.

Instinctively Max went round to the left and through to the restaurant and skittle alley, the reconstructed remains of the ancient chapel that the rest of the Inn was built around. It looked unexpectedly ordinary, with its simple wooden floor, rough stone walls and plain vaulted ceiling, but still a shiver ran through Max's whole body. He couldn't have described the feeling, but somehow it was as if suddenly the world in-

side his head had righted itself. He didn't know how, but instinctively he knew what the feeling was. It felt like he was home.

"Max? Max? Where *are* you?"

Max turned, to see his father enter the room.

"What are you doing?"

"Just looking around."

"It's time for bed Max."

Upstairs, his mother opened the door to the end room. It was just as Max 'remembered' it. The walls were lined with old-looking books, and every horizontal surface was covered in ornaments and other objects that, while not ornaments, obviously had some significance to their owner.

"This is Grandfather's room, isn't it?"

His mother gave him an awkward look.

"Yes, it... is."

"So where *is* Grandfather?"

"He's in hospital, lovey; you know that. Now get some sleep. New school tomorrow!"

The idea of going to school again after four years didn't help with the increased anxiety Max was feeling after coming off the medication, but both had been his decision. His parents didn't know about him not taking the pills, so he knew he just had to suck it up and get on with it. He also knew he had to get some sleep, even though his phone was beeping with message requests to rejoin the game he'd stopped playing back in Maes-G this morning. All that had to go as well, if he was going to deal with this thing.

*

CHAPTER THREE

"Max...? Max...? Wake up Max..."

Max came round slowly, and looked up from his pillow at his bedside clock, which said midnight. But then he looked up and gasped, for there, standing at the bottom of his bed was a tall, thin, elderly red-haired man. Max knew at once it was his grandfather.

"Grandfather? I thought you were in hospital..."

Percy looked askance at the boy.

"Grandfather? You can't call me Grandpa, after all we've been through?"

Max stared at the old man. All we've been through? But that was just in a dream... And anyway... Max had this thing about formality, about how to behave to his peers. No-one knew where it came from, it was just part of his thing. Dr. Llewellyn had tried for years to get Max to call him David, to try to break down the barriers, but he never did.

"I'm sorry I startled you Max, but I had to come and see you." Percy smiled softly at his grandson, and sat down on the bed, putting his hand soothingly on his shoulder.

"There's something I have to give you. Get up for a moment..."

Max got up off the bed, and then his grandfather pushed it to one side, before lifting up one of the floorboards and taking out an old box. He smiled at Max, handed him the box, replaced the floorboard and pushed the bed back.

"What is it?"

"Open it and see."

Max sat on the bed again, his heart racing, and slowly opened the box as if something might spring out of it. Inside was a thin leather-bound book, about the size of a large paperback, and another smaller box, the sort of thing jewellery might come in. Max looked nervously at his grandfather.

"What... what *are* these?"

"I think you know, Max."

Max opened the book, to find it was full of what looked like Mediaeval illuminations with strange writing underneath. Max had seen his grandfather use it, in his dream. He couldn't quite remember right now, but it had something to do with the Travelling. But the small box worried him more, because even though he didn't believe it, he knew exactly what was inside it. He opened the box very, very slowly, and then stifled a cry. Inside was a small Roman coin, a Saxon ring of ornately twisted silver tracery, and an oval gold Norman brooch with delicate geometric patterns surrounding a single large red garnet. Max instinctively touched the coin, and almost immediately let go of it in terror. For in the second or two that he'd touched it, the view out of the bay window changed from one of trees, fences and South Somerset Country Park signs to one of the high wooden walls of the first century inner stockade, burning with the fires of the Roman Demons.

"It's the Majyga!"

"Yes Max..."

Max's Grandfather had explained the Majyga to him, in The Dream. In the thirteenth century, the young philosopher Roger Bacon had begun to experiment with Alchemy, and especially in the legendary lost art of turning base metals into gold, but without success. But then a man came to him, and shared with him a great secret. Bacon took up a coin from his collection, one from the reign of the Emperor Claudius, and applied the new experiment. The coin still didn't turn to gold, but on picking it up, Bacon suddenly found himself transported to the first century. On returning, his visitor insisted Bacon repeat the experiment on two other objects in his possession, and thus The Majyga were born. The visitor was Max's grandfather, who had found the Majyga in the 1960s, and The Book, which Bacon had written, had told him what the Majyga were. It was the original of the so-called

Voynich Manuscript, the most notorious secret code book in the world, which Percy had been trying to crack for most of his life. He'd always suspected it had something to do with Bacon, even though the one in Yale Library had been dated to after Bacon's death. But this one was earlier, much better written and illustrated, and more importantly, containing a key to the code. Percy quickly deciphered it, and discovered to his amazement that it was Bacon's Time Travelling diary – where and when he went, and how he used the Majyga to get there. But when Percy used the Majyga to Travel back to find Bacon, he discovered that he had yet to create them, or write The Book. It was the first of many time travelling circularities that Max's grandfather Percy and Bacon created together over the coming years, as Time became ever more complicated, culminating in the battle at Ham Hill, when Percy finally realised his mistake after he had helped Bacon open the gates of Annwn.

Max stared at the objects in equal amazement and alarm.

"So the dream was all *real?* You *are* a *Time Traveller?!!*"

Max's head was spinning as he looked up from the old box and its contents at his Grandfather.

"Yes Max, it was all real, but I Travelled back to change it all, to make sure it didn't happen, and that you were safe. Then I tried to destroy the Majyga, but I couldn't do it – every time I destroyed them, they returned. I eventually realised that only you could do it, because you are The One. You must destroy them Max, find the Cross of Tofig, and lift the curse on our family."

Max stared at the Majyga again, as much in alarm as anything else.

"But how do I do *that?!*" Max looked up at his Grandfather again, but he was gone.

*

Max woke in his usual panic and looked around wildly. But after a minute or so the terror subsided, as it always did after The Dream. Except that wasn't The Dream – that was a new one. Max looked out of the side window to see the weak winter sun beginning to rise over Hedgecock Hill Wood and tried to control his breathing. It's OK, it was just a dream, it was just a dream, it was just a dream... He kept repeating the well-worn mantra until the shaking stopped.

A knock at the door made Max jump and his heart start racing again. But it was only his father.

"Max, can you come downstairs please?"

"Why? School doesn't start for hours yet."

"Please Max – it's important."

Max was a little taken aback. His father rarely said please, and only when something really *was* important. He put his duffle coat over his pyjamas and made his way downstairs. His parents were waiting for him in the little dining room to the left of the bar. The wood burner was going strong, and breakfast was laid out on the table.

"Sit down, Max," said his father in a kind of sad tone Max had never heard before. "There's a cup of tea there for you."

"Max, I'm afraid we have some bad news," said his mother, also sounding a little sad. "Your grandfather died last night..."

She trailed off at Max's reaction. Max's eyes had gone wide as she spoke, and now he was staring at the two of them in horror.

"What is it Max?" said his mother nervously.

"What time did Grandfather die?"

"What?" said his father, a little confused.

"What time did he *die?*"

"What...? I, I don't understand..." Ordinarily his father would have been short with him for using that insistent tone, but not now.

"What *time?!*"

"About midnight..." said his mother, also confused now.

36

"But..."

But Max was already out of his chair and racing back to his bedroom. In a moment he had pushed the bed aside, and levered up the floorboard. And then he stopped, and just stared, for what seemed like forever, not believing it was true. But, there it was. Not realising he was doing it, Max held his breath as he gently lifted the box out from under the floor, and opened it. He only touched the coin for a second, but it was long enough – long enough to know.

It was all real - Grandfather *was* a Time Traveller.

And so, it would seem, was he.

*

CHAPTER FOUR

Max had been sitting on his bed for an hour or so now, his knees curled up tight under his chin, just staring at the box, trying to work it all out. What are you supposed to feel about the death of a man you never met except in your time travelling dreams? He and his grandfather had had some amazing adventures together, and he loved him very much, in The Dream – but none of that was real. And yet, there were The Majyga in front of him, that had just briefly taken him to first century Britain. Max drew his knees even closer to his chest and tightly shut his eyes as impossible alternative realities whirled around his head. It can't be real, it can't be real, it can't be real, it *can't* be real...!

"Max, are you ready for school?" Outside the bedroom door, Max's father waited for an answer, but got none. Ordinarily he would have angered at this, but not today. "Max, come on, we have to go in ten minutes."

Max slowly unfurled, and looked around at the new school uniform he'd laid out on the bedroom chair the night before, the strange new reality still swirling around in his head. But he knew he had to stop it swirling. Right then - school. With such extraordinary possibilities filling his head, he knew he needed something ordinary, to get some perspective going.

"Coming Father." Outside the room, Owen sighed. Max insisted on calling them 'Mother' and 'Father'. No-one called their parents that, not these days. It annoyed them, and they suspected Max did it for just that reason. But he wouldn't say anything this time. Not today.

Max dressed quickly, put his duffle coat back on again, picked up his satchel, packed to obsessive perfection days ago, and opened the door.

"Sorry Father." Why was he saying sorry? He never said sorry. But for a moment there he *had* felt sorry, for his father, who'd just lost *his* father. Huh, he thought. This was a devel-

opment. Owen was equally taken aback, and for a moment they almost hugged, but the moment passed in an instant, ending in a light touch on the shoulder from father to son.

"Right then – school," said Owen lightly. "All ready?"

Of course the truth was that Max was anything but ready. His usual anxiety about this level of change was being seriously exaggerated by not having taken his medication for two days, but the events of the last few hours had momentarily made him forget all that. Now, the anxiety was back in force.

"It'll be fine Max – do you good to get some normality, eh?"

Max gave a half smile, and nodded. His father was right, for a rare change, even if he couldn't possibly understand why.

But as Max emerged from the Inn and headed for the car, he stopped for a moment, as he caught something out of the corner of his eye. A man in old-fashioned clothes was walking the other way. Max turned his head slowly, keeping the man in his peripheral vision, and watched him walk right through the low wall at the front of the Inn as if it wasn't there. And the Inn was different too, older, with no porch, and no outside tables. Huh. That hasn't happened in a while.

"Everything alright Max?" said Owen, getting into the car, as his son just stood, staring at nothing. Owen knew that look. Max shook his head to clear it, and focussed on his father, the car, and the present day. He answered his father's question with a shrug, and got into the car. The past was coming back. Max nodded imperceptibly to himself. You knew it would – that was the point of coming off the pills. Max caught a wave of panic just in time, and for a moment fought to control his breathing, but then it passed. His father didn't seem to have noticed.

As they drove down the steep hill towards Stoke sub Hamdon, Max kept his eyes facing rigidly forwards, concentrating on the present, but now and then, reality still blurred a little, as thousands of years of history began to return to the corner of his eye. To Max's surprise, he gave a little smile, realis-

ing that he'd actually missed all this. Five minutes later, after weaving through the narrow High Street, made narrower by rows of parked cars, they were at the school.

"So, you know where you're going?"

Max reached into his duffle coat pocket and pulled out a folded A4 plan of the school, waved it at his father and got out of the car.

"Alright then, see you here this afternoon." And with that, Owen drove off towards Yeovil Hospital, to start making arrangements for his late father.

Max looked at the plan of the school, double-checking where he was supposed to go, even though he'd double-checked it a dozen times already since they arrived last night. His usual obsession with researching anywhere new he was going was increasing along with his anxiety. Sure now, he looked up and headed towards the correct Tutor Room.

Hundreds of others were heading towards their own destinations, but one girl stood still, staring at him intensely. He looked at her a little self-consciously, but also a little curiously, searching his memory. Something about her long, deep red hair and Celtic-pale skin was familiar, but he couldn't work out why, and carried on towards his Tutor Room. As he passed her, she started to walk alongside him.

"You're new, aren't you?" she said, still staring at him. Max was getting more than a little unsettled now – girls almost never took any notice of him.

"Yes."

"Which Tutor are you in?"

"10RH."

"Me too. New teacher. Not sure what RH stands for. Come on, it's this way."

"I know." He held up his site plan. "I have a map."

"You're not from around here are you?" said the girl, still staring. "The accent...?"

"No." Max wasn't used to talking to girls either. "We just

41

moved from Wales."

The girl stared even more intensely now, her deep brown eyes a little wider.

"What's your name...?" she asked, as if she already knew the answer.

"Max Tovey."

The girl gasped now. "Max Tovey? Really? You're not... Percy's grandson are you...? From the Inn?"

"Yes. Did you know him?"

"What do you mean, *did?*"

"He died last night." The art of subtlety was not one Max practised.

Tears came to her eyes now. The news had been imparted so brutally. But she knew this boy, she just knew she did, and she knew it was his way. She just didn't know why she knew.

"I'm so sorry. He was such a lovely man. He was so kind to me and my grandfather when we first came to the Bubble."

"The Bubble?" Max had heard the name, but...

"Tinkers Bubble, you know, the eco-community in the woods. We've been there four years now."

Max's head was buzzing now. It was something about her voice. He'd heard it before, he just knew it.

"Where were you before?"

The girl gave Max a strange look now, as if she was wrestling with something in her head.

"I'm not sure. Something happened to us. We can't remember."

Max suddenly had a vision of a burning fort, and a girl, and an old man. "Save us Max!" No, couldn't be...

There was a long, slightly awkward pause now, and then they were at the Tutor Room, the last of their fellow students to arrive. They all greeted her in one way or another, obviously a popular girl, but then all stared at Max, some then giving him a greeting smile or nod, but others looking at him with the same confusion as the girl had. Max just sat down

42

next to the girl and buried his eyes in his satchel.

"This is Max," said the girl. "He's from Wales."

Several of the kids mouthed the word 'Max', their eyes a little wider. Max risked a look around the group, and didn't like the looks he was getting. These were more than just new kid at school looks.

"I'm Myvi by the way. Short for Myvannwl. It's Welsh too."

Now it was Max's turn to gasp a little. The name he knew, even if he couldn't place her face. It was the girl's name, in The Dream.

"No, not Welsh," said Max, trying not to think about it. "Old British, before they split into Welsh, Cornish, Irish and so on."

"How do you know that?" said Myvi a little nervously.

"Because I speak Old British, and Welsh, and..." He counted in his head. "...Saxon, Norman, Latin and Greek."

The Tutor Group's looks were divided now, some cynical, others impressed, but a third group looking increasingly uncomfortable.

"You speak six languages?" said Myvi in disbelief.

"Well, seven," said Max like it was no big deal, "if you count Klingon."

Some laughed now, but then went quiet as the door opened, and a tall, dark-haired man walked in. In his forties Max guessed, before really looking at him. But then he did.

"Good morning. My name is Mr. Hamandun, and I am to be your new Tutor."

Both Max and Myvi gasped now, then looked at each other before looking back at the new Tutor. That was a face Max knew very well indeed. He'd seen it so many times, in The Dream. He looked exactly like the man who saved him from the Demons. The man who turned into a giant dog.

With registration over, the Tutor turned to Max.

"Max, I'm afraid your first day at this fine institution is to be cut short – your Grandfather's funeral is to be in a few

hours, and you have been given leave to attend. You also are allowed to go, Myvannwl."

Max knew the voice so well. But it couldn't be. It's just a coincidence. *Has* to be.

"You are being picked up outside the school in ten minutes. So, I will see you later."

"Later?" said Max.

"There is to be a Wake at Tinkers Bubble I gather. I shall attend. I knew your grandfather well – Time it seems has finally caught up with him. I am sorry."

Max just outright stared now, but was jogged out of it by Myvi pulling at his coat sleeve.

"Come on Max, let's go."

Max and Myvi said nothing as they walked out of the school, nor for several minutes as they stood on the road waiting for whoever was picking them up. But then Myvi broke the silence.

"You've seen him before, haven't you?" She was looking right into Max's eyes now, as if daring him to say no. "Mr Hamandun."

"Yes."

"Where?"

Max thought hard about this, then came to a decision.

"I can't tell you."

"Why not?"

"Because you wouldn't believe me. You'd just laugh." Girls usually did, in his experience.

Myvi smiled at Max now, and touched his arm lightly. "I wouldn't, Max."

"Yes, you would."

"No, I wouldn't, because I think you saw him in the same place I did, and where I saw you. It was in a dream, wasn't it? A dream about Romans, and Demons, and Gurt Dogs – and Time Travelling."

Max just stared at her in amazement. "What...?!"

44

"I had it last night, and so did my Grandfather. And so did a good few other people. That's why they were all staring at you."

Myvi looked deep into Max's eyes now. "What does it mean, Max...?"

"I don't know." He had a horrible feeling he did though. He just hoped he was wrong.

But now their attention was distracted by an approaching noise. It sounded like people were banging tin cans together - but why would anyone be doing that...? As they looked down the road, they saw dozens of people approaching. They were all dressed in what looked like mediaeval costumes - smocks, woollen and leather jerkins, plain and striped baggy trousers and various styles of decorated hats – and all were banging cans, saucepans and other metal objects with an assortment of kitchen utensils. They were also all singing, very loudly, and although Max was no expert, many of them looked a little drunk. One of them was even riding a hobby horse. Despite everything going on in his tortured mind, Max started to laugh.

"It's a Tin Can Band!" Max had never actually seen one before but he knew what they looked like from his researches - they were a big part of Wessex folklore.

"That it is, young man," said the leader, a portly elderly man with a red face that probably had a lot to do with the flagon he was currently drinking from.

"They assemble at dawn, banging tins and other metal objects, and process through the town or village, waking its residents and demanding they join them in celebration." Max was quoting from memory.

"That we do   you must be Max," said the Tin Can Band leader.

Max was a little taken aback. Ordinarily most things he said out loud brought laughter or embarrassed glances. He either thought too much about what he was about to say be-

fore he said it and it came out in a mumble or he just said what was in his head without thinking about it at all and it came out weird, to other people at least. The problem was he lived in his head for so much of the time that he found it hard to judge how to talk to people. He didn't understand kids his own age or what they talked about, outside online gaming, and adults didn't understand why he was trying to talk to them on their own level. But not this time.

"Yes. But who are *you?*"

"My name is Brigadier-General Sir John Westenholme, and we have come to escort you and your grandfather to the Inn." Sir John now held out a silver urn for Max to take. Max looked at it for a moment, and then realised.

"Grandfather...?"

"It is indeed young man. In accordance with his wishes, he was cremated at zero seven hundred hours this morning, upon which I and this gallant band here proceeded to process from Yeovil Crematorium, via several accommodating watering holes, again, as per his wishes, and making a glorious racket as we went if I do say so meself. And now, to the Inn!"

"Wassail, wassail, and all wassail!" yelled the gallant band, obviously all equipped with their own tankards.

"You walked here from *Yeovil?!*" Max laughed again.

"We did indeed young man, although some danced, and others fell over a lot."

"Sorry," said an embarrassed wassailer at the back who by the looks of him had been wassailing since the early hours.

*

CHAPTER FIVE

Nick, the manager, had lit the fire and was checking the Wassail tureen when the front door opened and one of the younger barmen arrived.

"Morning Phil," said Nick. "Can you start organising the chapel? We're going to need all the chairs we can find."

"OK. Sad about the old boy."

Nick smiled sadly and nodded. "He had a good life though."

"He had a weird life is what *he* had. How did he *know?*"

The short-ish blonde-haired barman looked at Nick for answers, but he didn't get any as usual. Phil knew that Nick knew the truth about Percy's life, but he was fiercely loyal, and never gave anything away.

"Old people just know these things I guess," was all the answer he got. Among the Inn's staff Nick was the only one that knew the real answer – that the old man knew when he was going to die because he'd seen it happen. What Time Traveller *wouldn't* want to know?

Now the door opened again, and Max's father came into the bar, not looking very happy.

"What's going on Nick? I got to the hospital to be told that not only was my father's body not there, it had already been cremated and was on its way here!"

"Percy left detailed instructions."

Owen looked confused. "But he only died last night – how was it organised so quickly?!"

Nick had a lot to do, so decided to stop beating around the bush.

"*He* organised it, Owen."

They held each other's gaze for a moment while the ramifications sank in on Owen. So, Nick knew about the Travelling then.

"I see," said Owen. "But why wasn't I told? Why wasn't I there?"

"He didn't want you there Owen. He hadn't seen you for four years, since you banned him from seeing Max, after the, you know, 'incident', and he was still angry."

Owen sighed, and deflated.

"Now," said Nick, "they'll be here with the Urn soon, and there's a lot to do. So if you don't mind..."

"Oh, right. Sorry. What can I do?"

"Well, you could help Phil set up the chapel."

"Right. I'll just go and let Sarah know what's going on first if that's all right."

"Of course. Thanks."

*

The procession had reached the Inn, and burst through the front door.

"All hail here and prepare the way for Percy!" said Sir John, removing his Mr Punch hat, slapping it on the bar and accepting a top up into his wassail tankard that a grinning Nick decanted from the tureen on the bar.

Now Max entered, carrying the Urn, and followed by the rest of the procession, bells jingling on ankles, tins still being banged, and with a *lot* of hey nonny no-ing.

"What on Earth is going on?!" said Max's father as he rushed into the bar.

"It's a Tin Can Band!" said Max laughing.

Owen looked at the Urn his son was carrying and angered.

"This isn't funny Max – that's your dead grandfather you're holding!"

"And who might you be, sir?" said Sir John.

Max's father had a sudden shock of recognition. When he was Max's age, this portly man had been less portly, and his father's Commanding Officer.

"Sir John, it's me, Owen Tovey."

Sir John gave Max's father one of his best stares. "Ah, the

not so prodigal son. Well, now the old boy has gone, I suppose we have to suffer your presence."

Max looked at his father with a little pity – the Brigadier had obviously made him feel about four feet tall and six years old. He knew only too well how that felt.

"So what happens now, Sir John?" Max asked the Brigadier.

"Now my lad, we have one last wassail…"

"Wassail, wassail, and all wassail!" the crowd yelled, downing their drinks.

"…and then remove ourselves to the chapel, to remember your grandfather's life. Lead on, young man."

Max looked at Nick for guidance – he seemed to be the only sane person there. Nick smiled at him, and gestured for him to carry the Urn towards the chapel, which Max did, now followed by an entourage of gently chiming well-wishers.

But Max reeled as he reached the old chapel - the revelling noises of the present suddenly receded, to be replaced by the swirling and swelling sights and sounds of the past – every phase of construction, right back to when Joseph of Arimathea had built it in the first century, every generation of worshippers at this sacred place now whirled around him, the transparent tide of history ebbing and flowing, all jostling for position in commemoration of his grandfather, all celebrating his part in their lives, and their deaths, and their salvation.

Max was confused for a moment – so far since he had come off the medication and the visions had come back, his anxiety levels had been through the ceiling. But now as he mentally checked himself, this wasn't happening. If anything, he was feeling supremely calm. Weird.

They were all assembled in the old Chapel now, and the light-hearted air of earlier quietened into a respectful solemnity as the Brigadier outlined the mystery, to Max, that was his grandfather's life. Bright young scholar that entered Oxford at sixteen, brilliant army code-breaker, beloved pub

landlord in retirement, and of course teller of great tales from history, so real you could almost imagine he'd been there himself. Many others gave their own tributes – his grandfather had obviously been loved. But they equally obviously didn't know he was a time traveller.

*

The ceremony over, Max was standing outside the Inn, staring out over the fields below when a double rainbow appeared, the brightest Max had ever seen, the end of one on St Michael's hill, and the other on the Under Warren. Sir John laughed as he emerged from the Inn behind Max.

"We should go and dig up the pot of gold, eh lad?"

"There's nothing buried down there but the English dead," replied Max.

"English dead...?" said Sir John, unsuccessfully trying to conceal a faint smile.

"1068," said Max. "The last battle of the West Saxon Uprising. Against the Normans..." he added, for clarification.

Sir John looked down at the curious red-haired boy, not trying to conceal his smile any more.

"Very good, lad," he said as softly as his military brusqueness would allow. "Upstart Normans, daring to build a castle on our sacred hill! Right - off to The Bubble then!"

A cheer went up, and everyone started to head off towards the woods, filing past Max, nodding their condolences. Except for one, who just stood, a little way off, looking around him like he didn't know where he was. He turned to look at Max, and Max gave an almost cartoon double take – he looked just like his grandfather, only younger. Max shook his head – no, couldn't be. But when Max looked back, the man was gone. Max shrugged, and reverted to staring out over the fields, still trying to make sense of everything in his head. The break in the weather had been short-lived, and a great

mist was rolling in fast now, already enveloping the trees beyond the car park. But now Max noticed something in the mist, a huge white shape.

"What's that over there...?" said Myvi as she came out of the Inn.

"I don't know, a horse or something?" said Max, turning towards her. But then his attention was ripped away from whatever was in the trees by the old man standing with Myvi.

"No, it's not a horse," said the old man. Max knew the voice as well as he had known Myvi's when she first spoke to him. The long, thinning grey hair, the tall thin frame – Max suddenly had a flashback of the man standing by Myvi, waiting for him to get them away from the burning hill fort. In The Dream, he never saw their faces. But this time he did. It *was* them.

"Joseph...?" said Max tentatively.

"Hello Max," said the old man with a little foreboding.

Then the mist cleared for a moment, and they all saw that the shape was obviously not a horse.

"It's the Gurt Dog, Max!" exclaimed Myvi. "The Guardian of the Hill, from The Dream! But..." Myvi looked a little scared now. "But it *can't* be!"

But for Max, there could no longer be any doubt.

"I don't think it was a dream Myvi."

"What...?" she said weakly.

"I had another dream last night – my grandfather came to me in his old room, and told me he had changed the past, to keep us safe. He also showed me the Majyga, the Travelling Objects, in a box under his old bed. But now I don't think that was a dream either, I think it was a Fetch - you know, when people who arc about to die appear to their relatives? Thing is Myvi, the Majyga are really there, upstairs, in a box under his bed."

Myvi was just staring at Max now, her mouth open. Joseph just stared at the Gurt Dog, not believing what he was seeing.

"The Dream isn't a dream, Myvi – it's a memory of a past that's been changed. All that *really* happened. Grandfather really *was* a Time Traveller. And so are we."

Both Myvi and Joseph stared at Max now, but somehow they all knew that this made an insane kind of sense. As their worlds turned upside down, the gigantic White Dog slowly turned its gaze towards them and bowed its head, before disappearing.

*

The thick black over-laden rain clouds were now emptying themselves with great force all over the ancient escarpment as Nick led Max to Tinkers Bubble, the ramshackle self-built eco-community that had been in the woods for nigh on twenty years. The Inn was closed, and everyone had already headed there, to carry on celebrating old Percy's life, with music, and dancing, and a hog roast, and of course with their famous home-made cider, which they sold at the local markets, along with their vegetables, jams, bread, fruit juice and firewood, to help pay for the quirky but ground-breaking community's off-grid lifestyle. Myvi and her grandfather had called it home for the last four years, ever since Max had brought them from the chaos that was AD44 to the safety of 2010. But only now did they finally know this – that they had come from a past that had been erased.

Myvi and Joseph had tried to take Max to the wake, but he didn't want to go. He wasn't good at being sociable at the best of times, but especially not after what had just happened. But eventually Nick persuaded him to go. Max trusted Nick, somehow. He figured that if his grandfather had, then he should too.

"Let's take the middle path," said Nick, pulling the hood of his coat up. "It'll be more sheltered."

Nick and Max headed down from the top path, the relative

visibility of the winter-bare ash, beech and sycamore giving way to the enfolding gloom of the closely packed conifers that populated the lower stretches of Norton Wood. The path was narrower and muddier as rainwater tumbled down the fern-strewn hillside, but at least they had some shelter from the elements now roaring through the tree tops like high waves on a windswept beach.

Neither of them spoke much, partly because they were concentrating on keeping their footing on the increasingly slippery path, but truth be told, Max didn't talk much most of the time anyway. It wasn't that he didn't have anything to say, just that he found it hard to decide which of the myriad conversations swirling in his head were safe to share out loud. But finally he found one.

"So you knew Grandfather well then, Nick?"

"Yes, I did. He was a great guy."

Max suspected Nick knew more than he was letting on, and the events of the day now stopped him filtering his thoughts before he spoke them.

"So you knew about his..."

But Nick cut him off. "His other life? Yes Max, I did. He came and saw me too last night. He told me he'd talked to you. So, now you know."

"But..."

"How do I remember when none of the others do? Simple. I'm a Traveller too. But never mind that now - come on, there's a wake to go to!"

They were in the deepest part of the woods now, the hazy lights of Tinkers Bubble up the slope ahead of them. The rain was crashing down now, penetrating even the thick evergreen canopy above them. But as they rounded a corner, they almost bumped into someone half running the other way. Initial shock turned into apologies as they all recognised each other.

"Hey, how are you guys doing?"

It was Jack, one of the pub regulars, on his way back from The Bubble, still dressed in his pseudo Mediaeval finery. He was only in his early twenties, but he'd been coming here with his parents since he was a kid, and didn't give the strangeness that enveloped the place a second thought.

"Hey Jack," said Nick, smiling. "What are you doing going back so early? Have you drunk all the cider already?"

Max noticed it first. Jack suddenly looked... confused, like he was being forced to do something but didn't understand why.

"Jack?" Nick was a little worried now too.

Jack hung his head, and then slowly raised it, looking right at the two of them. But it was no longer Jack. His face had suddenly lost all its colour, and his now grey eyes were staring a thousand miles away. Before Max and Nick realised what was happening, he picked up a large fallen branch, wheeled around, and whirled it towards Max. But then came a voice, so deep it sounded like the ground itself was talking.

"Get him away from here, *now!*"

The branch that Jack was bringing down on Max now suddenly slowed in the arc that would have ended at his head. As Max turned to see where the voice had come from he saw something much more fearsome than Jack and his branch. But even though the massive White Dog was almost as tall as Max, somehow he wasn't afraid. For the first time, instinctively he began to trust the memory of his dream, and deep inside knew that this towering, slavering hound was there to help him.

As Jack's branch arced ever more slowly towards him, Nick grabbed Max's arm, and suddenly Max wasn't on Ham Hill anymore.

*

CHAPTER SIX

Max felt a little faint, almost like he'd just stepped off a boat and the world was still rocking back and forth.

"It will stop soon," said someone behind him. Max turned, to see a man with short, well-cut blonde hair dressed in a smart dark blue suit.

"That feeling in your head. It will stop soon."

Max looked around at his new surroundings, a white-painted room full of monitors, and a big window looking out onto what looked like hospital beds, their occupants seemingly asleep, attached to all manner of wires and tubes. A man in shirt sleeves came into the room and stopped and stared as he saw Max. "*He's* here?" said the man in alarm. He sat down at the monitors quickly, checking the sleepers' vital functions.

"It's alright Wilson – Stenton brought him in. He had to think quickly."

"Where am I?" said Max. "And who are *you?*"

"I am Major Willoughby, and you are in the TRD. Time Research Department. Welcome Max – we've been following your life since, well since it began really."

"Time Research Department?" said Max, a little cynicism creeping into his voice. "What, like a *government* department? Are you a secret agent or something?"

The Major laughed. "No Max, nothing so glamorous I'm afraid. This isn't Doctor Who."

Now Max looked closer at the occupant of one of the beds.

"That's Nick! What's he doing in that bed? He just rescued me from..."

"Yes, we saw. We can see everything The Dreamers do in these monitors here."

Max stared at the Major, then held his hand up, taking a minute to try to work things out. But he couldn't.

"Nick is a time traveller, as are the other five. Somehow they access the Multiverse - the infinite possible futures of

the Fifth Dimension, and the alternative Presents of the Sixth. Like you, they have something missing in their brains that makes us see Time as a straight line – but unlike you, they can't Travel when they're awake. Only you can do that, that we know of, except of course your late grandfather, and anyone who has The Majyga. And so they sleep, and dream, and through them we make sure the Past, and the Present, remains stable. Which we have done - until now."

"Where do they come from?"

"Percy found them shortly after he started Travelling himself," said the Major. "He was still working for Intelligence as a code breaker then. Things kept changing in history, and he couldn't work out why - then he found these guys. They didn't even know they were doing it at first, but slowly they realised, and started taking advantage, changing history for their own ends. Percy tracked them down, one by one, and brought them to us. We were a dream research establishment at the time, but he realised we – and these Travellers – could be put to work for the good of the world, changing it subtly to right historical wrongs."

Max was struggling. "So, you *are* government then...?"

"Well, a few people in various governments know about us, yes. But they don't interfere. We rather scare them."

Max looked at Nick again, confused. "But how can Nick be asleep here, *and* working at the Inn? He's what, a hologram or something?"

The Major laughed again. "No, he's very real, when he's there. He only got there yesterday, but the people there believe he's been there for years. It's the beauty of being able to manipulate time. If people believe enough that something is real, then it is."

Max looked back at the Major. "So... what's going to happen? What am I going to do now?"

The Major looked at one of the monitors, and then smiled at Max. "Now it's safe again, you're going to go back to your

grandfather's Wake and have a good time."

Max looked at the monitor, and saw the Gurt Dog take his giant paw from Jack's chest as the mist swirled around them both, and now all Jack saw was a dark-haired man helping him up.

"Mr. Hamandun? He really *is* a Gurt Dog?"

"They are one and the same. He is one of the Guardians of Time. He too has been following your life."

Max breathed out heavily. This was too much. "But what do I *do?!*"

"As your grandfather said to you last night, you must destroy the Majyga, find the Cross of Tofig, lift the curse, and stop Roger Bacon from opening the gates of Annwn. Basically, save the world."

Max just glared at the Major now, then erupted. "I'm *fourteen!* How am *I* supposed to save the world?!"

The Major smiled with a little embarrassment now. "I'm afraid we don't really know. All I know is what your grandfather told me, that you have to go back to the Majyga's Origin Points, where they were first lost. Percy tried, but he couldn't get to them – Time wouldn't let him, kept spitting him out. He was sure you could though. Sorry I don't know more. We'll help where we can though..."

The Major looked at one of the monitors, then leaned over one of the consoles and pressed a button below a microphone.

"Stenton, you can take Max home now."

*

For the first time in years, Max didn't wake up in a panic, but instead with a strange, slightly warm feeling inside. For once, his dreams had been like most other people's, a random, slightly surreal sorting of the previous day's events, which for Max was dominated by the Wake in the woods that had lasted well into the night, and that to his surprise,

he had actually enjoyed. The two dozen or so residents of the odd assortment of home-made wood, stone and canvas dwellings were beginning to realise that they shared a common past with Max, even if his grandfather had changed it to protect them all, and welcomed him into their midst with open arms. It was a new experience for Max, and at first he was a little nervous of it all. His condition had made him very shy, especially in the last four years, and he was now almost pathologically incapable of being sociable. But these people didn't care about any of that. Max didn't even notice it happening, but somehow they made him feel at home.

And then he was watching and listening in wonder and amusement as the Travellers recounted newly-remembered tales of adventures in history with old Percy. He laughed as they continued to Wassail, dancing around the billowing fire, the woods echoing with the tinkling of their bells. He looked on in delight as Myvi played and sang some hauntingly beautiful Celtic folk songs; and in the end, he even eventually allowed her to drag him from his seat to join in the dancing.

And then it was over, and he walked back to the Inn, alone, but safe in the knowledge that nothing would be allowed to happen to him in these ancient woods on this most magical of nights.

*

Max headed towards his father's car for the ride to school, to find his new tutor walking towards him.

"I am sorry Max, you would not have heard – you do not need to go to school this morning, for school is coming here, to the hill. A local history trip it seems. I was only informed yesterday afternoon myself. We are both new here!"

Max's father just shrugged, and went back into the Inn for an unexpected second coffee, but Max headed straight for his tutor, so many questions forming in his head he hardly knew

where to start. So he just waded right in.

"So I'm guessing Hamandun isn't your real name then?"

His Tutor let out a loud roar of a laugh.

"Rex Hamandun - King of Ham Hill," said Max. "Wasn't hard to work out."

"Oh, Max! Do we really have to begin again, after all we have done together? Is memory not returning to you?"

"A little, yes," said Max, "but I still have questions. So, you can just Travel at will?"

"Only when necessary - it is very tiring. The battle against Bacon's forces four years ago was almost the end of me, and I have only recently regained the strength to return."

Max stopped, and looked at his new tutor, his head reeling with the multiple impossibilities of the situation. He was talking to a man who he saw transform into a giant dog, one who saved his life almost two thousand years ago, which was also four years ago, and again last night, after the funeral for a grandfather he had never met, but who now it seemed he knew very well, in a dream that he now knew wasn't a dream, but an alternative past.

But then finally, Max realised that however impossible, he had to accept that it was all real, and that his world had changed forever.

He smiled, and nodded to himself. Right then.

"So why *have* you returned?"

Rex looked down at Max with a little pity. He didn't know exactly what was about to befall the boy, but he suspected enough to know it wouldn't be good.

"Danger comes to Hamandun once more, and I am its Guardian."

"Danger? What danger? You mean Bacon?"

"No, it cannot be *him*. Initially I thought it might be, but then realised I must be wrong. We defeated *him* and his forces, your grandfather destroyed the Majyga, and imprisoned Bacon in Annwn."

"So what *is* this danger then...?"

But Rex didn't have time to answer. As they rounded the last corner before the Frying Pan, as the area below the War Memorial had been known since before anyone could remember, there was suddenly an ear-splitting yelling and screaming as dozens of what looked to Max like sword and axe-wielding Saxon warriors charged down the embankment, heading towards a similar force of Dark Age British warriors charging at them from the opposite banks.

"What's going on?! Where have you taken me?!" Max yelled at Rex above the thunderous noise of the hand to hand battle now playing out just yards from them.

Rex just threw his head back and laughed.

"What?! Why are you laughing?!"

Before Rex could say anything a loud whistle blew, and the battle suddenly stopped.

"All right, all right, very good – you're getting the hang of it. Now, go to the first field, and we'll try the next part."

Max recognised the voice – it was Sir John. The 'warriors' all laughed, and started chatting away excitedly to each other in very modern English as they headed past Max on their way to the Warren Fields the other side of the hill fort. All except one, who was heading towards Max. But to Max's horror, as the 'soldier' got closer, he suddenly raised his sword and charged, screaming.

"What the – help!!" yelled Max, starting to run, but then suddenly the soldier pulled up and took off his helmet, to reveal that he was actually a she – Myvi, in fact.

"Not funny, Myvi," said Max, panting, but it didn't stop her laughing, nor Rex for that matter. But then Rex turned as a portly figure came towards them.

"Good day, Sir John," said Rex. "How go the Re-enactment rehearsals? Battle of Badon Hill isn't it? King Arthur's last battle?"

Sir John looked at Rex quizzically, as if he knew he should

know him.

"Do I know you, sir?"

Rex smiled at Sir John. "I am Rex Hamandun, Sir John, a new teacher at the school. But yet, I have been here for many, many years."

Sir John shook Rex's hand, and suddenly got a blast of recognition. "It is you? From the... Dream? How are you here?!"

"Do not worry, Sir John. I came merely to guide Percy safely to Annwn, and to ensure that all was well in Hamandun."

Sir John wrestled with what he was now realising was no longer false memory.

"And is it? We are still safe?"

"Of course you are, Sir John. We ensured it was so."

"Yes, well, we had better be. Come on you two, on to the fields..."

"I would like a little word with them if you don't mind, Sir John," said Rex. "I shall take them back to school."

"What? Oh, right, very well..."

The old soldier blustered past them, and hurried towards the fields, disappearing as the path took him behind the high mounds of the foundations of the ancient fort.

"He doesn't know, does he?" said Max after the old boy had gone. "That we're in danger."

"He doesn't need to know," said Rex, his voice deeper now. "No-one does - not yet. Not until *I* know what we are facing. But anyway..." His voice lightened again, and he smiled almost mischievously at Max. "If I am to be your tutor, then we should begin today's lessons!"

"Oh..." said Max, a little disappointed that real life needed to start again after the excitement of the last two days.

Rex led Max and Myvi to the centre of the stone circle that had been made to mark the Millennium and sat down next to the remains of a small fire, bidding the two teenagers to join him. In the distance, on the far edge of the Frying Pan, a digger started up at the new quarry pit; another seam of the

golden yellow Hamstone being dug out to build Somerset's new houses, and maintain its old ones.

"It's a bit cold to have lessons outside isn't it?" said Max, shivering a little, despite his thick jumper and duffle coat. "After all, it *is* January."

"Well, we shall have to warm ourselves then," said Rex with a little grin, as suddenly the cold dead fire sprang into life again. Max stared at the fire, and then at Rex.

"What, you can do *magic* as well?!" he said, barely believing what he'd just seen, even after the things he'd already seen in the last two days.

"That wasn't magic," said Rex. "Magic is for fairy tales. I merely brought the fire that was here yesterday through time."

"So this is *Time Travelling School?*" said Max, trying to hide hope behind outward incredulity.

"No, of course not, Max," said Rex. Max blushed instantly, his stomach suddenly in knots, feeling the kind of stupid he used to feel when he was at his old normal school, when he said things in class without mentally checking them first and people would laugh.

But neither Rex nor Myvi were laughing.

"But you know how to do that, don't you Max?" said Rex, deadly serious now. "You know how to conjure things up from history..."

"No..." Max shook his head, but then stopped shaking it, as a memory suddenly began to fade up in his head, a memory of a lost past, a memory of standing side by side with his grandfather, swords suddenly appearing in their hands just in time to... to...

Max dragged his gaze back from the hazy distance and stared at Rex, terrified by the horror of the memory.

"I have killed."

Rex just nodded, and sighed.

Max suddenly remembered more now, but it didn't make it any less terrifying. He had killed. His sword had stabbed

into a man's chest, and had ended his life, the man's life blood spurting out over Max's tunic, sword, and hands. And then the man fell to the ground, and Max pulled his sword from him, and swiftly attacked and killed another, and another, and another. So much death, and blood. He knew he had done it, but he just couldn't connect with the ten-year-old that had done that. And then full memory flooded back, the killing, the bloodlust of battle, and Max buckled, falling to his knees and sobbing uncontrollably.

"How could I do that?" he said, choking on the tears of memory. "I was *ten* – how could I *kill?!*"

"It was kill or be killed, Max," said Rex softly. "You know this now, don't you?"

Max stopped crying now, and wiped his eyes on the sleeves of his duffel coat, before looking up at Rex. Deep breath, more new reality. Yes, he knew. He just wished he didn't.

"I... had forgotten."

"You will need to remember, Max, if we are to win," said Rex, his voice deeper again. "Give it time, and you will."

"Yes, but how *much* time?" said Max. "What's going to happen? *When* is it going to happen?"

"That is the point, Max," said Rex. "We must stop it from happening at all." Rex's tone lightened again. "But, that is the future – now we must return to school!"

However, they both now realised that Myvi was crouched into a tight ball, sobbing even more than Max had been. It was a while before she unfurled. Rex tried kind words, but she remained tightly curled. Only Max's touch on her shoulder woke her from it.

"It's alright Myvi," said Max, somehow knowing now that it was.

Myvi took an age, but in the end, she looked up at Max.

"Really...?"

"We're safe."

"How do you know that?!"

"I'm not sure – I just do."

"Safe now, or safe forever?"

Max choked back a tear with a strangled laugh.

"I only just figured out the past Myvi – don't ask me about the future."

Now it was Myvi's turn to laugh, as much as she could, which wasn't much.

"What's going to happen Max?" Her eyes were wide, desperate, but Max just shrugged, so she turned to Rex. "Mr... Rex...?"

Rex's tone now forcibly lightened. "What's going to happen is that we are going back to school!"

And with that, the fire was instantly returned to the previous day, no doubt surprising the people who were sat round it when it suddenly went out.

Rex got up, but Max and Myvi just stayed there, by the now dead fire, both just staring at the ground.

"We'll be there in a minute," said Max, and Rex nodded. They needed some time to work all this out. He just hoped it wouldn't take too long, otherwise all was lost.

As Rex disappeared around the bend under the old fortifications, Myvi slowly got up, but then realised that Max was now crouching down again for some reason.

"Come on Max," said Myvi, trying to jolly her new friend up, but knowing her voice didn't have the conviction. "We'll be late – school time!"

But Max was now rocking gently and moaning quietly to himself. Myvi bent down to him, her turn to touch *his* shoulder lightly.

"Max...?"

"The thing about me, you see," said Max, still staring at the ground, "is I have this condition... Sometimes I don't make connections... Sometimes something can be staring me in the face and I just can't see it, but then later it just goes 'bang!', and I remember, and I realise, but it's too late."

64

"What are you talking about Max? Too late for what?"

But Max carried on as if she wasn't there.

"Sometimes it's just simple things, like forgetting to do something Mum has asked me to do, or forgetting I had homework until the next morning, or forgetting to tell Dad someone phoned..."

"So what is it *this* time, Max...?" said Myvi, a little nervous now.

"Rex said it couldn't be Bacon coming back, because the Majyga were destroyed. But they weren't. He doesn't know Grandfather didn't destroy them. I told you, they're upstairs."

Myvi's eyes went wide now. "What, you mean..."

"It *is* Bacon. He's trying to break out of Annwn. And he's coming to get me."

*

CHAPTER SEVEN

They'd walked back to the Inn after school. Max's father had texted to say he was going to be late picking him up, so Myvi suggested they walk. She walked to school every day anyway, through the woods, but for Max it was a new experience. He'd never been one for the outdoors much, but in contrast to the previous day there was a bright winter's sky, and he had to admit that with the sun casting pools of light through the bare-branched canopy, the woods did have a certain magic to them. The mud he wasn't so keen on, particularly the patch he slipped and fell into, to Myvi's amusement, and needed a complete change of clothes on returning to the Inn. Myvi had gone back to The Bubble to change her own, not because they were muddy, but because if they were going to be going back in time, she wasn't going to be doing it in her school uniform. She returned wearing a calf-length dress, leggings and a full length hooded coat. They were her 'old' clothes, which she now knew were genuine first century. Max in turn had changed into brown cords and a thick brown jumper. It wasn't perfect, but it was anonymous enough to pass. His school shoes probably wouldn't, but he didn't have anything else – Max had never worn trainers in his life.

They had reconvened out at the War Memorial, at the northernmost tip of Ham Hill, looking out over the Somerset Levels, luscious flatlands spreading out for miles below them. Once upon a time, everything they were looking at would have been under water at this time of year, from the Severn Estuary to the West to the legendary Glastonbury Tor to the North. Somerset used to be called The Land of The Summer People for good reason – for most of the winter it was largely uninhabitable marshland. But the land was drained centuries ago, and as the sun began to set on this cold but clear-skied 21st Century winter's day, the view was just spectacular, as the soon to be departing sun's orange glow bathed the hi-

bernating cider orchards down below, the rain-sodden water meadows of Muchelney in the far distance, and the still frosty hedgerows of the ancient field systems in between.

While the pills had kept Max normal, they'd also suppressed his visions, and his dreams, and therefore his *real* past - the past that he now knew was changed by his grandfather. Max had already accepted that The Dream was real, but it was taking longer for memory of his Travelling abilities to return. He knew that in his other past he could Travel like riding a bike. The now lost week he was with his grandfather four years ago was more like a year of actual Travelling. They went everywhere – the Battle of Hastings, the Fire of London, Wembley 1966, Dallas Texas 1963, so many famous moments in history. His grandfather had done such a great job of bringing out his innate Travelling skills that after only a few days he only had to think of a place and time and he was there. But that was then. His grandfather had also done a great job of erasing those memories, and what he hadn't wiped, the pills had.

"Shouldn't we tell them what we're doing?" said Myvi, looking a little tentatively at the three Majyga as Max opened the box.

"Who? Rex? He thinks they're already destroyed. And anyway, what can they do? Grandfather said only I could do it."

"So how do we destroy them?"

"We have to go back to when they were lost."

"And then what?"

"No idea."

"OK, helpful," said Myvi, flashing Max a little grin, and pulling her coat around her for warmth. "So how do they... work?" She had a hazy recollection of seeing Max use them before, but not enough to know what to do.

"I'm not sure – I mean, I remember a little, but not everything. I do know how The Coin works - you just touch it and you're right back in the battle, you know, in The Dream..."

"Don't think I'm ready for that yet," said Myvi, shivering at

recently returned memory.

"No, nor me," said Max. "We could try The Ring...?" Max gingerly picked up the ornate silver ring, but nothing happened.

"Maybe you have to put it on?" said Myvi.

Max had a sudden memory of doing so, and twisting it.

"You'd better hold on," said Max, shutting the box and putting it in his satchel. "Ready?"

"Not really." But she reached out and held Max's hand anyway. They looked at each other for a moment, memory returning of their friendship in the other past, then both looked away just as quickly, a little embarrassed.

Max turned The Ring slightly with his thumb, and reality blurred around them. Max instinctively stopped turning The Ring, and the world came into focus again.

"We're still on the hill," said Myvi looking around.

"Yes, but we *have* gone back a bit," said Max, indicating the War Memorial that was no longer there. Looking down into the village, they saw that it was smaller, with flickering gas street lights instead of electric ones.

"Victorian times, I'm guessing," said Max. "Not far enough. The Ring is Saxon – we need to go much further. OK, don't let go..."

Max turned The Ring more now, round and around his finger, and now reality buckled and roared, becoming a whirlwind of history flashing past too fast for their brains to register – and then to their horror Max and Myvi were lifted off their feet, and flung around the furious vortex.

"What's happening?!" shouted Myvi above the screaming, swirling winds.

"I think Time's trying to stop us - don't let go!" yelled Max.

"I wasn't about to!" Myvi yelled back, gripping Max's hand harder.

But eventually the maelstrom slowed, and subsided, and then finally stopped, leaving Max and Myvi to drop to the

ground, their heads reeling like they'd been thrown off a hundred mile an hour rollercoaster.

*

Gareth came back into the control room with his third mug of coffee that afternoon, and peered through the viewing window into the Sleep Room next door.

"Huh? That's not right..."

The Dreamers were all tossing and turning in their beds, the sensor wires attached to their heads flailing this way and that. Something was wrong – they shouldn't all be dreaming at the same time. Gareth checked the medication readouts. Something was definitely wrong – they should all be in deep sleep, not dreaming. He turned on the monitoring screens for all but his own empty bed and stared in alarm at what he saw. All five were having the same dream. Quickly he picked up the phone and pressed the first speed dial button.

"Major, you'd better get in here."

Moments later, Major Willoughby came rushing in.

"What is it Wilson?"

He stared intently at the monitors.

"Where is he?"

"Not sure Sir, but I think he's got through to one of the Origin Points."

Willoughby breathed out heavily.

"So Percy was right then - he is The One."

"Looks like it, Sir. Should I send Nick in?"

Willoughby looked at the scene on the monitors, and shook his head.

"I don't think Time would *let* him in. All we can do is watch, and hope."

*

They were on a different hill now, looking out over a different valley. In the distance was a small settlement of wattle, daub and thatch houses, and below them a small wood.

"I feel a bit sick," said Myvi, clutching her head to try to stop it spinning.

"I know - it'll settle down in a minute," said Max. "I remember this part now."

"So now what?"

"Well, I've been thinking about this," said Max, unbuttoning his duffle coat. The sun was glowing in a clear sky – it was obviously not winter here, wherever they were. "Bacon had these objects in his collection because they were lost somehow – here, somewhere, in The Ring's case. So if we find the original, and, I don't know, give it back to its owner, then it won't be lost any more, and Bacon won't get it, and it won't get turned into a Majyg."

Myvi thought about this for a moment, and then nodded. "Sounds like a plan. So how do we find the original?"

Suddenly there was a distant roar, down below the hill. Max and Myvi got up, and looked over the edge, to see two small armies racing towards each other, swords, spears and axes at the ready.

"I guess it's down there somewhere," said Myvi. "Max look!" Myvi pointed at The Ring. "Look at The Ring!"

Max looked down at The Ring, and saw that it was now glowing faintly.

"Maybe it can sense the other one," said Max. "Come on." Max started to walk down the steep slope towards the battle.

"Of course, we could wait till the battle's over," said Myvi, hovering hesitantly.

"No, someone will take it," said Max. "And then it will make its way to Bacon. We have to get there first."

"So *when* are we?" asked Myvi, as they made their way cautiously down the hill.

"Ninth century I'm guessing," said Max. "Those are Vikings

and Saxons." The Ring was glowing brighter now, and was beginning to hum quietly.

The Saxons had charged from the cover of the wood, but were now being beaten back into them by the overwhelming numbers and ferocity of the Viking attackers.

"We can't just walk into the middle of the battle, Max," said Myvi. They were only a few hundred yards away from the Saxon army's rear now.

"No, I know," said Max, thinking hard. If this was a video game, what would he do? Then he looked up, and smiled to himself. "Come on – up!"

"Really Max?" said Myvi, as Max started to climb up into a nearby tree.

"They're coming this way anyway," said Max as he climbed. "We'll just wait up here until the one with the original ring comes past."

Myvi shrugged, and followed Max up the low-hanging branches of the tree, until they were twenty or so feet up. The Ring was glowing stronger now, and humming louder. Below, the battle had reached them, as the Vikings furiously hacked and slashed their way through the rapidly collapsing Saxon defences. All around the tree they were sat in, valiant Saxons fell, until the cry went up to flee. The Vikings went to follow them, but a tall, powerfully built warrior yelled out, obviously their commander, telling them to leave the Saxons to their flight, and the Viking attackers fell back, retreating through the woods.

"I think it's safe now," said Max. "Come on." And with that, he began to climb back down the tree.

Once on the ground, Max started to pick his way around the fallen Saxons, trying not to look at them too closely – they weren't a pretty sight. He was concentrating on The Ring, which was humming louder and louder, and glowing ever brighter.

"There!" said Myvi, pointing at a dead warrior lying face

down, arms spread out, and a silver ring on one finger, which now also began to glow and hum.

Max bent down to get the ring, but then stood up again, a little shakily.

"What is it Max?" said Myvi.

"Nothing, nothing," said Max. "It's just that I've... never seen a dead person before."

"Yes, you have," said Myvi. "We both have, remember?"

Max smiled weakly at new returning memory. Yes, of course he had. And *he* had killed some of them.

"OK, but I've never touched one before..."

"Oh, for goodness' sake," said Myvi, and bent down, and took the ring from the man's finger.

But as she did so, and held it up for Max to see, the glow of the two rings suddenly got bigger and bigger, until they were two shining auras that now engulfed both Max and Myvi, while the humming had become a roar, as if the wind were screaming in sixty part harmony. Max and Myvi were being pushed apart, as if the rings were two powerful magnets repelling each other.

"I know what we have to do!" yelled Max. "Time doesn't want them to come together, but they must, Myvi!"

Max and Myvi both held out their rings and pushed as hard as they could against the force trying to keep them apart, as if they were battling hurricane-speed winds while pulling a truck. They pushed and pushed, and inch by inch they got closer and closer.

"Push Myvi!" yelled Max.

"I am!" Myvi yelled back. "I can't push any harder!"

"We *have* to! Come *on!!*"

And then, as if Time had had a change of plan, the rings were no longer repelling each other, but pulling towards the other with just as much force. Max and Myvi were both pulled off their feet as the rings came together, their brilliant auras now combining into a blinding flash of light, before

both vanished with a deafening crack, and suddenly the winds had gone, and Max and Myvi were left lying on the ground, both struggling to breathe.

They sat up and looked around, both still breathing heavily. Max looked on his finger, and then checked in the box.

"The Ring's gone!" he said exhaustedly. "We did it!"

Myvi smiled weakly at him. "One down, two to go. So, Brooch next?"

Max shrugged, still trying to get his breathing under control.

"Yes – just give me a minute."

But now Myvi looked past Max in alarm, then grabbed hold of his arm.

"We don't *have* a minute, Max – get us out of here!"

Max looked around wildly, to see a huge Viking warrior carrying a variety of souvenirs of war bearing down on them. He'd obviously ignored the order to retreat, and had gone on a one man plundering mission. Max grabbed the box from his satchel and pulled out the one thing he *knew* would get them out of there – The Coin. As the world buckled around them, all Max could hear was Myvi yelling "Max! What have you *done?!*"

*

74

CHAPTER EIGHT

They had landed on the northernmost tip of the ramparts of the fort, where almost nineteen hundred years later the War Memorial would be built. The Frying Pan was very different now to what it would be then though – where there would one day be grassed-over quarrying spoil mounds were now a collection of wooden huts, and at the far end, the single mound on top of which stood the inner fortress. The sun was setting over the Somerset Levels in the distance, and the trees and hedges of the lands below were glistening red green and gold. Autumn was upon Ham Hill. But neither Max nor Myvi noticed any of this. The only thing they noticed was that the fort *wasn't* on fire.

"Has the battle not begun yet?" said Myvi, memory of the other past now beginning to return, along with her memory of her life here at this place.

"I don't know," said Max warily. "Every time I touched The Coin before, I was instantly back among the fighting, and the Demons. Something must have happened."

"Maybe destroying The Ring has changed things?" said Myvi.

"Yes, it's possible I suppose," said Max.

"I remember... you using The Coin with The Brooch..." said Myvi.

Max searched inside himself, and felt the same memory. "Yes, I did. I think it did something useful..."

Max took out The Brooch, and held the two Majyga one in each hand, but nothing happened.

"No, I remember now – you have to pin it on," said Max, as he did so. "Then touch the jewel with The Coin."

But now Max hung his head for a moment, then looked out at the rapidly darkening Somerset Levels and breathed out heavily.

"What is it Max?" asked Myvi with a little concern.

Max didn't say anything for a moment, but then turned and looked at Myvi. "Sorry, it all just got a bit much."

"How do you mean?"

Max wasn't used to explaining what went on in his head. Even to Dr. Llewellyn it was a struggle.

"Oh, I don't know..." But he gave it a go. "Look, three days ago I was a scared kid playing games in my room, and now I'm Time Travelling to first century Britain. The medication is still wearing off - sometimes I'm forgetting to be scared, other times it just hits me in waves."

"So are you scared now?"

Max breathed out deeply again. "Yes. Of course. This is where it all began - The Dream."

Myvi smiled at him, and nodded. He'd told her some of this, as they walked home from school earlier. But now she gave a little laugh.

"Hey, how do you think *I* feel? I just found out I was *born* in first century Britain!"

Max gave a little laugh too now. "Yes, I suppose so. So, shall we try this Brooch/Coin thing then?"

"Can't hurt," said Myvi.

"Well, it might," said Max, holding out his hand towards Myvi's. "Just in case..."

Myvi smiled, a little coyly, and took Max's hand. Max looked down, concentrating on The Brooch, too desperately shy to meet her eyes. He knew they had been very close, in the other past, but that was different, they were only ten, and didn't think about those sort of things in that way. Not that Max did now – girls just didn't figure in his world. But now he was holding one's hand, his head was buzzing, and he just knew his face was bright red.

"Ready?" said Max, daring to look at Myvi now. She was grinning.

"I am if you are," said Myvi.

Max brought The Coin slowly up to The Brooch, and then

touched it to the centre jewel. There was a jolt, and the scenery changed. They were still sitting on the same hill, but they were several yards from where they were before.

"Yes," said Max. "I remember now. Could come in handy..."

Now, from the ramparts of the inner fortress, a single horn blasted out. Suddenly people began to emerge from the huts, carrying armfuls of belongings, or pushing them in small carts.

Myvi looked a little alarmed, a look of recognition on her face.

"What is it Myvi?" said Max, as people began to make their way to the eastern gates, beyond the inner fortress.

"That was the call to evacuate – they're all leaving!"

Then they heard another distant sound, a rumbling, thumping sound, and as it got louder, it was joined by the sound of rattling armour.

"Come on, quickly!" yelled the man on the inner fortress ramparts. "The Romans are here – we must leave *now!*"

Max and Myvi looked at each other in horror as the people below them made more haste towards the gates.

"I was right!" said Myvi. "We were early - the battle just hasn't started yet!"

But Max didn't look so sure. "I don't know Myvi – these people are packed up for leaving, not for fighting. And there's been no bombardment, no fireballs, like last time. Something *has* changed – come on."

"Where are we going?" said Myvi, already knowing the answer.

"To see the Romans – one of them has The Coin, and we have to find it."

Max stood up, and started to walk along the ramparts, keeping to the shadows of the wooden palisade that lined them all the way around this massive hill fort. Myvi shrugged, then stood up and followed. Soon they reached the far end of the inner fortress, as the last of its inhabitants made their

hasty way through the gates, leaving them abandoned. Max held his hand up for Myvi to wait, and then, as the very last ones left, he started down the rampart slopes towards the gates, and then out of them. What they saw the other side of them took their breath away. As hundreds upon hundreds of people flocked the other way, while others just stopped and stared, the entire Roman Second Legion marched in perfect unison across the Warren Fields towards the inner fortress.

"So now what?" said Myvi in a whisper.

"Speak Old British," Max whispered back. "Do you remember it?"

Myvi searched her memory, then nodded. But then Max looked at her curiously, like something had just clicked in his brain that he'd missed.

"Wait a minute - you speak English. I mean, *modern* English...!"

Myvi just stared at him. "Of course I do. It's been four years. We learnt. Max, get a grip!" She switched to her native tongue now. "What are we going to *do?!*"

"We're going to put our hoods up and mingle," Max whispered back, doing just that. They made their way carefully along the back of the watching crowd, until the Romans were only a few hundred yards away.

"There are no Demons, Myvi!" said Max in a more excited whisper. "And no Bacon, that I can see. We *must* have changed something!"

"Still have to find The Coin though, the original one."

"I think it's close," said Max, holding The Coin in the palm of his hand. Like The Ring, it was glowing, and humming a little. And as the Romans got closer, so the glowing and humming increased. As the General riding at the front of his Legion approached, it got brighter and brighter, and louder and louder. But then suddenly Max and Myvi were both dragged backwards, and pushed to the ground.

"Get down! You *know* what he said he would do if he saw

you again!"

Max looked up, and gasped as he saw them. It was Joseph, and the ten-year-old Myvi.

"Why have you returned?" said Myvi, staring at her four-teen-year-old self.

The older Myvi stared back at her younger self, and then at Max. It obviously hadn't occurred to her that she'd meet herself.

"Max – that's me. I hadn't thought... how is it possible? What's going to happen?"

"I don't know," said Max. "But I'd say if anything *was* going to happen, it would have done so by now."

As the General rode past at the head of his men, Max looked down at The Coin, which was glowing and humming at its brightest and loudest, but as the General headed towards the inner fortress, the glowing and humming became lesser.

"*He* must have it," said Max to the older Myvi. "The General. We have to get to him somehow."

"He will kill you on sight," said Joseph. "For so much he promised yesterday, when you were here before."

Max stared at Joseph now. "*Yesterday?*"

Joseph nodded. "Yes, yesterday. When Vespasian first arrived, to give us his terms."

Max decided not to tell them that he hadn't actually been there before, although obviously he would at some point. It would just confuse them, and they were obviously already confused enough. "So, do you know... what we are...?"

Joseph nodded again.

"You travel in Time," said the younger Myvi. "You told us not to resist when the Romans came, for you had seen us being slaughtered, in..." She was struggling with the concept now. "...in another future... We saw what you could do, and what you did to the Romans, and we believed you. So we are leaving."

"And so must you," said Joseph. "General Vespasian was

79

taken by surprise by you yesterday, but he will be doubly on his guard now. You will not get near him. You must come with us."

"Where are you going?" asked Max, still trying to work out a plan in his head.

"We are making camp outside the walls tonight, and then heading for Bryn Cwrdun, a day's walk to the North. The Chieftain of those lands has promised us sanctuary there. He has made peace with the Romans. We will be safe."

"Joseph! Why are you still here?! If Vespasian finds you he will crucify you!"

Max turned at the voice, to see a tall, broad man, with long dark hair framing his time-worn face, a long cloak over his wool and leather tunic and a gilt-handled sword on his belt. It was Chieftain Rhydderch, and suddenly Max was on the burning ramparts again.

"Run Max - the Demons are breaking through!"

Max shook his head, and he was back in the present moment, but the Chieftain was glaring at *him* now.

"*You?!* What are *you* doing back? You will endanger us all!"

"I have to get to Vespasian," said Max. "He has something of mine, and I could do with some help."

"And lose our heads? I do not think so. We have made peace with him, as you told us to, and have saved our lives. If you must go, you must, but you will be alone, and you will die alone."

"My Lord," said Max, trying to guess what he had told him the day before – what he *would* tell him the day before. "Did I tell you of a different future, of fire, and brimstone, and Demons?"

Rhydderch glared at Max again, but then nodded his head slowly. "You did, yes, but it did not happen."

"But it still could happen, if you do not help me. Was I not right about saving you?"

Rhydderch sighed. He knew the boy was right. How could

he not be right – he knew the future, however hard it had been to understand. In fact, he had been beginning to half believe that he had imagined it. But here was the boy again.

"Very well – but not until we have eaten. Are you hungry?"

Max hadn't thought about this before – Time Travelling has a way of confusing the brain into *not* thinking about it – but now as he *did* think about it, he realised that, in real time, it was probably the equivalent of the early hours of the morning. Yes, he was hungry.

*

CHAPTER NINE

Max, Myvi and Rhydderch crept around the edge of the fields, keeping as far away as possible from the hundreds of houses that populated them, now taken over as barracks by the Roman soldiers. They were each armed now, swords and daggers at their belts, but they were only three, and the Legion was five thousand plus. They had climbed the wooden walls on ropes, but they had not been defended – Vespasian was obviously confident that, their lives spared, the Britons would not think of attack. There were however guards on the gates of the inner fortress.

"How do we get in?" said Max to the Chieftain.

"Can you not get us in?" said the Chieftain. "Yesterday, I saw you vanish from one point and reappear at another."

"Hmmm," said Max. The Brooch had worked earlier, but he wasn't sure he could remember how to control it.

"Come on Max," said Myvi. "You can do it – you've done it so many times before. You just have to remember."

Max sighed. Yes, he remembered, but only vaguely. Myvi's memory was now returning faster than his own.

"Very well," he said, taking The Coin from his pocket, and holding out his hand towards Myvi, who took it. "Hold her hand, my Lord."

Max breathed in and out deeply a few times, trying to relax his body, and his mind, as he now had better memory of doing. Focussing on the walls of the inner fortress, suddenly he could see beyond them, albeit hazily.

"We need to get to the Great Hall – that's where he'll be," said Rhydderch. "To the back wall."

Max tried to picture the Hall. At first he couldn't see it, but slowly it emerged from the mists in his head. There were guards at the front, but nowhere else. Max breathed in and out again, controlling it until he was barely breathing at all, relaxed his shoulders, and slowly brought The Coin up to the

jewel in the centre of The Brooch, until they touched, but this time he kept them pressed together. The air around them began to swirl, until it formed a vortex that encompassed all three, and then, with a lurch, they were transported through the fortress walls and to the back wall of the Great Hall. Max took The Coin away from The Brooch, and he and Myvi took a moment to steady themselves. Chieftain Rhydderch, however, fell over, clutching his head.

"What happened?!" he cried, before Max quickly put his hand over his mouth.

"Quiet my Lord," he hissed. "You will raise the alarm!"

Max helped the Chieftain to his feet, and slowly his world stopped spinning round.

"It will pass in a moment," said Max, still holding the Chieftain's arm.

"Yes, it begins to," said the Chieftain, wiping his brow. "What was I thinking? I would rather have fought the whole Legion to get in here than do that!"

"You may yet have to," said Myvi. "We still have the guards to get past."

"No, we do not," said Rhydderch, recovered now. "There is a secret door into the sleeping chamber, where I am sure Vespasian will be at this hour."

"That's handy," said Max.

"If you build something," said Rhydderch, "always build in a way to get out quickly." The Chieftain felt along the wall, until he found what he was looking for, and took out his dagger, levering a piece of wall away. Suddenly, there was a door. He opened it carefully, peered in, and then beckoned the others to follow him in. Once inside, they immediately saw the General sleeping on a canopied bed at the other end of the chamber.

"So now you can find what you seek," whispered the Chieftain.

Max pulled The Coin from his pocket, which now glowed

very brightly, and hummed very loudly. Hoping desperately that it wouldn't wake the General, Max walked slowly towards the end of his bed, as The Coin was directing him to, until he came to a wooden chest.

"It must be in there," he whispered, before very, very carefully opening the lid. Inside, the chest was full of coins.

"How do we find the right one?" whispered Myvi. But they didn't need to – for just outside the chest, was one coin that had fallen out, now pressed into the ground by the General's boot. And it was glowing. As Max, Myvi and the Chieftain watched in amazement, The Coin began to glow, and hum, and then rise slowly out of the ground.

"What is this magic...?" said Rhydderch, a little afraid, despite himself.

The coin continued to rise, until it was at Max's waist. Tentatively Max held out The Majyga Coin in his palm under the one that was rising, until the two were touching. And then there was a blast of light, and both coins disappeared.

"What...?!" said Vespasian, waking suddenly, and on seeing Max, Myvi and Rhydderch, immediately called out.

"You?! I *told* you I'd kill you if I saw you again! Guards!"

Vespasian leapt out of bed and grabbed his sword as two guards with their own swords drawn rushed in. But then all three were stopped in their tracks as a strange glow began to form between them and Max and the others, a glow that was slowly taking form, and which, with a deep, deep growl, now became flesh, a huge man, easily seven feet tall, dressed in glowing silver armour, and carrying a long, barbed, razor sharp silver sword.

"You wish to destroy The Coin...?" came a voice out of it that was even lower than a Gurt Dog's. Max was staring wildly at the apparition, but somehow managed to nod.

"Then you must destroy *me*, for I *am* The Coin!"

Max ducked the first sword swipe, astonishingly fast for one so big, but one of the guards didn't, and fell instantly

dead.

"What *is* this?!" yelled Vespasian as he managed to parry a second blow, before leaping out of the bed chamber and into the Hall proper.

"Never mind what it is!" yelled Max, as he and the others followed the General, fleeing the demon soldier. "If you want to live, you'll have to help us kill it!"

More soldiers ran into the Great Hall now, until many dozens surrounded the Demon. No match for the Demon's lightening quick sword work, they fell as quickly as they arrived. Vespasian now ran up behind the Demon as it was occupied with two of his men and ran it through with his sword. Nothing happened. The Demon merely turned toward Vespasian and laughed.

"*You* cannot kill me!" it yelled, pointing its sword at Max and Myvi. "Only *they* can kill me!"

"I think we're in trouble," said Max, hugging his sword to his chest.

"You may be right," said Myvi, instinctively ducking a blow from the Demon, memory of many fights now returning to her. She rolled across the floor, parrying another blow, before bringing her own blade up at its sword arm, but it went right through, with no effect. The Demon laughed again.

"All they have to do is work out *how!*"

But now Myvi was pointing at Max's sword.

"Max! Your sword! It's glowing!"

The Demon growled low now, backing away as Max advanced towards it, his now glowing sword held out in front. He just hoped he could remember how to do this.

"How did you get it to glow?" said Myvi.

"I think I must have touched it against The Brooch!" said Max, slashing at the Demon, but the Demon slashed back, heavily, again and again, forcing Max to desperately parry time after time before falling to the ground. The Demon advanced on him now, and put its sword to his throat.

"You cannot beat me," growled the Demon. "The Coin is *not* for destroying!"

"Oh yes it is!" yelled Myvi, and before the Demon knew what was happening, with one movement she touched her sword to The Brooch then brought it up fast, taking the Demon's head clean off its shoulders.

The blast of sound and light this time knocked everyone off their feet, but then receded, and faded to nothing. After a moment, Max leant up on one elbow, looked around, then felt in his pocket. The Coin was gone.

Vespasian picked himself up now, held his sword out at Max, and looked at what guards remained alive.

"Take these abominations!" he yelled at them with what little breath he had left. "Take them and execute them! Now!"

But the guards weren't doing anything of the sort. Instead, they backed away, and fled from the Great Hall.

"Very well, I shall do it myself!" said the General, bringing his sword down on Max, but it didn't get more than half way before it was sliced in two by Myvi's still-glowing sword.

"I don't think so," said Myvi with what little Latin she knew.

"We must be going now, General," said Max in perfect Latin as he got up. "But thank you for your help."

"Wait," said Vespasian, sitting down on his bed, no fight left in him now. "You said yesterday you know the future. Do you know of mine?"

Max looked at the General with a little pity now. It wasn't his fault.

"Yes, General. You will conquer all of Britain for your Emperor, except the very North, and then in a few years you yourself will become Emperor."

Vespasian nodded, grateful at least that he would live a while longer.

"And what of Rome?"

"The Empire will last another four hundred years General, and then will be destroyed by barbarian hordes. But Latin

will still be taught in schools in two thousand years' time. Unfortunately."

Max held out his hand for Myvi, and as she took it, he touched the jewel on The Brooch, and they were gone.

*

CHAPTER TEN

The Brooch didn't take them to its Origin Point quite so easily as The Coin had done. As Max touched the jewel, they were whipped off their feet and hurled into the air, which almost instantly began to spin around them, rapidly coalescing into a raging, swirling tunnel of space/time, like a water slide with no end, and more stomach-churning twists and turns than any theme park ride designer could ever possibly imagine. The tunnel itself seemed almost alive, trying to spit them out at every moment, but Max and Myvi held firm, holding onto each other as tightly as possible as Time blurred and warped all around them, trying everything it knew to separate them, and spit them out. But in the end, it knew it couldn't, because it knew that Max was The One. Time had almost accepted its new destiny – but then it had one last idea of how to preserve its current path, and set them down, as roughly as it could, in a hay barn, from a great height. There was a lot of screaming, from both of them.

Max and Myvi actually passed out as they were deposited back into reality. When they came round, they realised awkwardly that they were still holding each other. After a lot of embarrassed coughing and half-begun sentences, they managed to right themselves in the hay, before trying to work out where they were. Hay barn, obviously, but where, and when?

They climbed down the hay bales into the barn, and found a door, with a shaft of moonlight coming through its ill-fitting and time-worn frame. Slowly and cautiously they pushed the large door open, and peered out.

"I know where this is," said Myvi. "It's Parsonage Farm in Stoke sub Hamdon. Used to be a Priory once. Come on..."

They emerged from the barn into the moonlit night, to immediately see that the grounds were being illuminated from the road by modern streets lights.

"That's weird," said Max. "The Brooch is Norman – this

can't be its Origin Point, surely?"

They went to the entrance to the Priory, as the National Trust now called it, and looked up and down the street. There were electric lights, certainly, but it didn't quite look like Max remembered it from the school run. It took him a moment to work it out, but then he got it.

"Those are all old cars," he said, indicating up and down the street. "Unless we're on a film set, I'd say we were sometime in the 1960s. But why...?"

"Who knows?" said Myvi, heading back into the farmyard. "But I'm guessing we need to be in there..." She was pointing at the Priory itself, and its mediaeval doorway. "Anything happening with The Brooch?"

Max looked down at The Brooch, and shook his head. No glow, and no humming.

"OK, let's go and see what we can find," said Myvi, heading for the old doorway. They paused nervously as they got to it though.

"Now what?" said Max.

"We go in, of course."

"We can't just go in – don't people still live here?"

Myvi just shrugged. Max looked along the long irregular line of leaded windows along the ancient building's street elevation. They were all dark. And then Max had a 'wait-a-minute' thought.

"No, it's OK – if this is the Sixties, then it was empty. The National Trust started renovating it in 1967, I think. I remember now – oh my God! This is where Grandfather found the Majyga!"

Myvi looked confused. "But they can't be here now – we just destroyed two of them. The Ring and The Coin at least don't exist, not now or in the past... or do they...?"

Max just shrugged. "I don't know any more Myvi – to be honest, it's doing my head in. Come on, let's just go in."

The door creaked as Myvi began to open it, causing them

90

both to jump.

"Careful!" hissed Max.

"I thought you said no-one was here," Myvi hissed back.

"I know, but, just in case..."

Max took the old iron door handle again, and slowly pushed the door open, stopping every time it threatened to creak. But eventually, he was inside. Max crept into the entrance porch, then looked around for Myvi, but she was still outside, looking nervous.

"Come on," said Max, beckoning her in.

"I don't know, Max – what if the Majyga *are* here? What if they came back, even if we did destroy them? They did it to Percy you said. And we still have one of them – what happens if the same Majyg is in the same place twice?"

Max shrugged. He had no idea any more. "I suppose there's only one way to find out..."

Myvi took a deep breath, and put one foot inside the door, as if something might bite it off. But then she gave a half smile, relaxed, and joined Max on the inside, before they went through another door to the right, and found themselves in what looked like it had once been a Great Hall. That use had obviously long since passed: the plaster on the stone walls was damp and crumbling, while from what Max could see by the moonlight coming in through the mediaeval mullioned windows, the large room was now a store room, mostly home to sacks of animal food and hay bales.

"So if the Majyga are here, where do we start looking?" whispered Myvi, but Max was already heading to the other end of the hall, disappearing into a small side room. Myvi followed, curious, treading softly so her footsteps didn't echo on the old stone floor. She found Max standing inside a large disused stone fireplace, reaching up inside. But then he emerged, looking confused, as he re-entered the main room.

"Grandfather said that's where he found them – but they're not there. And the Brooch isn't even close to glowing. Why

91

have we come here?!"

"I don't know, Max – "

But then Myvi suddenly went quiet – the front door had creaked, and someone was coming in. Max and Myvi looked at each other in alarm.

"Quick – hide!" whispered Myvi, and dragged Max down behind some hay bales. Max looked down at his jumper and gasped, then tugged at Myvi's coat.

"What?!" hissed Myvi.

"The Brooch is glowing, Myvi..."

Now it was Myvi's turn to gasp.

Max peered out and saw to his horror that whoever it was, was coming towards them. It was a man, wearing a long heavy coat, that much Max could see, but nothing else, as he was silhouetted in the moonlight coming through the window opposite. They both held their breath as the man approached, but he went to go straight past them and towards the side room they'd just been in. But as he passed, Max gave an involuntary gasp. He'd seen the man's face.

The man stopped suddenly, just the other side of the hay bales. He reached inside his coat, and pulled out a torch and shone it towards them.

"Alright, come out, whoever you are." It was said quietly, but forcefully.

Max and Myvi slowly stood up, and now it was the man's turn to gasp.

"Grandfather...?!" said Max in disbelief.

He was a few years younger than when Max had last 'seen' him, the night he died and came to him in the dream, Fetch, whatever it was, but there was no mistaking him.

"Max...?" said Percy, looking closely at Max. "Quickly - where have you come from? How old are you?"

"Fourteen."

"Huh - you were ten when I saw you this morning! What are you doing here?"

"We've destroyed The Ring and The Coin, Percy," said Myvi, looking very nervously at the old wooden box in the old man's hands. "And we're here to destroy The Brooch. But it didn't take us to its Origin Point, it brought us here."

Max's grandfather suddenly stopped, and stared at them in horror, and especially at The Brooch on Max's jumper, which was now beginning to glow and hum like neither of the other two had ever done.

"This *is* an Origin Point Max – this is where I found the Majyga. But later I realised that Bacon couldn't have left them here, because the Priory wasn't founded until after his time. So someone had to have put them here for me to find them – i.e., me. Which is why..."

Percy slowly opened the wooden box, to reveal all three Majyga, then pulled The Book from his pocket.

"But how can The Ring and The Coin be here? We destroyed them...!"

Max looked down at his jumper, but The Brooch was no longer there. He felt in his duffle coat pocket – The Book was gone as well. Max saw his Grandfather's Brooch and Book glow, then dim again.

"That's why The Brooch brought you here," said Percy. "So that you *couldn't* destroy it, and so the Majyga could be together again."

But then, after a deathly quiet pause, suddenly there was a crack so loud it shook the walls around them, and a great light shone through the windows. Max rushed across the room to look out.

"What is it Max?" yelled Myvi.

"There's nothing there!"

"What do you mean nothing?!"

"I mean, *nothing* – no buildings, no roads, no trees: no world!"

Myvi glared at Percy.

"What's happened?! Where are we?!"

93

Max's grandfather hung his head, sighed, then looked up at Myvi.

"We have caused a crack in Time."

*

In the woods, at Ham Hill, a great roar went up as Rex flickered between his three states – Gurt Dog, Tutor, and Ancient British King. He had missed his chance – he had taken his eye off Max, and now the moment was lost. Ham Hill, everything - past, present, future - had just stopped.

*

"What happened there?!"

All but one monitor had suddenly gone blank, and even Stenton's was only showing white light. With his C.O. looking urgently over his shoulder, Gareth's fingers were a blur on the console, but with no result. With the exception of Stenton in Bed 4, the Dreamers had all simultaneously relaxed, and gone into dreamless sleep.

But an eerie sound was now coming from the speakers, at first like a quiet squeaking, as if a mouse was behind a wall, but then it began to build, and build, until it became a deafening all-pervading screeching, like a hundred fingernails being scraped down a blackboard. Gareth pressed Bed 4's 'speak' button.

"Talk to me Nick – what's going on? Where are you?"

There was nothing, for a moment, but then Stenton's body twitched slightly in his bed, and an image of rough plastered stone wall flickered into life on his monitor.

"I don't know. I followed them into the grounds of Parsonage Farm, then it all went weird."

"What's that noise?!"

"I don't know, but it can't be good."

CHAPTER ELEVEN

"What's happening?!" yelled Max, his hands over his ears.

"The Anhrefnau are coming!" Percy yelled back.

"The what?!" Max shouted.

"The Chaos Bringers - arm yourselves!"

Percy held his arm out straight, closed his eyes, and suddenly his hand was holding a sword.

"Quickly – into the middle, back to back! They will be upon us at any moment!"

Max held out his own arm, and in an instant was holding his own sword. Percy grabbed them both and pulled them into the middle of the room so they each had their back to the others, ready for wherever the attack came from.

"Come on Myvi," said Percy. "You know how to do this!"

"Me?!" said Myvi. "But, *I'm* not a Traveller..."

"Yes Myvi, you are," said Percy. "Have you not realised yet?"

Myvi stared at Percy, but then suddenly her full memory flooded back, as if something had blown away the final piece from the dam.

"Think back to the past, see a sword, bring it to you!"

"Come on Myvi," said Max. "You can do it!"

Myvi shrugged, and held out her arm. She breathed out, and concentrated. Within a few moments, the otherworldly screeching was joined by the dreadful noise of war as in the corner of her eye Myvi saw a battle, Cavaliers in desperate hand-to-hand fighting with Cromwell's Roundheads, all around her. A shot rang out, and a Royalist soldier fell, his sword flying into the air, and into Myvi's outstretched hand.

And just in time - the Anhrefnau had broken through.

They came through the walls, pulling themselves through from their dimension to this, like they were pushing through a viciously thick hedge. But then, one by one, they were there, circling Percy, Max and Myvi, waving before them their short spindly swords, barely more than knives. Their teeth-filled

mouths, disproportionately big for their rounded, big-eared hairless heads, were drooling in anticipation of the killing to come, their short, thin, scaly bodies and their long thin arms and legs all poised, waiting for the moment to begin it.

"What are they?!" said Max, his sword out before him, daring the things to attack, pointing from one to another – there were a dozen at least there now – as they circled.

"They live in the depths of Annwn," said his grandfather, "just waiting for the chance to disrupt Fate, and bring disorder to Time."

"But what do they want?!" said Myvi, stabbing out at one of them, who reeled back, hissing.

"To kill us."

"I kinda guessed that," said Myvi, stabbing at another.

"It's not our time to die," said Percy, slashing one of the Anhrefnau's swords out of its hand, sending it scurrying back to retrieve it. "If they kill us, they will change the future."

"But anyone can do that, surely," said Max, swiping at another of the circling fiends. "Every decision we make changes the future."

"No Max, it doesn't – the future is set. Our every movement, every movement of every molecule is known in advance, by The High Guardians. The Anhrefnau delight in messing things up."

And then, as if one of them had silently sent a signal to the others, they attacked.

Max slashed and slashed as the Anhrefnau launched themselves at them relentlessly, but it was no good - they were too fast, too acrobatic, too much in synch with each other. But then something clicked in Max's brain. He remembered having a sword in his hand before, remembered the training he had received in that year-long week four years ago, remembered how instinctive it had become – and remembered how to kill.

Max leapt out of the defensive triangle and launched him-

self at one Anhrefn then another. In seconds one had lost its sword, another had lost its arm, and another its head. Max didn't stop to think, nothing in his head but attack, and survival. And then Myvi was with him.

"Alright Max!" she said, grinning as she despatched a Anhrefn that threw itself out of the wall sword first. It hit the floor, cut in half before it even had the chance to land a blow. Spinning round, she took another's head off its shoulders without even looking. "Come on Anhrefnau – you can do better than that!"

Percy was holding his own as well, dispatching Anhrefn after Anhrefn – but still they came, pouring out of the walls like wasps whose nest has been disturbed.

"They just keep coming!" yelled Max.

"Let 'em come!" Myvi yelled back, running another through.

But then it was if the walls were black with emerging Anhrefnau.

"Oh-oh," said Myvi, her head snapping round. "I think we're in trouble..."

But then someone leapt into the room, and within seconds the floor was covered in dead Anhrefnau, slain by the automatic fire that spat from his British Army issue SA80 assault rifle.

"Seriously, what's with the swords, Percy?"

The assault was suddenly over – what few Anhrefnau were left alive fled back through the walls. Percy looked at the new arrival and smiled wearily.

"Nicholas. Good to see the TRD is still on top of things."

Percy looked around, as if looking for a CCTV camera.

"Major, if you're watching, thank you. That was close."

Max looked at Nick, trying not to grin.

"Machine gun. Why didn't *I* think of that?" said Max. "But how did Time let you in here? It's an Origin Point isn't it – *the* Origin Point. And you too, Grandfather..."

97

"We have all been allowed in because you broke through Time's barriers, Max."

Everyone spun round, to see a tall, rugged man in monks' robe and haircut standing before them, a shotgun pointed right at them.

"Bacon!" Percy wondered why he wasn't surprised.

"Good evening to all of you. Put the gun down please, Stenton."

Nick did what he was told, and placed his weapon carefully on the floor.

"Now kick it over to me."

Again, Nick did as he was told.

Max's grandfather looked at the man before him with some confusion. That morning, in his time, they had been on the same side, showing the ten-year-old Max the sights of History. But this was obviously a different Time Path, and they were on different sides now.

"What happened to you, Roger?" said Percy, still confused.

"He turned, Grandfather," said Max. "There was a battle, on Ham Hill. He unleashed Annwn on the world – but you stopped him."

"I did?"

"Yes Percy, you and those infernal dogs."

"What do you want, Roger?"

"The Majyga, of course. And The Book. I have been imprisoned, in the dark bowels of Annwn, my mind screaming for revenge – but by your actions here you have freed me, old man. Time stands still, and my destiny begins anew. Now, give me the Majyga."

But the old man just laughed.

"You will never have them."

"Very well," said Bacon, pointing his shotgun at Max's grandfather. "Goodbye, Percy."

Bacon fired, but Percy suddenly vanished, to appear behind him, grabbing the shotgun before Bacon knew what

was happening and sending it flying back into time. Bacon whirled around and lashed out at the old man with his fist, but again, Percy vanished, to reappear immediately to Bacon's left, sending him flying with a blow of his own.

"I was always quicker than you, Roger."

"Maybe," said Bacon, jumping to his feet with a teenager's agility. "But you were younger then. Let us play, old man."

"Grandfather, no!"

"Don't worry Max, he'll soon be back in his chains."

Without warning, Myvi ran and slashed at Bacon with her sword, but he conjured up a shield from history and swatted her aside, sending her flying into the wall behind Max and Nick.

"Stay away!" Percy yelled. "I have this!"

Max went to launch himself at Bacon as well, but Nick grabbed him and pulled him back.

"No, Max," he said, in a tone that told Max he knew what he was doing. "I've seen your grandfather do this many times – he doesn't need any help from you."

So Max, Myvi and Nick watched from the shadows as the two old Travellers circled each other like two Wild West gunfighters, each waiting for the other to make their first move.

It was Bacon who went first, bringing forth a two headed flail and swinging the studded iron balls at Percy, but the old man countered with a plain wooden staff, wrapping the flail's chains around it and dragging Bacon to the ground with the momentum, before conjuring up a double-headed axe and swinging it down towards Bacon's neck, but Bacon was no longer on the floor, he was behind Percy, running at him with a Civil War pike. Percy wheeled round just in time, and grabbed the end of the pike, using Bacon's speed against him to throw him off his feet and into the end wall.

Bacon picked himself up, panting, and holding his hand up.

"I see you are still quick, old man."

Percy was panting too, truth be told.

"You haven't lost any of your speed either Roger. Can we not settle this another way?"

"No. I will have the Majyga, if I have to kill you for them, Tovey. I *will* fulfil my destiny, and the world *will* be mine!"

"No, Roger, it won't," said Percy, causing a ton of twentieth century animal feed to be transferred to the floor above, while bringing the sixteenth century false ceiling crashing down on top of Bacon amid a cloud of dust, and plaster, and food pellets.

Max went to his grandfather as he sank to his knees before the pile of debris that covered his adversary, coughing as the dust flew around the now enlarged room.

"Grandfather, are you all right?"

"Still, you can't call me Grandpa?" said Percy, as Max helped him to his feet.

"I'm sorry... Grandpa," said Max. "I, I have so many questions..."

"They can wait Max. Here..."

Percy took the box that contained the Majyga from his coat, and handed it to Max.

"You must have these. You must destroy them again, I'm afraid."

Max took the box and opened it, looking on the three small, but so powerful objects, and took The Book, which was the key to their use, and put it in his inside pocket again.

"But why me?"

Percy looked long at his Grandson, and smiled fondly.

"Ask your father, Max..."

"What do you mean, my – "

But Max's question was cut off by an eruption from underneath the pile of ceiling plaster and animal food.

"Those are mine, old man!" said Bacon, injured, woozy, but very much still alive. He threw himself at Percy, and with a conjured length of fence post, knocked him unconscious to

the floor, before drawing a dagger and holding it to Percy's throat. Nick dived for his gun, still lying on the floor, but with a wave of his hand Bacon sent him skidding across the floor to crash into the wall, knocking him unconscious too. Myvi charged once more at Bacon with her sword, but he easily deflected her, sending her flying into the pile of debris.

"Give me the box and The Book or he dies." Bacon glared at Max. Max knew he had no choice. He closed the box, and slid it along the floor towards Bacon, then reached inside his coat for the book.

In the corner, Nick came round, saw what was about to happen, and ran for Max.

"No Max...! Major, push The Button - NOW!"

As the box reached Bacon, and he picked it up, so Nick reached Max and grabbed his arm.

As reality was ripped apart around them, as the walls of the Priory faded to a fine mist, and as all there floated apart, their separate destinies beckoning, Max reached out desperately for Myvi, but both she and Percy were drifting away from him, screaming in desperation as they were washed away by the seas of Time.

"MYVI! NOOOOOO!!" screamed Max.

And then all became the most dark.

*

"Welcome back, Max," said Major Willoughby. "The world, as you knew it, is no longer there."

*

PART TWO

CHAPTER TWELVE

Below St. Michael's Hill, was only mist. Clouds were halt-ed in their journey, the bare tree branches motionless, and no birds sang. The world stood still, Time suspended. In the middle of the hill, the Tower no longer stood, in its place only grass. In this Time Path, it had never been built.

"What have you done, Blaiddud? The boy has changed ev-erything!"

Around the circumference of the hill's summit, their huge eyes glowing red as fire, stood nine massive white dogs, the Guardians of the Hills, and of Time.

As chief among them the Guardian of Caer Glasdun King Locrin spoke, the Gurt Dogs at once morphed into their Ancient British selves, eight Kings and one Queen, each in tunic, robe and crown, and each seated on an ornate stone throne, as if statues come to life.

The Council was assembled.

"I am at fault, my Lord," said King Blaiddud, "for the boy eluded me – I did not see his intentions until it was too late. He showed initiative, at least..."

"And that initiative has rent Time in two, and brought about a new world! How could you not have foreseen this?!"

King Blaiddud hung his head, then looked up again at his ancestor and fellow Guardian.

"His confidence had been shattered by his previous experi-ence, my Lord. I had not expected him to recover so quickly."

"And you still believe he is The One?" This time King Rhun spoke, once Blaiddud's father.

"I do, my Lord," said Blaiddud. "It will be different this time. Last time I underestimated Bacon. But in this new Time Path he is no longer a force."

"Maybe not, my son," said King Rhun. "But this new Path is very different and very terrible. And in it the boy does not exist!"

"And yet he does," said Blaiddud. "I can feel him. He is outside of here somehow, but exist he does. He will find a way back."

"We cannot allow it!" said King Mynyr. "It is an abomination – he will break the very fabric of Time itself! And as for Bacon, he may not play a part in this Path, yet he is still imprisoned in the deepest dungeons of Annwn, ever searching for a means of escape. The boy may once more provide those means!"

King Locrin rose, and waved his descendants and fellow Guardians to be calm.

"It is futile to debate this until the boy returns to the world – *if* he returns."

*

Max looked around the TRD anxiously.

"What happened?"

"We don't *know,*" said the Major. "All we know is that the world has shifted onto an entirely different Time Path. We only just saved ourselves – who knows what the world is like out there."

"You don't know?!"

"No Max – we are outside Time now, in Limbo if you like. Who knows if we will ever return. We are hoping you will help."

Max suddenly panicked. "Where's Myvi?!"

"We don't know that either. It's possible she was thrown back to her own time, of course. If she was lucky."

"I have to go and find her!"

"I agree – but there's a problem. Here, let me show you."

Major Willoughby took Max out of the monitoring room, along a corridor, and down some stairs into what looked like an entrance hall. All in all the place had the feel of a doctor's surgery – it reminded Max a little of Dr. Llewellyn's practise,

in fact. As the Major reached for the front door handle he paused, and turned to Max.

"Now try not to be too alarmed at what you see out there. We're pretty sure it isn't real."

Major Willoughby opened the door, and suddenly the air was full of screaming, and all around were flames; great, billowing nebula of fire, like they were in an unformed Universe, flaming gas clouds light years across swirling ferociously as stars formed cataclysmically inside them.

"We need you to go out there, Max," Willoughby shouted over the apocalyptic noise. "We can't - but you can, and then we can follow you, and get back into Time, whatever it looks like now."

"I'm not going out *there!*" Max yelled back. Willoughby shut the door again, and the screaming stopped.

"You must, Max - you must find a way to change things back, get the old Time Path back. If you stay here, we will all slowly cease to exist - including you. We've lost one Dreamer already..."

"Wait a minute," said Max, his mind full of competing nagging questions. "The Cross - isn't it at Waltham Abbey? Why couldn't Grandpa just go and get it?"

"Because it isn't there - it disappeared in the sixteenth century. All your grandfather knew was that it no longer exists on this Earth, but is somewhere else, protected by Time. But not even he could find it."

Max decided to deal with that one later - other more pressing questions were nagging now.

"OK, so why can't *you* go out?"

"They won't let us."

"They? Who's 'They'?"

"We don't know. There are voices... Only you can help us Max. You will be safe - they have promised it."

"They *have?!*"

"Yes Max - they've been asking for you."

"But..." Max's head was in a spin. As if in a daze, he went to the door and opened it again, and again, there was screaming, and fire.

"Come to us, Max..." It wasn't just one voice, but many, all in deep, calm, almost soothing harmony, somehow perfectly clear amid the screaming choir. Max had a nagging thought in the back of his mind that the voices reminded him of something, or someone, but...

"You will be safe, I promise..."

This time it was just one voice.

"Rex...?"

"Yes, Max."

Max closed his eyes, and tentatively put one foot outside the door. He felt around – there was solid ground out there. Not daring to look, the screams of Limbo drowning out even Max's never-ending thoughts, he stepped out of the door.

And then the fire and screaming vanished, leaving Max on a misty hill top, a huge white dog looming over him and smiling.

"Rex!"

Max couldn't but hug him, but as he pulled away, he gasped. Rex was not alone. Around the hill stood eight other Gurt Dogs, their flaming red eyes all staring at him.

Rex returned to his place in the circle around the edge of the top of the hill, and as Max stared at the giant dogs in astonishment, they morphed into their human forms, their original human forms, and now nine ancient Monarchs sat on nine ancient thrones.

"Who *are* you?!" Max was staring particularly at 'Rex' now. He was younger than when he last saw him – in fact none of them looked more than twenty. Like all the others, he wore a floor-length white robe and cloak, a jewelled sword hanging from his belt, and an ornate bronze crown on his head.

"Are you a King...?" asked Max incredulously. Probably not the correct form of address, but when Max forgot to edit

what he was about to say in his head he wasn't good at correct form.

"We all ruled once, Max," said Blaiddud, "and now we are the Guardians of the Nine Hills. We are the descendants of the High Guardian Brutus, the first King of these isles, and the Overlord of Time. I am King Blaiddud..."

Blaiddud gestured at each of the Kings as he named them. Max knew he knew the names, but for a moment he couldn't place them. Locrin son of Brutus, Madawg, Gwendoleu, Mynyr, Efroc, Brutus Darian-glas, Lleon, and Blaiddud's father Rhun Baladr-bras. But then Max remembered – they were the mythical first Ancient Kings of the Mediaeval Welsh 'Chronicle of the Kings of Britain'. Mythical, and fictitious. And yet here they were, all but one bowing to him.

"Why do you bow to the boy?!" said King Mynyr angrily. "He brings us nothing but trouble."

"Because we are in his hands, my Lord," said King Locrin sternly. "You would do well to pay your respect."

"I will do no such thing!" spluttered King Mynyr.

"You *will!*" The ground shook as Locrin spoke, and forced Mynyr to bow to Max against his will.

Max felt strange, a growing sense of empowerment welling up inside. Max had never felt empowered in his life, except when playing video games. But inside, Max now realised that his normal rules no longer applied – his normal rules being mostly hiding from the world and not making waves. But what was it that Locrin had said? We are in his hands – his hands. Whatever this new world was, it seemed to depend on him, almost revolving around him. Previously, that would have scared him so much he wouldn't have come out of his room. But now, his words, his actions, seemed to command some kind of respect. Just like before.

"Enough," said the High Guardian, getting up from his throne and approaching Max. "It is time that you return to the world, boy. But be warned – it is not what it was. Your

109

actions have brought such a change that we fear for Annwn itself. You must restore the world that you once knew or we are all lost."

"*Me?* But how?!"

"You will know once you are there," said King Locrin.

So many questions were whirling around in Max's head he didn't know where to start. The all-powerful Guardians of Time needed *him* to sort the world out. Him - Max Tovey. Fourteen-year-old Max Tovey. The teenage anxieties weren't quite buried yet.

"I can't do it on my own. I need Myvi. Where is she?"

The Guardians passed glances between themselves.

"Perhaps he is not ready after all..." said Queen Gwendoleu.

"He is ready – I know it," said King Blaiddud. "But, perhaps he would be best aided in his endeavours with the girl by his side."

"Very well, Blaiddud," said King Locrin, "let it be done, and let us be gone."

"Wait a minute," said Max. "What about this Cross I'm supposed to find? *You* must know where it is, surely?"

"We do not," said Blaiddud. "But we do know it is not in this new time. We would sense it if it was. If you can return the world to the old time, *then* you can try to find it."

"Good fortune to you boy," said Locrin. "The future, and the past, is in your hands now."

As the ancient rulers rose from their thrones as one, Max started to panic.

"Wait – you can't leave it like that! You, you said..." - what was it he'd said? Oh yes – "you said 'my actions': what have I done? *How* is the world changed? What do I have to *do?!*"

But they said no more, and, with a flourish of their robes, vanished into the mist, leaving Max alone on the hilltop, below him now a vista that he recognised only too well. The flooded fields, the occasional pocket of raised wooden stilt houses, and in the distance, the vast hill fort with its miles of

wooden palisades looming up out of the waterlogged Somer-set Levels meant only one thing. He was back at first century Ham Hill.

*

CHAPTER THIRTEEN

The walls of Caer Fandwy rang with laughter and song, as the great and the beautiful of its people feasted. Far below its vast, lofty walls of shimmering golden stone that follow the hill's undulating contours the fields glittered, and the trees and flowers waved balletically in the soft, ethereal breeze that tempers the eternal sunshine of Annwn, the world within a world where live all those that have gone before, that lives alongside the world of mortals, their sadness that they will never know its beauty until their time is over.

But all is not beauty in Annwn, and Mynyr, once High King of the mortal world and now Guardian of Caer Ochren, was not there to feast nor to sing. He wasn't noticed as he slipped through a small door and began to descend a narrow stone staircase. The steps wound down and down, twisting and turning until finally they widened, and opened out onto a natural stone platform above the torch-lit gloom of The Depths, where there is only cold, and the all-pervading sound of the moaning, wailing and screaming of the Demons and the Damned. Mynyr paused briefly at the bottom of the steps to gaze out into the seemingly endless and bottomless cavern that stretched beyond sight into the distance, and below. This was not a place he would normally even contemplate visiting, but he had no choice. Annwn was in danger, and he did not trust his fellow Guardians' plan of action. The boy must be stopped.

Below him stretched myriad stone staircases, each winding perilously down into the countless murky shadow worlds of despair where lay captive the lost dark souls and their Demon tormentors. Mynyr took a breath, and set off downwards into the screaming gloom, either side of him an endless drop into the sickening void.

The staircase itself split into countless others on its way down, but Mynyr knew where he was going. In the end he

found himself at a small cavern, but was taken aback at what he saw, for here were no Demon guards, no tortured screams, only a man, sitting at a wooden writing desk.

"My Lord Mynyr," said the man, turning. "To what do I owe this pleasure?"

Mynyr looked curiously at the man. He was old, his beard long and grey – unlike every other inhabitant of Annwn.

"You wonder at my countenance, my Lord. It is the misfortune of the dead that once in Annwn they are forever young again, without the wisdom of age. It is my misfortune that when I was cast into this place, I had grown old, but had not yet died. I am spirit, and yet I am flesh also."

"But why are you not in chains?"

But Mynyr soon had his answer, for as he approached, he was suddenly thrown back by a cloud of snarling teeth and slashing claws that vanished as quickly as it had appeared.

"*They* are my chains, my Lord. Now, what may I deduce from your presence? Hmm, I sense discord – you are not here officially I suspect...?"

As Mynyr told the imprisoned philosopher of the terrible new future that had been created, Bacon's expression remained unchanged and unsurprised, even when Mynyr told him that, in the new past, he had never learned to Travel, and had died unrecorded by history.

"And yet here I am, my Lord," said Bacon, still expressionless, "my memory of a life that seems now gone still intact. Now, what do you want of me?"

"I want you to kill the boy – but in the past, so that this new future shall not exist."

"I see. But why can you not do this yourself?"

"I cannot do it – Time will not allow it."

"So why would it allow me?"

"Because in this new path, you as a Time Traveller do not exist. You will go unnoticed, for a while at least."

"So, will you release me then?"

"You know that I cannot – it is beyond my powers. But I can show you a way to be there in spirit at least."

"Intriguing – do come in. And before you protest, I know you can – I know what you are."

King Mynyr took a step towards Bacon, and again the Demonic force field appeared, but this was his plan – to size up his enemy. With a swirl of his cloak, High King became Gurt Dog, and roared deep and ferocious at Bacon's jailers, forcing them to retreat, screaming, allowing him into the cavern.

"What is it that you write, Bacon?" said Mynyr, who had remained in Gurt Dog form. He peered at the manuscript on the desk, which seemed to be some kind of illuminated work.

"Oh, a little something to while away the time, my Lord – it is merely a diary. Now, you were going to show me something...?

Mynyr nodded slightly, and gave out a long breath, and before them formed a cloud, which hung in the air, before clearing, to reveal a scene. It was Max, and ahead of him, the first century hill fort of Hamdun.

"I know the place well," said Bacon. "But how do I get there?"

"I will show you," said Mynyr, and now the scene changed, to another hill fort, but this time dead lay all around, as two Roman officers surveyed the scene.

"It is a year after the Romans invaded, and they are now conquering the South West of the Isle, destroying all resistance. Hamdun will be next. You recognise these men?"

"Of course," said Bacon smiling. "That is Vespasian, commander of the Second Legion, and beside him, his second in command. It was his mind that I took over the last time."

"And you shall do it again," said Mynyr, "only this time you shall win, and the old Time Path shall be restored."

"Except that I have a better way, my Lord..." said Bacon.

"And what is that?" said Mynyr, turning to Bacon as the image vanished. But Bacon had vanished as well.

"Bacon! Where are you?!" roared the Gurt Dog Mynyr looking around wildly. He *cannot* have escaped!

"I am inside you, my Lord," came a voice inside Mynyr's head, "and I shall conquer you. I was powerful when I was imprisoned here, and I am twice as powerful now."

"Nooooo!!" It was as much of a roar as a scream, and as two spirits battled for one body, that body flickered between forms - King, Philosopher, Gurt Dog - and lightning flashed and unearthly screams echoed around the cavern as the spirits distorted, twisting and struggling desperately for dominance.

And then it was over, and the Gurt Dog lay on its side, panting with exhaustion. Slowly it raised itself up and shook its head, before giving out a great, rumbling roar that once again sent the Demon jailers scrambling away, allowing the massive hound out of the cavern before closing behind it.

"And so it begins, again."

*

CHAPTER FOURTEEN

The sun was low in the sky and what felt, to Max, like an autumnal chill was settling in as he sat and stared out from what would one day be called St. Michael's Hill towards the giant Eastern gate of Hamdun Fort. Max guessed it was autumn anyway, as leaves were still on the trees and bushes in the fields below. The slopes of the great hill, however, had no trees, as they would one day have, but covered only in bracken and small bushes, so as not to give potential attackers any cover. And as Max knew only too well, attackers were coming. He guessed the inhabitants of the fort knew this too, because the beacon was burning at the high end of the hill where the War Memorial would one day stand, and down below hundreds upon hundreds of people were heading towards the safety of the fort from all around. Max's plan was to mingle with them and get into the fort that way. But as he went to stand up, the world started to spin, and he stumbled, and sat down again with a thump. His head was suddenly full of noise, and the enormity of his situation suddenly flooded over him. What are you doing here?! What have you just done?! Did that all really happen?! The Romans are coming for goodness sake – you're fourteen, you can't fight *Romans!* Max tried to stand again, but his legs were jelly - but worse, as he peered down the slope of the hill, the world started spinning again and he had to almost throw himself backwards to stop from fainting and falling down the hill.

"Stop it!" he yelled to himself, as he shook his head violently to try to stop it spinning. He started deep breathing, in through the nose, out through the mouth, in, out, in, out. He knew what this was – this was a panic attack. He hadn't had one of these since... since before he went on the medication. But of course he wasn't *on* the medication any more.

"Come on, stop it you idiot!" He had found that talking out loud was often a good way of stopping these attacks – if you

live in your head too much, as he did, your head can start to play tricks with you, start putting thoughts in you that make no sense, but which increase the sense of panic. Shouting out loud helped distract him from them.

"Come on Max, get a grip – it's just a panic attack, you've had them before, you *know* how to deal with them."

And now, slowly, the panic began to subside. Max tried standing again, and it was a bit better. He looked over the side of the steep hill, and the world wasn't swirling around nearly so much.

"Come on, you can do this – you *have* to do this! You have to save Myvi from the Romans! Come ON!!"

He'd initially dismissed the idea of Travelling into the fort, in case he materialised in front of someone and they took him for a Demon or a witch or something. He could take someone's clothes, but that would involve knocking them out, and Max wasn't sure he could actually bring himself to do that – and anyway, whoever's clothes he took would eventually raise the alarm. He had no choice – he'd *have* to Travel there, to Myvi's hut. If he could remember which one it was.

Max relaxed his body, breathed out, and let his focus blur. In his mind's eye he began to see the inside of the fort, and the hundreds of wattle, daub and thatch roundhouses filling much of the first of the three huge fields in neat, orderly rows, like a first century housing estate. People were coming in from the other fields, spades, hoes and rakes over their shoulders from a long day's farming. Max thought he saw Joseph outside one of the huts, but the vision began to fade.

"Come on Max, concentrate!" Max berated himself, and the vision became clearer again. Now he was seeing inside the hut, and remembered it, all the familiar possessions, especially Joseph's long grey cloak. This *must* be the one.

Max took a deep breath, and exhaled slowly as he zoomed in on the hut, picturing the inside in his mind, the simple straw mattresses, the fire, and the large cooking pot hang-

ing from the roof in the middle, and then Max breathed out heavily, closed his eyes, hung his head and held his arms out as if about to dive. As he opened his eyes again, reality bent and swirled around him like a dust storm in a fish-eye camera lens and Max was sucked through the vortex that centred on Myvi's hut, and then he was *in* Myvi's hut, trying to keep his balance, but he couldn't, and fell over onto a pile of metal plates, causing them to clatter across the hut. Max held his breath in fear of someone having heard, but no-one came. He breathed out, and sat down on Myvi's bed. The fire was still going, the warm, homely smell of stew emanating from the cooking pot hanging over it. Max suddenly realised he was hungry, very hungry – he did some quick mental calculations, and realised *why* he was feeling so hungry – he hadn't eaten for a day in *real* time, since he was last here in fact, which in theory was tomorrow here, although all that could have changed now. He hadn't slept either, for that matter. That's the problem with Travelling through Time – you lose track of it. Max took a bowl and ladled it full of stew, eating it in a couple of ravenous minutes, before his eyes could stay open no longer, and he fell fast asleep.

*

"Hey! What are you doing in my bed?!"

Max woke, slowly, and peered up at the person doing the shouting. It was Myvi, and Joseph was right behind her. They both looked puzzled, as did Max for a moment – Myvi was younger than when he'd last seen her. But then he woke up properly and remembered - this was 44AD, when they'd first met, when they were only ten.

"Oh, sorry Myvi," said Max. "I must have fallen asleep."

But Myvi and Joseph just stared at him, both now looking quite alarmed.

Max quickly realised why, and said it again, but this time in

Old British. But still they stared. And then Myvi screamed.

"HELP!!"

Multiple options ran simultaneously through Max's head, none of them good. As Joseph drew his short sword, without thinking Max grabbed the grey cloak hanging from the wall and threw it over Joseph before barging him over and racing out of the hut – straight into the arms of two large armed men.

"Grab him Owain!" snarled the smaller of the two men. He was still much bigger than Max though, and looked a *lot* stronger.

"Got him Gwydion," said the larger man, grabbing Max by the arms and lifting him off the ground while the other put his face right up to Max's and glared.

"Who are you? Where have you come from?"

"My name is..." In a split second Max realised he couldn't give them his real name – Max was originally short for Maximus, a Roman name.

"...Blaiddud!" It was the first name that came into his head. "I've come from Caer Maidun – the Romans are coming!"

"We know they are," said the one called Gwydion. "Why do you think the beacon is lit?"

"And anyway," growled Owain, still holding Max off the ground, "the survivors from Caer Maidun and all the other forts the Romans have attacked got here *days* ago - why are you only here *now?*"

"I think he's a Roman spy, Gwydion," sneered Owain.

"Yes, I think you're right Owain," said Gwydion with a nasty grin as he leant even closer to Max's face. "And you know what we do with spies, don't you?"

"N-no..." stuttered Max, although he had a fairly good idea.

"Put him down, Owain – we'll take him to the Chieftain," said Gwydion, and with that the two men grabbed one of Max's arms each, and marched him away.

"Myvi! Joseph! Help me! *Myvi!!*" But she did nothing. Max

sighed, and almost began to cry, knowing that despite everything they'd been through, *this* Myvi didn't know him. Max slumped as he was taken away. Myvi was the only real friend he'd ever had, and now that was all gone.

Myvi, for her part, just stood at the door of their roundhouse, looking confused.

"How does he know our names, Myvanwyl?"

"I don't know, Grandda – maybe he *is* what they say, a spy?"

"But he is so young, only a few years older than you."

"You know what they say about the Romans – they stop at nothing."

But Myvi didn't look convinced. She stared after the boy as the two warriors took him towards the inner fortress in the distance, at the centre of the vast hill, where their Chieftain resided. And then she made up her mind.

"I think he needs help, Grandda."

Joseph looked at the young girl, and her resolute expression. He knew that even at ten years old she was rarely wrong about things. She had been through so much, since he had found her as a toddler under the bodies of her parents after the last great battle with the Belgae tribe. Ever since then, she had displayed an intelligence far beyond her years, and Joseph, wise as he was, had long come to trust her judgement. Joseph wasn't even her grandfather – he had rescued her from the slaughter and brought her up. He and his followers had only just arrived from Judea at that point, but something told him he had to look after her, and so he made his home at Hamdun. It was a good base from which to spread the Gospel. She knew all this, everyone knew this, but she still called him Grandda.

By the time they reached the Great Hall, the huge wood and thatch meeting place that dominated the inner fortress, there was already a large crowd surrounding Max and Chief Rhydderch. Looking past the Great Hall out over the northern spur of the hill, Max saw hundreds, possibly thousands of

people, a temporary camp of refugees from the Roman brutality, gathered here to make a last stand against the invaders at this, the greatest of all the ancient fortresses.

Joseph and Myvi pushed their way to the front; on seeing them, the Chieftain gave a slight bow of the head, and the crowd grew back slightly in deference to the old man.

"Good day, wise Joseph, Myvanwyl," said Rhydderch with some solemnity. "What have you to do with this spy?"

"He is not a spy, my Lord," said Joseph gently but forcibly.

"And yet he knows your names – maybe you are spies too, eh Arimathea?"

"My Lord..." But Rhydderch cut Joseph off with a wave and a half smile.

"I know you are not, Joseph – and yet it is still a puzzle, but one to which I may have the solution."

The Chieftain gave a slight gesture to Max's captors, at which Gwydion quickly drew a knife and held it at Max's throat, bringing a startled cry from the increasingly nervous Time Traveller. Of course, there was an easy way out – he could just Travel his way out of trouble, but as long as this warrior kept hold of him, he'd have to take him with him, and then he'd be a very *frightened* warrior with a knife to his throat.

"Now boy," said Rhydderch in perfect Latin, "if you do not reply to me, I shall have your throat cut."

"No please – I can explain!" said Max in alarm, also in Latin.

"Aha!" exclaimed the Chieftain, speaking British again. "So the boy speaks Latin!"

The crowd closed in again, their mood darkening, sure now they had a spy amongst them.

"But so do you!" said Max indignantly.

"Ah, but I am a Chieftain – it is my job to know the language of my enemy. You are but a boy."

"Leave him alone!" said Myvi. No-one had seen her sneak

around behind Gwydion, but now her dagger was at *his* throat. The advantage of being a ten-year-old girl is that no-one expects you to do things like that, although in Myvi's case they shouldn't have been surprised.

"Myvi!" said Max in relief. "You *do* know me!"

"No," said Myvi. "But I will not let them kill you for being something you are not."

"All right Myvanwyl," said the Chieftain, "put the dagger down – you could hurt someone."

"I know I could," said Myvi in a growl a ten-year-old shouldn't be able to produce. But the showdown was suddenly interrupted by a cry.

"The Romans are here!" One of the Outer Gate Guards was now racing towards them from the inner fortress gate.

"How many?" yelled Rhydderch.

"About twenty!" the Guard yelled back as he came nearer. "At the South Gate!"

"Twenty?" said Rhydderch curiously, almost to himself. "An advance party maybe?"

"Probably," said Joseph. "They must not find me here – if they did, they would surely crucify me as they did our Lord."

"I know, Joseph – do not worry, they shall not find you," said Rhydderch. "Well, we had better go and see what they want I suppose. All right Myvanwyl, put Gwydion down, Gwydion, let the boy go." The Chieftain gestured at Max's captor, and Max was released. But now he was staring at Joseph.

"*What* did he call you, Joseph?"

Joseph looked confused.

"He called you Arimathea! *You*...are Joseph of *Arimathea?* Who took Jesus down from the cross?"

"Yes, but..." said Joseph, even more confused now.

"Why did I never know that? After all this time?!"

"But we have only just met," said Joseph.

But before he could say anything else, Max had a stab of realisation that he was about to give himself away, and quick-

ly went quiet.

"Never mind all that," said Rhydderch. "Right you," he said, growling at Max, "*you* come with me. Gwydion, follow me to the gate, and bring the Guard. Owain, make things ready."

*

CHAPTER FIFTEEN

Rhydderch took Max's arm firmly, but not roughly, and marched him down the hill from the Great Hall towards a chariot that sat by Joseph's small wooden chapel next to the gate, where one day Max's grandfather's Inn would stand. Climbing in, he stood Max by his side as he took the reins. The two ponies snuffled as the bits pulled back against their mouths.

As Gwydion mounted his own chariot, he gestured at a group of men who had followed them.

"Chieftain's Guard, follow me!"

The men, all with bows and arrow quivers on their backs and swords at their belts, leapt onto horses tethered by the gate, before following their Chieftain and his two chief warriors out of the inner fortress and towards the South Gate.

"Hey, wait for me!" said Myvi, vaulting up onto a large grey horse's back.

"Myvi, no..." said Joseph, but he knew protest was futile.

"*Yes*, Grandda," said Myvi firmly. "Yaaah!" Myvi slapped the horse's rear and shot out of the fortress. She quickly caught up with the others, drawing alongside the Chieftain and Max.

As they raced towards the South Gate, Max looked at Myvi almost with amusement. She was exactly as he remembered. In the great battle that now hadn't happened, but which now may be about to happen again, she had fought as fiercely as any man, accounting for many Roman soldiers, as well as a good number of Bacon's Demons.

"How do you know me?!" yelled Myvi.

"I can't explain, not now!" Max yelled back. "But I will, I promise!"

They reached the gate, at the very far tip of the great hill fortress, past the hundreds of roundhouses in the first field, past the countless cows, pigs and sheep that populated the middle

field, and along the path to the gate that split the final field of crops in two. They dismounted, and climbed the gatehouses, before filing out onto the crenellated wooden parapet that topped the giant iron-reinforced wooden gates. Max stood next to Chieftain Rhydderch, with Myvi on his other side, while the Guard stood either side, their bows aimed right at the Roman soldiers below.

There were two dozen of them, the setting autumn sun glinting off their perfectly polished armour. At their head were two soldiers on horseback, obviously officers, and the leader of them obviously very high ranking judging by the ornate decoration on his breast plate and the fur cloak hanging over his shoulders.

"Vespasian!" exclaimed Max under his breath.

"That's *Vespasian?!*" said Rhydderch, part in awe, part in alarm, but both were soon replaced by suspicion.

"How do you know, if you are not Roman...?"

"I saw him, at... Caer Maidun." It was easier than the truth, that he had seen him right here, in a past that no longer existed, and tomorrow, in a future that may or may not now happen.

"Hmmm..." The Chieftain obviously wasn't convinced.

But what was alarming Max more was not the General, but the man slightly behind him, obviously his Aide de Camp. He was there before as well, but the last time he had been taken over by Bacon. But it couldn't be, not this time. Rex had told him that Bacon, the Time Travelling Bacon, didn't exist in this Time Path.

"General Vespasian!" bellowed the Chieftain.

"You know me?" called the General.

"No, but your little spy here does!"

Rhydderch hoisted Max up by the back of his duffle coat and dangled him over the parapet. "Shall I give him back to you?"

"Noooo!" screamed Max involuntarily, then checked him-

self. He was frightened, but underneath he was fairly sure Rhydderch wasn't going to throw him over the edge.

"I do not know this boy," said Vespasian calmly. "We have come to discuss your surrender. I would highly advise you to let us in. If you do not, I will return with my Legion, burn your fortress to the ground, and leave not one of you alive."

Rhydderch sighed, let Max down, and gestured to the Gate Keepers. He knew only too well what had happened to Caer Maidun when they defied Vespasian's Second Legion. But Max caught him glancing a sly look at Gwydion as he gave the order. What was he up to?

"Let them in."

The huge tree trunk that barred the gates was lifted from its iron brackets, and as the gates were swung open, the Romans climbed the steep ramp that led to them, and entered, to be greeted by Rhydderch and his men, now down from the parapet, but still with bows drawn.

"Tell your men to lower their bows," said Vespasian calmly. "We do not intend violence, unless you seek it."

The Chieftain gestured to his men, and they relaxed their bows, but still kept hold of them, just in case.

"Are you the King of this castle?" asked Vespasian.

"We have no Kings here, General - I am Rhydderch, elected Chieftain of the people of Hamdun and its surrounds."

Vespasian saluted in the Roman way, putting his fist to his chest.

"Well, Chief Rhydderch, I am giving you formal warning that my Legion shall take your fortress. You have one day to gather your people and your belongings and leave. If you do not, well, I have already explained the consequences..."

"I am not disposed to leave, General," said Rhydderch with a smile.

Vespasian sighed, and gestured through the gate. As he did so, the air was suddenly full of the sound of feet marching, and wheels rolling.

"Rhydderch, what do you see out there?"

The Chieftain walked to the gate, and peered out. He already had an idea what he was going to see. From the trees at the other side of the fields, below the gate, now emerged the entire Roman Second Legion, thousands of battle-hardened soldiers and dozens upon dozens of giant Onegars, Ballistae, Battering Rams and Siege Towers.

Vespasian turned to the other officer.

"Tribune Bassianus, how many would you say we were?"

"A little over five thousand, General," said the officer.

"Impressive," said Rhydderch. "Five thousand you say?" The Chieftain turned to Gwydion. "Gwydion, how many do *we* have, all in all?"

"I'm not sure, my Lord," said Gwydion, trying to keep a straight face. "I'll ask. Owain!" he yelled across the field. "How many are we now?"

And then, from over the brow of the middle of the sloping field rose thousands of jeering, yelling and screaming warriors, all waving their weapons above their heads in defiance. Gwydion turned back to Rhydderch and Vespasian, who was scowling now.

"That many," he said matter-of-factly.

"You will not find us such an easy fight as Caer Maidun, General," said Rhydderch. "Men from all over the area are here now, eager to avenge your attacks on their homes. And God is on our side," said Rhydderch, deadly solemn now.

Vespasian angered. This new cult was causing enough problems in Rome, and he was determined to crush it here before it caught hold. They would revert to their old Gods soon enough.

"Your 'God' did not protect Caer Maidun, nor Eggardun, nor Pilsdun or the rest, and neither will he protect you, regardless of what the rebel Arimathea and his so-called Christians may have led you to believe. But have it your way, Rhydderch - we shall go, but we shall return, and we shall

destroy you, just like all the others."

Vespasian turned to go, but then turned back again, looking a little confused now.

"Oh, and I shall take the boy."

"What?" said Rhydderch. "So he *is* your spy then?"

Max looked at Vespasian struggling with his thoughts. He'd seen that before, when Time was being messed with. And then he saw it. Behind Vespasian, his number two Bassianus was flickering. It was almost imperceptible, as if someone had taken a few frames out of a film, and Max was the only one who spotted it. But then Max was the only other Time Traveller there. It took one to know one.

"Yes, it would seem... that he is..." said Vespasian, still looking a little confused.

"I'm *not* his spy," said Max between his teeth, pointing at the Commander. "And *that* man is not what he seems."

Bassianus dived for Max, but Max dodged out of the way.

"Grab him you idiots!" Bassianus yelled at the soldiers, but before they could move, the Chieftain's Guard had their bows aimed again, and Myvi had her dagger at Bassianus's throat.

"Leave him!" she snarled, but then Bassianus vanished, to reappear behind Rhydderch, his own dagger now at the Chieftain's throat. Everyone just stared in horror now, Romans and Britons alike. Everyone except Max of course.

"How did he do that?" said Gwydion, as shaken as the rest. "What is he?!"

"He is a Devil!" said some of the Roman soldiers.

"No, he's a Time Traveller," said Max. "Just like me." And with that, Max also vanished, to reappear behind Bassianus, holding a large rock. But before he could bring it down on his head, Bassianus vanished again, reappearing behind Max, his sword to his back.

"This is the end, Max," said Bassianus in modern English, and thrust the sword... into thin air.

"Bacon!" exclaimed Max, now opposite the possessed sol-

dier. "How did you escape Annwn?!"

"You'll never know!" said Bacon, swinging his sword at Max.

"Max, catch!" A sword flew through the air towards Max. He grabbed it just in time to parry the blow.

"Thanks Myvi!" said Max, then stopped and turned. If people were staring before, they were doing so doubly now, for there in the middle of them all stood Myvi - the fourteen year old Myvi.

"Myvi...?" said Max, also staring, but smiling. "How did *you* get here?"

"I don't know – I don't remember anything after the Priory. Time must have sent me home I guess – but look out!"

Bacon swung his sword down at Max again, but Max ducked the blow, and brought his own sword up underneath the Roman breast plate and into Bacon's stomach. Bacon staggered, and fell to his knees, but then looked up and smiled.

"You can't kill *me!*"

"No, but we can send you back to where you came from!" said the older Myvi as she stabbed her own sword down into the back of his neck. The body of Bassianus crumpled to the ground, but it wasn't over yet. From out of his body came what at first looked like steam, but then the steam took form, at first of Bacon, but then it changed to another – to Mynyr, the Guardian. As both Britons and Romans cowered in terror at the sight, unearthly screams flooded over the fields as the two spirits battled for supremacy. But this time the Guardian of Caer Ochren won.

As everyone stared in horrified disbelief, before Max now materialised Mynyr, in his human form.

"I apologise, Max," he said in a soft but deep voice. "I was wrong about you. I allowed my reason to be subverted by Bacon – I know now that he was manipulating me all along. But no longer – he is back in Annwn again now, and will trouble you no more. And now you must return to your own

time – what will happen here will happen. You have a greater task in hand."

And then, to a collective gasp from all, Mynyr swirled his cloak around him, and disappeared.

No-one was staring at Myvi more than Myvi herself, of course. The younger girl slowly approached her older self.

"Are we a Traveller in Time also?" said the younger Myvi.

The older Myvi smiled at her younger self. "Yes, we are."

"But how can we both be here?"

"I don't know – I suspect Time is a little confused. But probably not for much longer..." Then she turned to Max and smiled right into his eyes, and took his hand and squeezed it. "I thought I'd never see you again."

Max looked into Myvi's deep brown eyes and also smiled, if a little awkwardly. He still wasn't used to being liked by a girl. But, she was back, and that was all that mattered. But there were things to do now.

"Look, Myvi," said Max, turning to the ten-year-old Myvi, "we must go, but it's possible we may return, tomorrow. If we do, please try not to have me killed as a spy."

Despite everything, the young Myvi managed a little laugh.

Now it was the Chieftain's turn to pluck up courage.

"You say you journey through Time, boy..."

"Yes," said Max, smiling at him. "And yes, I know what will happen here. Do not fight – you will not win. Save yourself and your people."

"Sound advice," said Vespasian rather shakily. "We shall return tomorrow. And if you *are* here, boy," he said, glaring at Max, "Time Voyager or Demon or whatever you may be, I shall kill you."

And with that, the General turned and led his terrified men back out of the gate.

"Shall we?" said the older Myvi to Max.

*

131

It was dark when they got back to the Inn, and at first they didn't notice the differences. The building was the same, the view out over the Under Warren to East Stoke seemed the same. But something was different.

"They've taken all the outside tables away," said Max.

"There are no cars either," said Myvi, peering round at where the car park used to be. "Or car park..."

"And no light coming from the Inn," said Max.

"Curtains are drawn," said Myvi, looking at the window.

"Are we in the right time?" said Max. "It looks more like the Inn did in the nineteenth century."

Just then, they began to hear a loud rumbling noise in the distance, like an old propeller-driven plane, but much louder. And then they saw it.

"What's *that?!*" said Max, looking out over the fields below. It looked like an old-fashioned navy ship, all iron sheet and big rivets. Except it was flying. A searchlight lit up on its deck, which started scouring the land below it.

"What are you doing?! Get in here!" came a voice behind them. "Quickly, before they see you!"

"Who's 'they'?" said Max.

Max turned, to see a man silhouetted at the door of the Inn, beckoning desperately for them to go in.

"The Romans of course!" said the man, stepping out slightly. "Come on!"

Now Max saw him properly. He was thirty years younger, but it was most definitely his grandfather.

*

PART THREE

CHAPTER SIXTEEN

The Inn looked very different inside – before, the main bar was all one room, but now it was split into two smaller ones. Max's grandfather beckoned them through the right hand door, and they entered the bar. The fireplace was the same, and the stone floor, but that was about it. Behind the bar were just two wooden barrels, rather than the rows of metal ones, a few bottles standing next to them, and beside them, an old-fashioned manual till, with press-down typewriter-style keys. On the walls were oil lamps, the ceiling above them stained black with their smoke. Nowhere was there any evidence of electricity.

"I told you – it's the nineteenth century," whispered Max.

"With flying ships?" Myvi whispered back. "No, we're in the right Time – just a new Time Path."

"Now then you two," said Percy, turning back towards Max and Myvi. "What were you doing out there after dark? If that ship had spotted you, it'd have been the end of you..."

Percy gave a slight gasp as Max and Myvi pulled back their hoods. Max and Myvi looked at each other, both having seen the look of recognition on his face. And now he just stared at them warily.

"What is it?" asked Max.

"You know us, don't you?" said Myvi. "You've seen us before."

"No..." said Percy. "Of course I haven't!"

"Yes you have, Percy," said Myvi, a little more forcefully now. "There's no point denying it. We know what you are."

"I don't know what you're talking about! And how do you know my name?!"

"Because," said Max, "where *we* come from, you're my grandfather. Or you *were* anyway."

"*Were?*"

"You died a few days ago. You were a lot older than you are

135

here."

This really got through. Percy suddenly looked a little faint, and sat down heavily at one of the wooden tables.

"You're a Time Traveller, Percy – just like us. *Aren't* you?"

Percy sat back and dropped his head, and breathed out deeply, before eventually looking back up. "Yes. Last night, I dream-travelled, and saw you here, outside the Inn, but... it was all different like. There were people, lots of people, and strange metal machines sat next to the Inn... And there was a dog, a right Gurt dog..."

"The funeral!" said Max and Myvi in unison.

"I *thought* I saw you there!" said Max.

"But how did I get there – it was like a whole different world..."

"It was, Percy," said Myvi, sitting down next to him and holding his hand. Percy just stared at her. As his eyes went ever wider, Max and Myvi laid it all down - Time Travelling, the Multiverse, Bacon, the alternative 2014, the whole nine yards.

"But who's this 'Bacon'?" said Percy, still a little shocked.

"*Roger* Bacon," said Max. "You know, thirteenth century philosopher and alchemist, founder of the modern scientific method – you were obsessed with him."

"Never heard of him, boy."

Max stared at Percy for a moment, and then slapped his forehead.

"*That's* what happened at the Priory!" he said, turning to Myvi. "Bacon got the Majyga, so Grandfather couldn't hide them there for himself to find, so he didn't discover he could Travel, so didn't go back to find Bacon!"

"Of course!" said Myvi. "And if he never found Bacon, then *he* never discovered Time Travel, never learned the ancients' secrets, and never wrote his influential works. That would have changed things a *lot*."

Percy was looking very confused now. "But, I *am* a Travel-

ler..."

Max and Myvi looked at each other, also confused now.

"He's right," said Myvi. "So that theory doesn't work..."

"Yes it does," said Max. "In *this* Time Path, he knows he's a Traveller, so he doesn't *need* the Majyga."

Myvi thought about this for a moment, the variations of Travelling reality twisting around in her head until it began to hurt. But in the end she realised that, yes, Max was right.

"Yes," said Myvi, nodding, "that must be it. So," she said, turning back to Max's grandfather, "tell us about *this* world then, Percy."

"Yes," said Max. "Like, why are there Romans in flying ships?"

"You really *aren't* from this time, are you?" said Percy.

Percy told them what he knew – that for a little over five hundred years, this world had been ruled by a New Roman Empire, at its head, an Emperor-Pope descended from the infamous and ruthless Pope Alexander VI, otherwise known as Rodrigo Borgia. Somehow they had discovered how to cheat gravity, and built a huge fleet of floating battleships, with which, within a very few years, they conquered the known world.

"They discovered negative gravity in the fifteenth century?!" said Max incredulously.

"Not they – one man, who was working for Cesare, the Pope's – the *Emperor's* son." Percy looked around as if someone might have heard him not giving the Emperor his correct title. "It was that Leonardo da Vinci."

"Oh, OK," said Max. Yes, OK, da Vinci *was* a genius, but... "But even so, he never even got his *helicopter* to fly – how on earth did he make a Negative Gravity Engine? That's science fiction stuff!"

"Oh, that's simple," said Percy. "Because he discovered something else first, didn't he..."

"Don't tell me," said Myvi. "Time Travel."

"Exactly. He learned the secrets of history, but also of the future – and put them all to work in the service of his master."

"Wasn't there any, you know, rebellion?" said Max.

"Oh, all the time – but no-one knows about it, not even those who rebel. The Romans have an army of Travellers that simply change history back again."

"And no-one knows the difference?" said Myvi. It was all very familiar.

"That's right. People are happy. The Empire's rich, there's food and work for everyone, no-one knows any different. World hasn't changed for nigh on five hundred years, but if there's food on your table and money in your pocket, who's going to complain?"

"Wait a minute," said Max. "If the Roman Travellers make sure this knowledge is kept from the people, how come *you* know about it?"

"Only we Travellers know. Once we realised our dreams were about a world that had been changed, we began to figure out the truth."

"*We?*" said Max. "How many are there?"

"Hundreds, maybe thousands across the world. We do what we can against the Romans, but you know what, they're better than us. Our little victories are just wiped out the next day."

"Do you only Travel in your dreams?" said Max.

"Of course – no-one can travel while awake. Only The One That Is To Come will do that."

Myvi shot Max a concealed grin, but she didn't conceal it well enough. Percy looked wildly from one of them to the other.

"What? Are you *actually* here, and not dream-travelling? Are *you* The One?"

Max blushed and scowled at Myvi, who only smirked more.

"There are those that believe he is The One, yes," said Myvi. "He's not convinced though."

Percy's eyes were wider than ever now.

Max looked like he was wrestling in his head. "Oh, I don't know – it's just an old superstition... But, no, no, hang on, you *can* Travel awake Grandfather, at least you could in our time. *You* taught *me!*"

But before they could say anything else a door slammed and a young man ran into the bar from the back.

"The Romans are coming!" he shouted, before stopping suddenly in front of Max in surprise. They both looked at each other, sure they'd seen the other before, but...

"What have you done, boy?!" Percy shouted back at him.

"We got into Yeovil Fortress and blew up three Ironclads. We were almost out, but - "

Percy suddenly angered. " - but the RTs spotted you, didn't they? You *fool,* boy!"

But now they all froze. The sound of throbbing steam engines began to fill the air, their deep rumbling beginning to shake the old building as the ship got ever nearer. Percy ran to the window and peered through the curtains before turning back.

"They're here!"

Max looked out now, and saw hovering above the Inn a huge Ironclad, steam churning from its funnels into the night sky, soldiers swarming down ropes towards them.

"We can fix this," he said to Percy, grabbing Myvi's hand, before glaring at the young man. "When *was* this?"

"What?"

"When did you attack the fortress?"

"Wha – er, I don't know, about sunset I suppose. Why? Who are you?!" said the young man, before turning to Percy. "Who *is* he?!"

"I'm your son from another time Owen," said Max, and then he and Myvi disappeared.

*

139

CHAPTER SEVENTEEN

"We're still at the Inn."

"Well, outside it, obviously." said Max.

"Yes, Max," said Myvi with a raise of one eyebrow. He had come so far in the last few days from the scared introvert she'd first re-met at the funeral, but sometimes his inability to understand any kind of subtlety still surprised her.

"But two hours before," he continued, oblivious. "Gives us time to get to the Fortress and..."

"So why didn't you just Travel us straight to the Fortress?"

"No, can't do that – the, what did Grandfather... Percy... call them - the RTs might spot us. Sounds like the Romans have some kind of Traveller Detection or something."

"Who knows, Max – it's a whole new world."

"Exactly. Can't be too careful. No, we're going to have to walk. It's not that far, as the crow flies."

Myvi raised her eyebrows at Max again, as if to say 'well *you* can walk...' But then they heard the sound of horses neighing nearby, and Myvi looked around and grinned.

"No, I've got a better idea..."

Max looked where Myvi had been looking – it was the building that had once been the chapel, and in their time a skittle alley. This time around it was obviously stables.

"But I can't ride a *horse!*" said Max.

"Yes, you can Max – you rode loads of horses, before? Come on, you can do it – it's just like riding a bike!"

"Except bikes don't bite and kick you when you're not looking," mumbled Max as he followed Myvi to the stables.

*

Myvi had quickly saddled the two horses. Max tried to help, but she quickly told him to stop 'helping'. It took a few attempts for Max to get up into the saddle, but, with a bit

141

of pushing from Myvi, he finally made it. They took the old Camp Road, now little more than a dark tree-lined track, and headed towards Yeovil, coats buttoned up tight against the January cold. Going via Montacute would have been slightly quicker, but Myvi wanted to keep off the main roads into the town.

After a little while, they reached the ancient village of Odcombe. It was smaller than Max remembered it, but then he realised there were no modern houses there. The ham-stone cottages that were there were all dark, their curtains all drawn for the night time curfew. Like the Inn, the village seemed to Max like a mediaeval film set, with not a trace of any of the modernities of the other 2014 – not even tar-macked roads.

"At least no-one will hear the hooves and raise the alarm I suppose," said Max as they trotted along the dirt road through the sleeping village. He still wasn't comfortable on the horse, not the least because it was big and he wasn't. But he was managing to stay on, so far.

They saw the smoke long before they saw the Fortress, a huge grey cloud hanging over the plain below what used to be the heavily populated hills of Yeovil. They weren't any more. As they looked out over the river plain that once housed in-dustrial estates and Westlands helicopter factory, all Max and Myvi saw were clusters of small stone houses clinging to the high ground here and there, a few hundred at most in all. Of the populous if somewhat downtrodden town of the other 2014 there was no sign. The Romans first put a villa on this plain nearly two thousand years before, and this was where the new Romans had placed their vast steam-powered, iron and stone Fortress, as they had all over the known world.

"What's that noise?" said Max.

"The Fortress," said Myvi. Even though it was the best part of two miles away, the grinding and churning of its steam engines was still very much audible.

"No, not that noise – *that* noise..."

They both looked up into the skies, as from the cloud covering the valley emerged a small dark shape that began to fly slowly around the perimeter of the town.

"Patrol ship?" said Max.

"Looks like it," said Myvi. "We have to get off the road, *now.*"

Myvi backed her horse up, then urged it on at the hedge that bordered the slope down into the valley, jumping it with ease before stopping and turning.

"Come on Max!"

"I'm not doing *that!*"

"You have to – come on!"

Taking a deep breath, Max backed his own horse up, then squeezed his heels into its flanks like he'd seen in films. "Come on horse – yaaah!"

As the horse bolted forwards, Max held onto the reins for dear life as it sailed over the hedge, tilting Max backwards so hard he almost fell off, but then they were over the hedge and now he fell forwards, only staying on by clinging desperately onto the horse's neck. But the horse didn't stop, but instead charged down into the valley below.

"Hey, wait for me!" yelled Myvi.

"I would if I could!" Max yelled back, now slightly more upright, but still with no control over the horse. Myvi urged her horse into a full gallop, and as she gradually came alongside Max, she grabbed hold of his reins and slowly brought his horse to a halt, before guiding it up the northern slope of the field towards the safety of the tree-lined hedge.

"They shouldn't spot us if we keep to this hedge," said Myvi. "And, you're welcome."

"Sorry," said Max. "Thanks."

"Not all your memories coming back, then."

"Not horse-riding ones, no."

The ship continued on its patrol, but obviously hadn't spot-

ted them. Max and Myvi crept their horses along the hedge-line towards the Fortress, until they were level with its western wall, which, like the rest of the vast perimeter, towered thirty or so feet above its surroundings, the distant churning of the steam engines that powered the Fortress now a hammering wave. The Fortress was nearly a mile long, a small town unto itself. At one end was a massive factory, a forest of smoking chimneys piercing its roofs, there to serve the dozen or so humming and throbbing Ironclads of various sizes that hung in the air within its inner walls. But it was the far end of the Fortress that grabbed Max and Myvi's attention. They hadn't seen it earlier, from the road, because it had been obscured by the clouds of smoke. But now they did.

"It's like something out of Star Wars!" said Max, staring in amazement at what looked for all the world like someone had recreated Mont St Michel in iron and glass, a massive inner conical fortress whose blackened metal outer walls spiralled up into the sky like a Demonic helter-skelter. The slopes of the inner streets were lined with houses of all shapes and sizes, their riveted iron walls pierced by the glow through their narrow windows, while at the very top, an enormous chimney belched out smoke from the machinery deep within that presumably powered the whole building.

"Looks like they *have* invented electricity after all," said Max.

"And keep it to themselves, I guess," said Myvi. "So now what?"

"We find my... we find Owen."

As they got nearer to the Fortress, Myvi pulled up.

"We should leave the horses here," she said, dismounting and tying the reins of her horse to a tree branch. Max got off his own horse, albeit with rather less style, and did the same.

"Don't worry guys," she said, patting the horses on their flanks. "We'll come back for you."

They set off cautiously down the slope towards the Fortress,

144

but they only got a few yards before they were knocked off their feet, as one of the larger Ironclads was ripped apart by a huge explosion. Max and Myvi threw themselves over the hedge as the night sky was lit up by a massive fireball, while hot metal fragments rained down all around.

"I guess we found him," yelled Myvi over the noise of several smaller secondary explosions. "Come on Max, get us in there!" she said, grabbing hold of Max's hand.

"But we're not supposed to be Travelling!" said Max as a second, smaller ship erupted violently into flame.

"Too late to worry about that – come on!"

The noise of the explosions was now beginning to be matched by the sound of people screaming orders and firing weapons. By the sound of it, the Romans had also invented machine guns.

Max stood up, took Myvi's hand, and let his focus blur. In his mind's eye, the towering Fortress walls fell away, to reveal the fighting behind. Hundreds of Roman soldiers, dressed in what would have been state of the art black combat gear in the other 2014, poured out of the Tower to back up their colleagues currently firing at anything that looked like a saboteur. Max finally spotted Owen, crouching with another man behind the burning wreckage of one of the Ironclads. They were also dressed in black, both with long hooded coats. But they weren't armed, and worse, there were soldiers heading towards them from all directions. Max blocked out all other thoughts, especially those concerning what he was actually going to do once he got in there, and focussed his mind solely on Owen. The air began to bend and buckle around him as the space-time vortex between him and Owen coalesced into a swirling tunnel. Max held out his arms, and prepared to be sucked through the dimensions towards the man who may or may not one day become his father – but then, rather than Max Travelling into the Fortress, Owen and the other man suddenly materialised on the grass in front of them. Max's

focus snapped so violently back to the there and then that he fell over backwards.

Owen and his friend looked wildly around them in alarm, and then stared wide-eyed at Max.

"Did *you* do that?" Owen demanded of Max.

"Yes," said Max getting up a little shakily. The effort of getting Owen and the other man out of the Fortress had taken it out of him. "But I don't know how – that's never happened before."

Myvi just smiled to herself. *He's getting it back, and then some.*

"Are you cloaked?" said Owen.

"What?"

"Are you *cloaked?* Against the RTs? If you're not, we're in even worse trouble than we were in *there!*"

"I don't know what you mean."

Owen looked at Max in amazement.

"You don't know what cloaking is? And yet you're obviously a Traveller. You carry something that shouldn't be here - it confuses their tracking system, stops them recognising you as a Traveller - mostly anyway."

"Owen," said Myvi grinning, "we *are* something that shouldn't be here!"

"How do you know my name?" said Owen.

"And what are you doing with our horses?" said the other, pulling his hood back. Or rather, *her* hood. Now it was Max's turn to stare. It was Sarah, the girl who may or may not one day become his mother.

"No time to explain!" said Myvi, looking back at the Fortress as half a dozen patrol ships launched into the blazing night, before heading for the horse she came on. "Let's go!"

"But they'll spot us!" said Sarah.

"Then we'll have to ride quick enough so they don't!"

But Owen was the first to the horses.

"You," he said in Max's direction as he leapt onto his horse.

"Up behind me."

"My name's Max."

"Alright then, Max, up behind me. You, go with Sarah," he said to Myvi, and put out an arm to help Max up behind him.

Sarah in turn leapt into her own saddle, and Myvi leapt up behind her, over the horse's rump.

"You've done that before..."

"Myvanwyl. Myvi for short. Yes, many times."

"Yaaah!" Owen kicked his horse into an almost instant gallop as Max held desperately onto his cloak, and they charged as fast as the horses could go along the hedge line and up the slope to the Odcombe road. But it wasn't fast enough. A searchlight beam wafted around the valley floor before zeroing in on them.

"They've spotted us!" yelled Sarah.

"Faster!" yelled Myvi, slapping the horse's rump. But it was no good – the patrol ship was roaring towards them now, the circle of the searchlight beam getting ever larger and ever nearer. And then the firing started. As both horses flew over the hedge at the top, bullets hit the earth all around them, throwing up a cloud of splintered soil. Owen and Sarah both weaved their horses along the road as they obviously had done many times before, but the bullets were still getting closer. Side by side the horses raced through Odcombe village, bullets thudding into the dirt road and ricocheting off the stone walls of the cottages that lined it.

"Max, *do* something!" yelled Myvi.

"Like *what?!*" he yelled back, still only barely hanging on to Owen's cloak.

"Get us out of here!"

"What, four people and two horses?!"

"You know you can!"

Max breathed out deeply, then held out his hand to Myvi.

"OK, I'll try – hold on!"

The patrol ship was right above them now, its front gunner

taking particular aim, and firing. But the hail of bullets hit the empty road.

Both horses reared madly, confused and terrified as they found themselves running along a completely different track to the one they were on only seconds ago. Myvi held on to Sarah as she fought to bring her horse to a halt, but Max's grip loosened, the effort of that much Travelling weakening him so much he fainted, and fell backwards off the horse onto the grassy edge of the hill opposite the Inn, tumbling over and over down the near vertical slope towards the field below.

*

When Max came to, he was lying in a bed – an unfamiliar bed. He sat up in a panic, but then looked out of the window, and saw the familiar fields of Ham Hill. Max smiled, and sighed deeply. He was in the Inn, just in a different room. He was home again. He *knew* it - it *had* all been a dream!

But as Max got out of bed and looked again at the scene outside, he realised there were no benches in front of the Inn, and no street lights in the distance. Max slumped back down onto the bed again. He was still a million miles from home.

*

CHAPTER EIGHTEEN

Cardinal Vellucci looked out over the city from the window of his Imperial Palace apartment high up on the Quirinal Hill. The sea of sienna walls, roofs, domes and spires below glowed in the winter sun, the haze of steam emanating from the giant chimneys that ringed the city dissipated by a brisk north wind. Everything was as it always had been in Rome, never changing, preserved in Time's aspic for five hundred years. But now danger came. The gangly old white haired Cardinal knew something had happened - he could feel it. Like all Travellers, whether they knew it or not, Vellucci was connected into the Gaiasma, the global collective consciousness that allowed Time Travel in the first place. He sensed something was wrong, not because he could see it in his mind's eye, but because he couldn't. He knew something was there, but it was invisible to him, and that worried him. Vellucci was one of the great Roman Travellers, and his instincts were almost never wrong. Those instincts were now telling him that whatever it was he couldn't see was about to bring their world crashing down, a feeling that was reinforced when there was a furious knocking on the door to the apartment. Moments later his colleague Cardinal Masenna ran into the room, a nervous look in his eyes. Vellucci didn't even need to ask. He just knew. But he asked anyway.

"What is it, Francesco?"

"It is the Holy Emperor – he commands an audience..."

"Yes, I suspected he might. How is he today?"

The younger Cardinal faltered, trying to choose his words without causing offence, and without causing any danger to himself.

"He... he is excitable... He says that the end is coming. What does he mean?"

Vellucci looked gently on his young colleague. He was clearly terrified.

"I suspect he means exactly that."

"But how? What is to happen to us?"

"That is for the Holy Emperor to say. But he has been wrong before."

Now Masenna just stood there, transfixed, his mouth slightly open. His superior had said openly that the Holy Emperor was fallible.

"Yes, I know Francesco, now you must report me for what I just said. Whether you do or not, is of course up to you. But if the end is to come, what will it matter either way? Now go, do what you must. I shall repair to the Hall of the Holy Emperor."

The younger Cardinal backed away from his elder colleague through the open double entrance doors, and then turned and fled.

Vellucci shook his head slightly, touched the large gold cross hanging down over his scarlet cassock, and sighed deeply. The Hall of the Holy Emperor was a terrifying enough place as it was, but if the Holy Emperor himself was even more unbalanced than usual, as it sounded that he was, then he didn't rate his chances of seeing another day very highly.

The Imperial Palace was a vast building that took up almost the whole of the summit of the Quirinal Hill, the highest in Rome. Unlike the Rome of Max's time, the Imperial Palace was the centre of the Catholic capital, not the Vatican, and unlike in Max's time, this Quirinal Palace was built for protection, not show. Pope Alexander VI had it built shortly after he declared himself Holy Emperor in 1503, moving in Papacy and Government in their entirety. The fifty foot thick Castle walls and their accommodation formed a vast square around a central quad, each wall over a quarter of a mile long and five storeys high. In the centre of the square stood the Hall of the Holy Emperor, a highly ornate stone inner Palace now protected by a giant metal dome, connected to the outside walls by a network of metal tunnels, both tunnels and

dome being impenetrable to bullets, explosives, and especially to Travellers.

It took a good twenty minutes for Cardinal Vellucci to get from his apartment in the western wall to the entrance to the dome. Few people in the Palace were allowed even this far, but Vellucci was one. As he approached the dome through the western tunnel, he marvelled, as he always did, at the construction. The curved walls of both tunnel and dome were made from metal a foot thick, and yet, when required, they could be as transparent as glass. One of da Vinci's many, many discoveries all those years ago, and one put into great service by the Emperor.

Vellucci reached the end of the tunnel, to be confronted by a solid wall of metal, but as he approached, the whole wall slid sideways to allow him in.

The Cardinal stepped through the doorway into a second, shorter tunnel that led to the older building inside. The tunnel splayed out at the end, until it formed a surround to two large iron-reinforced wooden doors, original to the Palace. These in turn opened as Vellucci approached them, to reveal the Audience Chamber, a huge room by most standards, dominated by the Imperial Throne in the centre, itself covered by a large transparent metal dome. Behind this were two vast doors that led to the Great Hall itself, where no man entered and returned. The rest of the Audience Chamber was decorated as would be expected for an Imperial Palace, walls lined with huge paintings and tapestries, floor covered in the finest carpet, and every piece of detailing possible covered in gold. But there was no furniture. No-one sat in the presence of the Holy Emperor, and if they did, the two eight foot tall Demon guards standing and snuffling menacingly either side of the throne dome ensured they never did it again.

Vellucci said nothing, but knelt, still and silent before the throne, waiting for the Holy Emperor to arrive, silently praying the two Demons remembered he was friendly. Then the

151

dome covering the throne began to fill with billowing grey clouds that quickly darkened, and now thunder clashed and lightning flashed against the inside of the dome until the throne became almost completely obscured. But then the storm subsided, and the clouds cleared a little, to reveal the old, portly, but powerfully built and majestically robed form of His Imperial and Apostolic Majesty, the Holy Emperor Alexander VI, not a descendant as the world believed, but Rodrigo Borgia himself, now in the five hundred and ninth year of his imperial reign.

The Emperor didn't speak for a moment, but instead just sat, his head resting on his fingertips as if in prayer, his book as ever on his lap. Vellucci didn't look up. No-one ever looked up when in the presence of the Emperor, until he commanded it. It was hard enough just knowing that the world was ruled by the living spirit of a man who should be five hundred years in his grave, but actually seeing him had sent many before mad. But now he spoke.

"The One has arrived in our time, as I predicted he would. He will find us, eventually, and all will end. I have seen his time, and know his destiny."

There was a long pause, broken only by the Emperor's shallow breathing.

"You may speak, Vellucci."

Vellucci coughed nervously. "Is there nothing we can do, your Imperial and Apostolic Majesty?" Vellucci still didn't look up.

"I didn't hear you, Vellucci, your gaze was towards the floor. Look up, man – look at me."

The two Demons growled a little, a deep rumbling that sounded like an Ironclad was flying overhead. Slowly, Vellucci looked up, to see his Imperial master scowling at him, and kneading the hem of his gold-lined white Papal robes with one hand and clutching a large wooden cross that hung from his neck with the other. The cross is new, thought Vellucci.

152

"Now. Repeat."

Vellucci took a very deep breath.

"Your Imperial and Apostolic Majesty, I asked whether there was nothing that we can do? It is one person, and we are Rome."

Vellucci held his breath for what seemed like an eternity as the expression on the old man's face went through half a dozen changes, none of them good. Finally the Emperor settled on a mood. Vellucci breathed out as he realised it was defiant, but not towards him.

"Your Eminence, we shall throw all the forces of your world and mine at his coming, we shall fight until the last man is dead and the last soul is destroyed, but we shall not win. We shall put great armies and great spirit forces in his way, but he will circumvent them all. I sought to protect your world from him by imprisoning the Guardians of the Gates, who I believed were assisting him, but still he is here. These last days great battles have taken place in the Otherworld, but I have triumphed. The Lord Gwynn ap Llud is in chains, his cross is mine, and I now rule there as well as here. But even this was to no avail, for *still* he came."

Vellucci had just managed to stop his eyes going wide at the news that the Emperor was now Ruler of the Otherworld. Lesser men than the wise Cardinal would on that news now believe that the Devil was ruling the world, but Vellucci knew things weren't that simple. The Emperor was not the Devil: his determination to do everything in his now obviously much augmented power to keep his Empire in charge of the world had often necessitated deeds that might be seen as evil, but he was not himself evil, of this Vellucci was sure. Unless...

"Who is he, your Imperial and –"

"Vellucci, under these circumstances, 'your Majesty' will suffice."

"Yes... your Majesty. Do you know who he is, or *where* he is?"

153

Now the Emperor gave a deep sigh.

"I will admit, your Eminence, that I have not seen him, but as I know that you yourself do, I feel his presence, and know that, because I cannot see him, he is here."

Vellucci gave a bow. "Your Majesty knows my every thought."

"I know *everyone's* every thought Vellucci. Now, go, prepare your armies, and find him. Our one hope is that he has not yet gained his full power."

The clouds returned to the throne dome, lightning flashed once more, and then the Holy Emperor was gone. The Demons remained though. They never moved, ever, unless provoked - and no-one even thought about provoking them - guarding the portal by which their master moved between this world and the Other. In Max's time, Pope Alexander VI had actually died in 1503; in this path, da Vinci's early experiments accidentally caused a rift in time, opening up a gateway in this room to the Otherworld. With da Vinci's help, the Pope, by then greatly ailing, entered this gateway, never physically to return, but never quite to leave either, nor age, using the power of the Otherworld, or Annwn as Max knew it, to maintain his power over the Empire, and over his own mortality.

Cardinal Vellucci stood up, and slowly backed out towards the door, which opened as he approached. It wasn't that tradition demanded you reverse out of the room, but no-one who entered could ever bring themselves to take their eyes off the two Demons, just in case. In fact, only two other people were party to the secret of the undead Emperor - Cardinal Masenna, who had earlier informed him of the Emperor's wish for an audience, and the elderly and increasingly fragile Cardinal Arezzo. Ordinarily Arezzo was not to be concerned with even relatively important matters of state, but in this instance all three of them would have to convene. As he exited the metal tunnel into the outer castle, Cardinal Vellucci

hailed a passing secretary and commanded him to ask both men to hasten to his apartment. It was going to be a long day, and no doubt a long night also.

*

CHAPTER NINETEEN

Max was woken by Percy.

"Come on, Max – there are some people I want you to meet."

"Wha...?" said Max blearily. "People...?" He looked around the room, to see daylight poking through the thick green curtains.

"What time is it?"

"Midnight."

"Midnight? But it's light outside..."

"You're still asleep, Max."

Max sat up on his elbows and stared at Percy.

"What...? Is this a dream?"

"No. I'll explain shortly – come on."

Max got out of bed to find he was still dressed. But as he looked around for his duffle coat he got the shock of his life. He saw himself, still asleep in the bed.

"Grandpa...?!"

"Percy, remember? It's alright boy, you're Dream Travelling. It was the only way."

"Only way to *what?*"

"To show you what you are Max. Now hold my hand."

Max took Percy's hand, and suddenly the world twisted around him as he and Percy flew through the swirling void.

"Where are we going?!" Max shouted above the roaring of the Space/Time maelstrom.

"Somewhere safe – don't let go!"

The next thing Max knew he was standing next to Percy at the top of a sloping cobbled street, ahead of them a jumbled line of stone and timber mediaeval shops and houses, their mostly half-timbered upper floors hanging out over the un-paved street below. It looked all too familiar, but at the same time very different to his memory of it, as if, like everywhere else he'd seen so far in this alternative 2014, nothing had

changed since the Sixteenth Century. But it was very different to the barely developed Yeovil, almost prosperous, with dozens of people bustling along the street, in and out of the various shops. They weren't the shops of Max's time of course – no charity shops, nor expensive clothes emporia here, just butchers, bakers, cobblers, blacksmiths and the like, and, of course, taverns.

"I remember this place," said Max as he followed Percy down the street. "You brought me here once, in the other time. It was nice." Max paused. "Why are we in Sherborne?"

"We're not," Percy replied. "Well, we are, but we're not. This is *our* Sherborne, our refuge outside of Time, somewhere to meet where the Romans can't find us."

"Did you... *make* this...?" said Max, looking in wonder at the chocolate box scenes around him. But now that he looked a little closer, he could see it. The Sherborne of his time was one of the quintessential English towns, the mediaeval layout and character of its core still perfectly preserved within its more recent expansion, but this was almost *too* perfect. *This* Sherborne shimmered slightly at its edges, as places do when they are there by force of will alone; and now he looked beyond the end of the ancient centre, there *was* no beyond.

"*We* made it," replied Percy, shaking the hand of yet another passer-by. Everyone they saw seemed to know Percy – and each one also gave Max a smile, as if they knew him too. "The Travellers. Everyone you see here is a Traveller. It's a real place, but we locked it away outside Time in a shared dream. We come here when we need to discuss something together – or sometimes," he said, turning and smiling at Max, "we just come here because it's nicer than the real world."

Max smiled back. He got it now. "It's your shared Happy Place, isn't it?"

Percy laughed, and patted Max fondly on the shoulder. "Aye, that's it boy."

But now Max heard a commotion behind him, and turned,

to see that everyone was following them. At first he startled, the effects of his PTSD still not quite gone, despite everything that had happened since.

"Grand –" Max corrected himself. "Percy...?" said Max, nervously indicating behind them. But Percy just laughed, and patted Max on the shoulder again.

"Nothing to worry about boy – we're all friends here."

As they passed more shops and houses, more and more people flooded out onto the street, all smiling at each other, and at Max, and chatting away to each other with joy.

"They've Travelled from all over the world to be here to-day," said Percy loudly over the growing clamour.

"But why?"

"So they can hear how you're going to save them of course!"

"What?! But..."

But Max got no further – as they reached the old Conduit at the bottom of the communally imagined Cheap Street, they were greeted by a huge mass of cheering men and women, who all crowded round, eager to get a better view of Max, and as one they surged along Half Moon Street towards the great golden-stoned Abbey, Max's feet barely touching the ground. Max tried to struggle free of the crush as panic started to rise, but before he knew it he had been hoisted up to shoulder height as the crowd poured through the Abbey's great Norman doorway and up to the dais on which sat the High Altar, where Max was delicately set back on his feet before the crowd retreated to the main body of the Abbey, their commotion now almost at fever pitch.

Hundreds of questions were being yelled at once at Percy, and at Max, the noise echoing around the old Abbey, amplifying manyfold as it bounced off the magnificently painted fan-vaulted ceiling and back around the cavernous interior. Percy tried to calm everyone down but the Travellers were just getting more excited. Max couldn't take any more, and buckled under the furious roar, falling to his knees, his hands

clasped to his ears, but still it couldn't be blocked out. He was in a full-on panic now, his heart racing like it had never done before, the blood boiling in his head. He screwed his eyes tight, trying to focus on the room at the Inn where he still lay sleeping, trying to wake himself up, but it was no use. The noise pervaded his every thought, jamming any attempt to escape. In a last desperate effort to purge the fear from his head he leapt up, and screamed.

"WHAT DO YOU WANT FROM ME?!!"

There was an almost instant quiet now, and the crowd stared at Max, their expressions a mass embarrassed realisation of what they had been inflicting on the boy who would save them.

Max stared around, his head still boiling, his eyes still wide in equal fear and anger, as if daring any of them to ever speak again.

After a long, piercing quiet, one man came forwards from the throng, and bowed his head at Max.

"Why are you *bowing* to me?" said Max, still ravingly angry. "I'm not a Lord or anything – I'm just a *boy!*"

The man, tall, with long greying hair and an almost floor-length leather coat, looked a little embarrassed.

"Our apologies sir – "

"And don't call me 'sir', either – I'm Max. *Just Max!*" Max was calming a little, but not much.

"Our apologies... Max... but you must understand, we are all overjoyed at your coming, knowing that we shall be free at last from the Romans."

Max's anger flared back to a place he barely recognised. "And how am I supposed to do that?! I told you, I'm just a boy! You can't *do* this to me!" This last screamed as Max crouched back down, hands over ears again, and eyes screwed tight shut.

The man looked confused. "But, but Percy said..."

There was a long, long moment, as Max slowly opened his

eyes, and stared viciously at the obviously deeply shocked man.

"What? That I was The One That Is To Come?!"

"Well, aren't you?" came another, rather more familiar voice. Max was suddenly ripped from his anger, and plunged into confusion instead. He looked wildly around the crowd; and then he saw him. But before Max could say anything, Nick shook his head slightly and put his finger to his lips.

Max calmed now, and tried to breathe properly again. "I, I don't know – it's what everyone keeps telling me, but..."

"Can you not Travel awake, as He will?" continued Nick. "And are you not a descendant of Tofig, as He will be? And have you not Travelled here from a different world, as He will?" At each of Nick's questions, the crowd replied with resounding affirmation, as if they were in a modern-day evangelical church.

"Well, yes, I suppose so..." said Max weakly, before turning to Percy. "How do they know all this?"

Percy smiled. "Because I told them all, when I summoned them to Assemble."

Max needed help, and Myvi was no doubt still asleep in her own bed. More than anything else, he needed to know just what was going on.

"You sir," he called out to Nick, moderating his language to fit with what he supposed those assembled would respect. "Would you please come forward?"

The crowd parted as Nick moved through it, and curious looks followed him to the Altar. Everyone was looking at everyone else to see if there was anyone that recognised him, but obviously no-one did. A murmur began to build among the Travellers.

As Nick reached Max, Max beckoned for him to join him and Percy on the dais, before turning to the crowd.

"We shall be but a minute... Erm... I believe there may be a way... Erm..." Max couldn't think of anything else to say, and

panicked. "...talk amongst yourselves..."

Max introduced Nick to Percy as quickly as he could without getting into too much detail, but sufficient for Percy to know exactly what his other self had done in Max's time.

"What's going on Nick? Is the TRD *here* now? Can you get me back to my proper time? What's with this new Roman Empire?" Max fired these and many other questions at Nick in a rapid hushed whisper, but it still wasn't quiet enough to quell a suspicion among the crowd that all was not well, and they began to advance on the dais, one word on their lips – Roman. The man who had before spoken first was at their forefront.

"Why do none of us know this man?" he said to Max.

"Er, er, he's not *from* here," said Max a little anxiously. The Travellers were not looking welcoming. "But he's a friend, I promise!"

The murmur became slowly louder, and more threatening.

"We believe he is an imposter, a Roman Traveller, and as such cannot be allowed to leave."

"No, he's not, really!" said Max. "He's *not* an RT - you *must* believe me!"

"We do not, sir," growled the man, the crowd behind him now positively menacing. "We believe he *is* an RT, and if you vouch for him, then you must be one too."

"What? No!" said Max, looking to Percy for help.

"Percy, tell them!"

"No Max, *you* tell *them*," said Percy firmly. "This is why you are here. Tell them everything you told me. If you are to lead them, you must take charge. Now."

Just then there was a loud beeping sound. The Travellers looked around, but could see no source for the noise. Max didn't connect for a moment, but then gave a half smile, put his hand in his duffle coat pocket, and pulled out his phone. He'd forgotten all about it. The beeping was the low battery warning. Max looked up at the crowd defiantly.

"Let me show you something from my time," he said loudly, then pressed the screen a few times, before holding it up, and, hoping the battery would last long enough, regaled the crowd with his favourite piece of music, 'O Fortuna' from Carl Orff's 'Carmina Burana'. The jubilantly soaring piece inspires awe in most who hear it, but when played over a piece of technology that shouldn't exist to hundreds of twenty-first century mediaeval time travellers, Max could have told them he was a God and they would have believed him.

Now he had their attention, Max told them everything. By the time he was done, they had a plan. The Commander of the Yeovil Fortress had been recalled to Rome, to account for his inability to capture those that had attacked his Ironclads. The plan was simple – to hijack the Commander's ship, fly to Rome and destroy the Emperor.

And then the Travellers dispersed, quietly, as Max had asked, to return to their sleep, to await his instructions.

Just as the last of them disappeared, Percy looked a little anxiously at Max.

"Can we really do all that?"

"Of course we can," said Max, now feeling empowered again. "We're Toveys – we can do *anything!*"

After they'd stopped laughing, mostly to cover their nervousness at the task ahead, Nick took Max's arm with one hand, and Percy's with the other.

"Come on Max," said Nick, looking up at the TRD's virtual camera. "I think we need to go and see the Major."

And before Percy could say 'who's the Major', all three vanished.

∗

The TRD looked exactly the same, except there were now only three Dreamers, including Nick, now no longer with them, but here in his bed, sleeping deeply. Max reeled from

the almost instantaneous journey from the Travellers' construct to wherever this building was now, and had to be steadied by Major Willoughby. Percy, however, showed no signs of Travelling sickness, and was looking around the TRD with a mixture of amazement and fascination.

"So, Max tells me I created this, Major?" said Percy, peering at the monitors, all three of which were now blank, as the Dreamers slept deeply, exhausted from getting Nick into the Travellers' secret world.

"Yes Sir," said Willoughby, himself a little phased by being confronted by a Percy at the same age as he had been when he had indeed created the TRD, but in a completely different time path.

"Fascinating," said Percy, reaching towards one of the control panels, before Willoughby gently restrained him.

"Sorry sir..."

"But don't touch, eh Major?" said Percy, grinning. "We've never discovered how the Romans Travel - perhaps *this* is their method..."

"We believe it is, yes, or something like it, although we have yet to fully penetrate their defences. But the question is what do we do now? You come from a world that threatens existence itself; your Emperor, as far as we can tell, is rather more than you knew."

Max and Percy stared with alarm as the Major told them the truth of the undead Emperor.

"I know," said the Major. "And he is about to unleash all the Demonic forces at his disposal to stop Max getting to him, seemingly quite happy to destroy the world he commands to do so."

"Ah, but we have a plan, don't we Max?" said Percy, trying to get his head back to some kind of normality, such as it is for a Traveller.

But Max wasn't listening, lost in his own thoughts.

"How did Leonardo da Vinci discover Time Travel?"

Percy and the Major both turned to him with a little surprise at his quick recovery.

"Straight to the point as ever, Max," said the Major, giving Percy a look.

"I mean, I'm supposing you can't get me back to my Time from here, Major?" said Max matter-of-factly.

"No, I'm afraid not Max. Only you can do that. We just don't know how."

"So, how *did* he?"

"Well, from what we've gathered so far, he discovered an arcane book that gave him the secrets. Percy's book, from your Time, but how it got into da Vinci's Time path we have no idea. The Emperor keeps it with him at all times. It's what gives him his power."

Max gave a half laugh, and reached into his pocket.

"What, you mean *this* book?" said Max, holding up his original of the so-called Voynich Manuscript.

The Major stared at Max now, in alarm at first, but then, with a little excitement building.

"You *have* The *Book?!* I thought Percy destroyed it!"

"I've never seen that before in my life!" said Percy.

The Major looked at Percy with apology.

"Sorry, I meant the other Percy, in Max's time."

"Don't apologise, Major," said Percy. "I'm just as confused as you are."

"I'm not," said Max, smiling at both of them. Now he knew how they were going to do it. "When we were in the Priory, two of the same Majyga being in the same place caused a crack in Time that brought me here. If the two Books were brought together, maybe it would cause another one and things could go back to normal."

The Major looked at Max, and at the small, but now obviously immensely powerful book that he was still holding up. He knew what Max was about to say, but he still had to ask.

"So what are you saying Max?"

"I'm saying The Book and I have to get to the Emperor."

CHAPTER TWENTY

Max woke in a panic again, and this time seeing the familiarity of his bedroom didn't help. He was most definitely still not home. Someone knocked on the door, gently, but it still made him jump.

"Yes..." said Max tentatively.

The door opened – it was Myvi, dressed in what looked like a Victorian lady's night dress, a floor-length white affair with a lot of broderie anglaise, and much too big for her. Max failed to stifle a snigger.

"Don't laugh," said Myvi, but still smirking anyway. "It's all there was. Your Grandmother's, apparently."

Max sat bolt upright now. "*My Grandmother's?!* Is she...?"

"No, I'm afraid not Max. She died giving birth to Owen in this time as well. I'm sorry."

Myvi sat down on the edge of the bed and smiled gently at Max. He'd been through so much in the last few days, and yet here he still was, unscathed. She hoped.

"Percy told me what happened last night. How are you feeling this morning?"

Max thought about this for a moment, and then came to a conclusion.

"Tired."

"I know what you mean," said Myvi, smiling. "Hard work this Time Travelling."

"Tell me about it!" said Max, not noticing that Myvi was making a joke.

"Joke, Max," said Myvi, and Max blushed. "There's a dressing gown on the end of the bed, and some clean clothes. Sarah's washing *your* clothes, although I said she should have burned them..."

"What? Why?"

Myvi sighed. Still no closer to getting sarcasm.

"I was joking again, Max. There's a bath run for you. When

167

you're dressed, there's some breakfast downstairs."

"Can't I have breakfast first? I'm starving!"

"No Max," said Myvi, holding her nose. "Bath first."

Max scowled. "Are you saying I smell?"

"Max, you've been Travelling for three days straight in the same clothes and without so much as a face wash. Yes, I'm saying you smell!"

Max scowled again, but then sniffed under his arms and recoiled.

"Ah. Yes. Maybe I will have a bath after all."

They both laughed, then Myvi touched Max's hand lightly before getting up to leave.

"See you downstairs, Max."

"OK."

*

Deep, deep down in the forgotten dark halls of Annwn, where even Demons feared to venture, nine Guardians languished in nine Obsidian dungeons, their bodies, minds and souls in chains, doomed by the new dark ruler of this Otherworld to an eternity of torment. But not even the power of the undead Emperor could contain them completely, for though they were in different, dank caverns, still they were able, with supreme effort, to hear each other's thoughts, if only for a short while.

"They are seeking us, the boy and the girl."

"They will not find us – He will not allow it."

"And yet he is allowing us our thoughts at this moment – perhaps he is distracted. We should try to respond."

"We *must* try to reach the boy, and the girl...!"

"Very well."

Nine black holes now slowly glowed, as the Guardians drew upon every ounce of their restrained power, to send one of them above, however briefly, to try to get help.

*

"It's not working," said Max, breathing heavily after his exertions. "I can't see him. Anywhere."

Max had decided that they needed help – that they needed Rex. And so, after a huge breakfast that had only just begun to fill the hole left by three days of Travelling on almost no food, and dressed in old clothes of Owen's and Sarah's that made them look like something out of a Dickens film, they had set off through the woods for St. Michael's Hill.

As the autumn winds lashed the top of the Hill around the two seated teenagers, Myvi stretched out her hands to Max.

"Take my hands, Max – maybe together we can get through to him. The hill has never been without its Guardian – he's here somewhere."

Max took Myvi's hands, and both bowed their heads, and closed their eyes, trying to picture their friend, the High King Blaiddud. The wind swirled around them now, causing a mini maelstrom of leaves to fly in all directions.

"It's no good!" Max yelled above the deafening noise.

"Yes it is Max – look!"

Myvi was pointing at the leaves, which now seemed to be forming a shape in the air, a shape that now slowly coalesced into a giant head. A giant head of a giant white hound.

"Rex, is that you?!" Max yelled.

The head opened its mouth slowly, and let out a low, rumbling, ground-shaking roar.

"It is - it's him Max!" Myvi screamed, looking up with joy at the enormous leaf head.

"The High Kings are imprisoned," said Rex, in a voice almost as deep as his roar. "The Emperor seeks you out, to destroy you. He cannot yet see you, but I see your plans – *you* are to go to *him...?*"

"With this!" shouted Max, holding up The Book. "Will it

work? Will it put everything back where it was?"

"I do not know," said the head of Blaiddud. "Our foresight is blocked, our powers violently constrained. But..."

The head reared up now, and let out an ear-splitting roar of pain, the leaves blowing apart, before slowly coming together again.

"He has discovered our deceit," said Blaiddud, grimacing in agony. "Go to him, Max, in his Great Hall, where he is most..." Another scream of pain. "...vulnerable..."

One final scream rang out, so piercing that Max and Myvi had to cover their ears, but still it rang around their heads like fingernails on a thousand blackboards, and then the giant leaf head exploded into a cloud of fragments that showered down onto the hill top. He was gone.

Neither Max nor Myvi said anything for a while, or even moved, though the grass they sat on was still wet, both of them just staring out into the distance over the flooded fields of the Somerset Levels, never drained by the new Romans.

Max was the first to speak.

"So now what?" he said, getting up and pulling his duffle coat tighter around him against the cold. Myvi stood up as well, and started heading back down the hill.

"Now we go to Rome."

*

While Max and Myvi tucked into a second breakfast, Percy, Owen, Sarah and three other men were sat around the other sides of the large old table in the bar discussing how exactly they were supposed to hijack an Ironclad.

"We have enough people inside the Fortress," said Thomas, the older of the three men, also the one who had questioned Nick's presence in the Abbey that night. All three men were obviously fellow Travellers. "They could let us in tonight, and we could get on the ship before the Commander flies for

Rome."

"Maybe," said Cyrus, the older of the other two, maybe ten years older than Owen, with a similar wiry build, but taller, and with dark hair. "But even if we were not found by the ship's guards, we are still only six against dozens."

"Eight," said Max through a mouthful of bacon, indicating himself and Myvi.

All three men looked at Max, and smiled politely.

"I meant six adults. Six fighters," said Cyrus. "No offence."

Max's head was suddenly boiling, and before he knew what was happening, another him was behind Cyrus, a knife to his throat.

"None taken," said the other Max. Everyone just stared in amazement, none more so than Myvi, as the other Max disappeared again.

"What did you do there Max...? And how...?!"

Max was equally confused. "I, I'm not sure. I got angry, and then..."

"It was a projection," said Cyrus. "I've only ever seen that once, and that was one of the Roman RTs.

"Your powers are strong young man. Very well then, eight," said Cyrus, nodding his apologies to Max. "But my point still stands – even if we overpowered the whole crew, that would leave just eight of us to fly the ship, and none of us know how."

"Why can't we just Travel up into the ship as it's leaving?" said Seth, the youngest of the three, but by far the largest, if not the brightest. He was very handy in a fight though. The other two sighed.

"Because, Seth," said Thomas, obviously not for the first time, "the RT would spot us immediately."

"Is he going with the ship then, the Yeovil RT?" said Percy. "Because if he is, then –" But Cyrus cut him off.

"No, they'd never leave the Fortress unguarded against Travellers. Rome is sending a special one apparently."

171

"The obvious thing to do is Travel back and replace all the crew with Travellers who are now trained to fly the ship," said Max matter-of-factly, mopping his plate clean with his last piece of bread. The others all looked at him awkwardly, not wanting to criticise, but at the same time... Percy broke the silence.

"Max, that would cause shock waves so big the Emperor himself would come and 'deal' with us."

Ordinarily that kind of rebuke, however gentle, would have sent Max into a psychological huddle, regardless of whether or not he knew he was right. But to Max's surprise, this time it didn't.

"But if you're cloaked..."

"Yes, I know," said Percy, "but our cloaking objects aren't strong enough to cover that level of time meddling."

"Well, you need stronger objects then," said Max, pulling out his phone and putting it down on the table. As he did so, it gave out one last terminal beep and shut down. "Something that *really* shouldn't be here."

Everyone watched in alarm as Max took the phone apart with his breakfast knife, component by component, until it lay in dozens of different pieces.

"There," said Max, pushing the pile towards Percy. "Give everyone a piece."

"But you've broken it, your... whatever it is..." said Seth.

"It's more use this way," said Max. "I mean, what's the point in having a mobile phone when you're several dimensions away from anyone to talk to on it?"

The others may not have understood what he was talking about, but what they *did* understand was that they now had a plan.

*

Commander Fiorento looked out nervously over the black-

ness of Fortress Yeovil from his sparse quarters at the top of the iron and steel-glass Tower. In the distance, an Iron-clad was being prepared for its journey, its decks lit up by the yellowy glow of the maintenance crew's steam-powered arc lights. He had been in this backwater for too long, and was happy to grasp at any chance of being relocated, even one as risky as this.

"Are you sure he is here, your Eminence?"

"Not here Commander, no, not in the Fortress. Not yet. But he is making ready."

"And I am to be the bait..."

"Precisely."

Cardinal Vellucci felt no pity for the old Commander – he was too experienced to have not foreseen the sabotage of the other night, and the Emperor was quite rightly demanding his head.

"And if I do this, the Emperor will give me a new post? That *is* what you said."

"If you fulfil your role, he may look favourably upon your request, yes."

"*May...?*"

"Yes Commander, *may.*"

"And if I don't?"

"You know the alternative."

Fiorento sighed. He'd had a good life, until he was posted here. But he had never complained, not once, even though he knew that the mistake that got him the posting was not his. You don't complain. Ever. And now it was him against this, whatever it was that was coming.

"And you say he is just a boy, your Eminence?"

"Outwardly, yes. But from what I saw last night in the Travellers' so-called sanctuary, I am certain that he is The One."

"But how did you penetrate their defences? We have been trying for years with no success. And how did they not know you?"

"Commander," said Vellucci, hard steel now in his voice, "I did not rise to this position by accident."

Fiorento flushed bright red, and gave a deep bow.

"My apologies, your Eminence - I didn't mean..."

The old Cardinal glared at the old soldier as he straightened up.

"We have done our job Commander, now you do yours, or it is your life."

And with this, Cardinal Vellucci vanished. Fiorento breathed out deeply, steadying himself on the arm of a nearby chair as his knees went weak. But as quickly as he went, the Cardinal reappeared, giving the Commander such a shock that he fell into the chair.

"One more thing Commander," said Vellucci, now leaning over Fiorento menacingly. "I am accompanying you on your trip tomorrow. You may not know me at first, but I will make myself known to you."

"Of, of course, your Eminence..." The Commander gave as much of a bow as he could from the chair. When he looked up, the Cardinal had gone again. No matter how long he had lived with it, nor how much of a part of life it was, Fiorento had never got used to the Travelling. Give him a tank battalion and a straight fight any day. The Commander rose from the chair, went over to the dark wooden sideboard, and poured himself a large drink. He was pretty sure he was going to need it.

*

CHAPTER TWENTY ONE

"So is everywhere like that?" said Max, peering out over the darkness of Fortress Yeovil from the relative safety of the hedges on the slopes above. They had waited until nightfall before making their way from the Inn. Nick had driven them in Percy's carriage to the Odcombe edge of the plain before leaving them to walk the rest of the way and returning to Ham Hill. They still had an hour before the Commander flew for Rome.

"Like what?" said Percy.

"You know, devastated and, I don't know, grungy?"

"No, most places are pretty prosperous – the Romans like to make their money out of us. But some places, especially those that rebelled, are left as ruins, as an example. And Yeovil, she rebelled greatly."

"When was that?"

"Oh, way back," said Percy, adjusting his small telescope, looking for signs of their co-conspirators, who were to let them into the Fortress. "Back when we still had Kings and that. The last one, old Henry the Eighth, put up a hell of a fight against Rome he did, but they still conquered us, like everywhere else. You couldn't fight flying ships with bows and arrows. But enough now."

It had taken a lot of work, years in Travelling time, for Percy and the others to go back in time and retrain all the Yeovil Travellers so that, at this precise point, they were now a fully-trained Ironclad crew. In real time, of course, it was a matter of a split second. It didn't make Percy and the others any less tired, but they hid it well, their strength honed by years of rebellion. But, to Max, Percy seemed worried. Max suspected that, despite their precautions, the Travellers still couldn't believe that somewhere along the way their activities hadn't been spotted by the Romans. But, despite their understandable paranoia, their cloaking did seem to have

175

held, the pieces of Max's smartphone they all now carried seeming to have worked.

An owl cried in the distance, once, twice, three times.

"That's the signal," said Percy quietly, still sweeping the Fortress for signs of their allies from inside, and any Romans who might have discovered them. "There," he said, folding up the telescope, putting it back in the pocket of his Roman Naval jacket, and pointing to the Fortress wall. "Let's be going then."

Percy led the way down the slope towards the high iron and stone wall, as Max, Myvi, Owen and Sarah followed, all similarly in Roman Naval uniform, purloined by Percy on one of his Travelling trips. Max felt uncomfortable without his precious duffle coat, but after much ribbing from Myvi, he had been persuaded to leave it at the Inn.

They reached the wall, where they discovered Thomas holding open what looked like a hinged section of six foot thick wall.

"Took some making I can tell you – had to go all the way back to when it was first built and alter the plans," whispered Thomas in response to Percy's compliments. Sarah was the last in, and Thomas silently closed the secret door behind them, before flickering slightly. The door no longer existed. "Can't be too careful..."

The Ironclad fleet hovered menacingly ahead of them, stretching out for half a mile. All were dormant, except for one, lights glowing dimly through portholes, while dozens of maintenance crew busied around on and below deck, making her ready for flight. On the ground, other men pulled trolleys full of large wooden crates of ammunition towards the underside of the ship. That was their way in. Five of them had been emptied of their ammunition. Max hadn't been happy with the idea of being nailed inside a crate, but after much long-suffering persuasion from Myvi, he had accepted it was the simplest way to be smuggled on board.

Slowly and cautiously they crept towards the crates, and as they got close, the loading crew suddenly all left their trolleys to return to the supply depot. It had all been pre-arranged of course, but it didn't make any of them feel any less nervous. Thomas lifted the lid of the first of the crates, and beckoned Percy forwards.

"You first, Percy..."

Percy didn't say a word, but climbed into the crate and lay down, as Thomas pushed the few real nails that had been left back down through the lid and into the crate. One by one the others allowed Thomas to do the same, until at last it was Max's turn. He didn't offer any complaint, and lay down in his own crate, but his head was full of one abiding thought - if someone *wasn't* on their side, if somehow the Romans had got wind of their plans, being nailed into a crate bound for the bowels of an Ironclad might not be the best idea.

Max had a momentary panic as he felt his crate move, but quickly realised it was being winched into the Ironclad. He knew the plan – they'd gone over it many times that day. He told himself over and over that it was all going to be all right, but he'd never been good with confined spaces.

"It's all right Max," came Myvi's voice, but it was very soft. Max was confused for a moment – she couldn't be talking to him from her crate, not at that volume. But then he realised, she wasn't talking to him, she was thinking to him. They hadn't done *that* before...

"Just keep it together, you'll be fine. We'll be fine."

"But what if – " thought Max.

"No what if, Max. You're ready for this, you know you are. Just remember who you are."

"I'm trying..."

"They won't know what hit them Max, trust me."

And then the engines thundered into action, and the ship eased from its moorings and up into the night sky, bound for Rome.

177

"Myvi...!"

"Calm down, Max. You *are* The One. Believe."

*

"He is coming."

"Yes, your Majesty, I see it too. I am with them."

"Bring him to me."

"Your Majesty, I'm..." Vellucci realised instantly that this was an error. Never in his forty years of service to the Emperor had he ever even thought about questioning him. The Cardinal mentally prepared himself for the end. But nothing came. And then it did.

"Your Eminence, his arrival will redeem you, for now nothing else will."

*

Owen prised up the lid of the crate, and looked inside at its occupant. He shot a look at Myvi beside him. Myvi stifled a laugh, reached into the crate and shook Max gently. Max slowly opened his eyes and peered up, to see Myvi grinning and shaking her head.

"Max, have you been asleep all this time?"

Max rubbed his eyes, and sat up, looking around. Percy, Owen, Sarah and Myvi were all stood over him, as well as Thomas and Cyrus, and one he didn't know, but as he was smiling as well he assumed he was on their side.

"What...? No, erm, well, maybe, I mean... Are we there yet?"

Percy laughed, but quickly caught it.

"Nearly Max – we are almost upon Rome. It is time for the next part of the plan to begin. Time to take the fight to *them.*"

But as Max stood up, he knew things were very wrong.

From all around his peripheral vision shimmering translucent black things flew. He widened his eyes to try to snap away from imagined terror, but still they came, small, but slavering ghost Demons, with whirling arms and claws, but almost no bodies, just drooling heads and piercing eyes. There were five of them, and each one flew towards each one of them like a guided missile. The others screamed as they saw them too, but there was no time to react, as the tiny Demons latched onto their foreheads and buried in deep, numbing their thoughts, and their resistance. Max struggled, and tried to mentally scream louder than his attacker, but it was all in vain, as the eyelids of his soul were slowly gummed shut.

"Keep quiet, and you will live," said Thomas, his voice now deep, calm, and chilling. "Resist, and they will destroy your mind."

As Max was helped up and out of the crate, he saw, through the mist brought down upon his vision by his Demon mindcuffs, his co-conspirators standing deadly still, as if terrified to move, and just in case, a dozen men with guns surrounding them all, a dozen men that he recognised from the Abbey the other night, a dozen fellow Travellers, who were obviously no longer so, if they had ever been. Thomas came forwards and helped Max out of the crate, but he was no longer Thomas. Now he was tall, and old, and wore a red robe.

"Master Tovey, I am Cardinal Vellucci, first counsel to his Imperial and Apostolic Majesty the Emperor. So good to make your acquaintance. Now, if you would come with me please...?"

Max's first instinct was to Travel out of trouble, but the moment he tried, his head felt as if it was being split apart by a hundred claws.

"I'm afraid your powers, whatever they are, are of no use any more," said the Cardinal. "The Garcharwyr feed on your resistance – the harder you struggle, the sooner they will drain your mind. But thank you for trying – it has confirmed

my suspicions that you are of no threat to us after all. Your friends here were even less so. Pitiful, that they thought they could deceive us. Whatever they think they can do, we can *always* undo. And now, you shall have the greatest honour."

"What... what's that...?" said Max, trying to keep both mind and body as still as possible.

"Why, you shall meet the Emperor of course. He has waited a long, long time for your coming, and is very much looking forward to your going, if you understand me."

Max understood him only too well. And then the world went into tortuous contortions around them all, the like of which even he had never seen, as the Cardinal, with a mere wave of his hand, took them all with a physically sickening lurch from the Ironclad directly into the Imperial Palace. But in the split second before they were hurtled through the void, a thought entered Max's head, and suddenly he knew all was not lost. The Book. The Cardinal didn't know about The Book – if he had, he would have taken it from him, but there it was, still safe in the inside pocket of his jacket. But now Max mentally slapped himself – doh! By thinking this he had revealed himself!

But then... nothing. Nothing was happening. These 'Garcharwyr' didn't seem to have heard that thought, and so couldn't see The Book. His mind was somehow protecting The Book from them. Or maybe, The Book was doing the protecting.

*

CHAPTER TWENTY TWO

Max had never been actually sick from Travelling before, but then he had never been Travelled with that much power before. As he knelt on the floor of the Audience Chamber, still more came up, as it did for all the others, excepting Myvi, who was still standing, seemingly unaffected, although still with the vacant look on her face brought about by the Demon in her mind.

"Kneel with the others!" said Vellucci in a voice from the depths, pushing Myvi to her knees. She didn't resist, nor even look at Max, only at the floor.

Cardinal Vellucci was the only one to accompany them into the Chamber. He had no need of guards any more – the Garcharwyr in their minds, and the Emperor's two Demon guards, would ensure that escape for his captives was impossible. Now, as the clouds gathered in the giant glass dome before them, Vellucci knelt down also, awaiting the arrival of his master the Emperor; the cracks of lightning out of his sight signalled that he was now amongst them.

"You have done well, your Eminence - a flawless operation. I am of a mind to forgive your earlier transgression."

Vellucci breathed out in relief as silently as he could.

"I am forever in your debt, your Imperial and Apostolic Majesty."

"Get up Vellucci, and bring him to me."

Max felt a firm hand on his upper arm as he was dragged to his feet. He looked up for the first time, and stifled a cry at his first sight of the undead Emperor and his slavering Demon guards. Must be strong, he thought, before a stabbing pain in his head made him stop thinking.

As Max was pulled towards him, the Emperor leaned forwards in his throne.

"So, this is The One, is it?" said the Emperor with a cruel smile, before bursting into laughter. Even the Demons

looked a little alarmed at this, and shuffled awkwardly on their clawed feet. But Max just stood still.

"Really Vellucci, *this* is the redeemer prophesied in The Book?" said the Emperor, holding up the book he kept on his lap always, then laughed loudly again, before leaning right up against the inside of the dome, his face and Max's inches away.

"How did the elders ever think that *you* could defeat *me?* Eh, boy?!"

But Max didn't answer, instead concentrating all his efforts on the crashing glory of Beethoven's Eroica symphony that he had on permanent loop in his head, in an attempt to disguise his true thoughts from the Garcharwyr, and from the Emperor.

"Nothing to say, boy?!" said the Emperor, angering now. The Demon guards stopped shuffling now, looming instead over Max, their drooling jaws slowly opening, revealing rows of jagged, blackened teeth and fat, slime-covered forked tongues. But then the Emperor suddenly sat back in his throne, and they relaxed a little.

"Very well," said the Emperor, looking at Vellucci. "Your Eminence, we shall employ what powers he has in the service of the Empire. I shall bring him into the Great Hall – he and his friends shall join all those other Travellers who have tried and failed to defeat me. I look forward to meeting him in person."

"Very well, your Majesty," said Vellucci, bowing deeply, and as he did, the clouds flooded into the dome, and lightning flashed once more, and the Emperor was gone. And now so too was Vellucci, backing out of the chamber.

"The Lord have mercy on your souls," said the Cardinal, a look almost of sadness on his face. "For the Emperor will not." And then he was gone.

Nothing happened for a moment, and the others slowly stood up and looked around the chamber, and at each oth-

er. But they didn't have time to say anything, as they were suddenly forced by their mental captors to walk towards the huge doors behind the throne dome, which now swung open. There was a collective gasp of horror at what Max and the others saw stretching out behind the doors – this was no Great Hall, not in any earthly sense anyway. Behind the doors stretched a seemingly endless fire-lit cavern, its roof beyond sight, its distant walls dripping with water and blood. As Max and the others stared in dumbstruck terror, they saw also thousands upon thousands of people in myriad concentric circles, all lying suspended over the fiery abyss below, their heads all connected by countless wispy tentacles that glowed with the thoughts passing through them to the centre, a vast, billowing mass of swirling cloud and pulsating light. And before this, on a giant, malevolently ornate throne, sat the Emperor, no dome protecting him, for he had no need of protection from the real world now, for neither he, nor Max and the others, were *in* the real world any more.

None of them were capable of speech, but even had they been, they would have had no chance to say anything, as suddenly their feet flew up from under them, and they were floating horizontal towards the circles of Travellers, for there was no doubt this was what they were, like a gigantic and horrific version of Major Willoughby's TRD.

As Max floated towards an empty space in the outer circle, he was conscious of the Emperor getting off his throne and floating towards him. Beethoven raged ever louder in Max's head as he fought to block even the slightest thought from detection. Max came to a rest, hovering between two others, blank but terrified expressions on both their faces, and now the same ghostly feelers attached to their heads also whipped out and suckered onto his, sending his thoughts directly into the throbbing core, which had the strange effect of filling the cavern with the symphony still thundering in his head. And now the Emperor was upon him, leaning over him and smil-

ing a ghastly smile as Max's head jolted with pain.

"It is no use Max – you cannot block your thoughts from me. Give in, and the pain will be over. Your resistance is at an end – you are now in my service."

Slowly, Max moved his hands up to his chest, palms together. The Emperor laughed.

"You can pray all you like boy, but God will not help you, not *here*."

But just as the symphony now filling the air was reaching its crescendic climax, in one swift movement Max pulled out his book and held it up in front of the Emperor's immediately alarmed face, before pressing it against the one held by the Emperor, clasping their hands together with all his might. The Emperor tried to pull away, but Max held firm, as suddenly a piercing sheet of light blasted out from the books, engulfing them both.

The Emperor screamed. "NOOOOOOOOOOOO!!!"

"Get out of here Myvi!" Max yelled. "And take as many as you can with you – I *know* you can!"

The Demonic tendrils attached to Max and all the countless others snapped away from them, now flailing around the cavern like a million screaming snakes, and the Garcharwyr fled from their heads in terror as the core began to glow yellow, then red, and expanded faster and faster until it exploded with massive force, and suddenly Max and the Emperor were falling into the void, still clasped together. But as they fell, the Emperor's five hundred years suddenly came upon him in a rush, and, with one last unearthly scream, he exploded in a shower of bone dust. Max fainted, seeing no more of his fall.

*

Max came round, slowly, and everything hurt. He lifted his head up carefully, and tried to work out where he was. Just as carefully, he propped himself up on his elbows. The ground

was entirely rock, and everything around him was black. But there was one spot of light, in the near distance. Max pulled himself painfully up, first to his knees, then to his feet. His head spun at first, but he steadied himself, and headed towards the light. There was no memory of how he got here, wherever it was that he was, only the knowledge that he was still alive. At least, he assumed he was. He was thinking after all, even though his thoughts had nothing in them but the light ahead of him.

"Who knows, maybe I'm dead," he said to himself. "I should be, after that..." Max stopped, with fearful memory of what had gone before returning with a crash. But it made no sense – how did he survive that? Again, he thought that maybe he hadn't.

"But if this is Heaven," he said to himself, looking at the nothingness that was all around, "then we really have been seriously misinformed!"

The ground sloped down as he walked, gently at first, but then steeply, and became less solid, as if he was walking in mud. Still the light drew him, and then he was upon it, an opening in the rock that illuminated the narrow path that Max had come along. Looking back at the endless, cavernous depths, and the narrow causeway he'd just walked along, Max was glad he hadn't been able to see where he was.

Behind the opening was an old man, dressed a little like a mediaeval monk, but with long grey hair and beard. The old man looked up as Max slowly and cautiously approached, and smiled, but not with any friendliness, more as one would smile when you know the person you're smiling at is as doomed as you are. The old man put down the quill with which he was writing, and stood up from his desk. Suddenly Max had a sharp pang of recognition, but this was followed by a long confusion as he struggled to remember anything at all. But then one word crashed into his head like a bullet as the old man spoke. Bacon.

"Welcome to the Underworld, master Tovey."

*

CHAPTER TWENTY THREE

As the mist swirled around the edges of St. Michael's Hill, eight Kings and a Queen sat once more on their thrones.

"He has freed us, by his actions, as I said he would," said King Blaiddud.

"We should not have doubted you," said King Locrin. "But now you say one more must be freed, in order for Time to be restored. It is a dangerous path, releasing *him*."

"Indeed, my Lord," said King Blaiddud. "And yet, I am afraid, necessary."

"But how might we do this?" said King Rhun. "It is not in our power surely?"

"The Emperor is fallen," replied King Locrin, "but our master Lord Gwynn ap Llud is not yet restored. Until we can bring that about, the power of Annwn rests with us."

"Nonetheless, we must be on our guard," said King Rhun.

"Very much so, my Lord," said King Locrin.

*

"You have The Book – *my* book," said Bacon, indicating his work on the desk. Max stepped towards the cave entrance to get a better look. This was not the middle-aged Roger Bacon that had tried to kill them in the Priory, but instead an old man.

"I would advise you not to come any closer," said Bacon.

"Why?" said Max, taking another step, but nothing happened. Max walked to the desk, and peered at Bacon's work. It was indeed the same as his book.

Bacon looked at Max, astonished, then at the entrance.

"Strange..." he said, edging towards the entrance. But again, nothing happened.

"What?" said Max.

"There should be Demons," said Bacon, still puzzled. "They

are my jailers. Something must have happened."

"The Emperor is dead," said Max. "I killed him, with The Book. I was hoping it would take me back to my old time, but I'm here instead."

"With The Book? Well, I knew it was powerful, but not *that* much so!"

"But how?" said Max.

"You *do* know what this book *is,* Max, surely...?" said Bacon.

"Of course," said Max. "It's your Time Travelling diary. Grandpa told me."

"It is much more than that, Max. This book is the ultimate Majyg. I am writing it now, here in Annwn, and yet I would not have got here had I not been shown The Book in the first place by your grandfather. I am curious to see the finished work again - may I...?"

Bacon held out his hand for Max to give him The Book, but Max shook his head and backed away. Putting the two books together was what had got him down here in the first place.

"Do not worry, Max – this book is not yet finished, so there is no danger."

Max shrugged, and went to take The Book out of his pocket, but then took another step back as memory flooded back of exactly who Bacon was and what he had done.

"I'm not giving it to *you!*" said Max. "Who knows *what* you'd use it for!"

"I mean no harm, young Tovey, but, under the circumstances, I suppose I must understand. You have progressed much since I saw you last. Very well, perhaps you could just hold The Book up and show it to me? I will stand away."

Max thought about this for a moment, saw no reason why not and slowly took it out of his pocket and held it up. Bacon motioned for him to flick through the pages, and then held up his hand for him to stop.

"Ah yes, of course; *that* is what that page looks like. I was

not sure of my memory. You know what it is?"

"You asked me that already – it's – "

"No no, that page."

Max looked at the page. It was a series of ornate circles, four of them connected to one large one in the middle. Each circle had strange designs on them, while the central one had an image of a castle upon it. He had no idea what it was – he had never really studied The Book since he had found it underneath his grandfather's bedroom floor.

"It is a map, Max, of how to get into Annwn, but also how to get out. It is also a map of how to get to the key, to The Cross that you seek. Do you see, the nine hills, and the nine castles – they are the nine Gate Castles of Annwn."

Max looked again at the page, but still wasn't quite sure what he was looking at.

"This page and those that surround it are the key to finding The Cross, the journey that must be taken, and the four that must take it."

"And who *are* the four?"

"You, of course, your mother and father, and your grandfather."

"Not you?"

"No, I am merely the one who shows the way. The last time, I believed I was the one, that I would create and rule the perfect world. But I was wrong. Do you remember that time?"

"Yes. My dreams are full of it."

"My apologies. Do you hate me for it?"

Max dug deep for a moment, and then remembered.

"You tried to kill me. Many times."

"And yet you live, while *I* am in here."

"No, wait a minute!" said Max, getting angry with Bacon now. "You're the reason I got so messed up inside, *and* the reason the world is as it is, *and* the reason I'm in here!"

Bacon smiled a little.

"Yes, I am sorry about that also. But I have had a long time

to think, waiting for you to arrive."

Max got even angrier now, but then stopped dead in his mental tracks. "What? You knew I was coming? *Here?*"

"Of course – as soon as you arrived at the Inn on Hamdun Hill for the second time, it was inevitable. And now I must get you out again and make amends."

"How?"

"Well, you take your book, and give it to me, the younger, unknowing me, so that the correct time may begin again."

Max scowled at the old man, but then stopped, realisation setting in.

Bacon gave a half smile.

"Had that not occurred to you?"

Max closed his eyes, hung his head, and sighed very deeply. In all the excitement, and the terror, the most obvious had been staring him in the face, and neither he, nor anyone else, had seen it.

"I shall assume from your countenance that it had not," said Bacon, his smile fading. To his surprise, he actually found himself feeling sorry for the boy. But now Max raised his head again, a new realisation having dawned.

"No, wait a minute – you're just trying to trick me into giving you The Book!"

Bacon smiled again.

"Of course you have every right to believe that. But I am afraid you must trust me."

"Why should I?"

"Because, Max, I am the only one who can show you how to get out of here."

*

"Are you sure this is wise my Lord?" said King Locrin. "The Emperor may be dead, but his Demon supporters are loyal. They will follow them."

190

"It must be done my Lord," said King Blaiddud. "Remember that we shall be there to help them. The prize must surely be worth the risk?"

King Locrin thought hard, but then reached a conclusion.

"Very well, let it be so."

⁂

"So, which way then?" said Max.

"Up," said Bacon. "It is always up from here."

But as they stepped out of the cavern, they found themselves no longer in the depths of Annwn, but instead on a dusty cobbled street crammed on either side with a hotchpotch of very old, mostly timber buildings. Except that they didn't look old.

"Well, that was easy," said Max, but Bacon was staring around in confusion.

"I didn't do that..." said Bacon. But now there came a cry.

"Out of the way!"

They both looked around madly, then darted to the side of the road just in time to avoid being run down by a horseman as he cantered by. The world suddenly spun around Max, and he sat down heavily on a nearby doorstep and clutched his head. Travelling consciously, when you're in control of your destination, takes enough out of you, but when someone Travels you from the depths of the Underworld without even a moment's notice, recovery can take a while. After a few minutes Max opened his eyes again, and looked up. The world seemed to have stopped spinning. Beside him, Bacon had obviously had a similar reaction.

"What happened?!" said Max, staring at their new surroundings. "Where are we?!"

Bacon looked up slowly, but then suddenly he was smiling. He knew exactly where they were.

"Oxford," he said, standing, and still smiling. "We're in Ox-

ford."

"Really?" said Max, curious, also getting to his feet. It didn't look anything like the Oxford *he* knew, all gleaming golden-stoned colleges and churches.

"This is *my* Oxford, the town in which I spent much of my life, before I learned of Travelling. Someone is helping us, it seems – someone who wants the old Time back as much as we do."

"Rex!" said Max joyously. "It's the Guardians – they must be free!"

But then there came a deep growling sound. Max and Bacon both looked around slowly to see two huge, drooling Demons stomping towards them. It was the Emperor's guards.

"And so is the rest of Annwn!" said Bacon. "Run!"

As they hurtled down the cobbled street, the walls of the numerous houses and shops seemed to melt as a cloud of Demons of all ghoulish shapes and sizes flooded out from their dungeon dimensions and hurtled on feet and wings towards their prey, their only thought, vengeance for their master's demise.

"I think Time has realised what we are about to do!" Bacon yelled at Max, as both hacked at flying, screeching pursuers with conjured swords. "Do you see that tower on the bridge down there?"

"Yes...?" Max yelled back.

"Get us inside it!"

"I can't do it while we're running – I need to concentrate!"

"Then we had better run faster!"

But now from the direction of the Tower came more, huge beasts, silhouetted by the dazzling low winter sunset, the pounding of their massive feet shaking the ground as they raced towards the two Travellers.

"We are trapped!" yelled Bacon as the still silhouetted beasts got ever closer. But now Max gave out a strangled cry of joy as the sun finally went down behind the bridge, reveal-

ing the nature of the beasts hurtling towards them.

"Get down!" yelled Max, dragging Bacon to the ground just in time as the nine massive hounds leapt over them and into the now screaming Demonic mass.

"It's the Guardians!"

"Into the tower, quickly!" Bacon shouted over the squealing terror of the hellish battle now behind them.

Their way was now clear, and, as they reached the tower on the river that was home to Roger Bacon, at this moment an unremarked young teacher, Time accepted its new destiny.

*

"We're back Major," said Gareth, as an image began to form on the main monitor. "The kid did it!"

Major Willoughby peered at the image and smiled, before breathing a huge sigh of relief.

"How are the boys doing, Sergeant?"

"All fine," said Gareth, indicating the Dreamers' readouts.

"Better send Nick in," said the Major.

"Why him?" said Gareth.

"Because I think he'll want to be there," said the Major, pointing at the image on the monitor, "given that that's the Prince of Wales Inn."

*

Max woke slowly, but with a confusing sense that he was moving, or at least in something that was moving. Opening his eyes blearily, he realised he was in a car. His father's car. And now his father smiled over his shoulder.

"We're back, Max."

"Had a good sleep?" said his mother, also smiling.

Max stared at both of them, and then at his surroundings. It was the same car, but that was about it. His parents were

not only being nice to him, they were both ten years younger than when he last saw them. But that wasn't all. As the
car pulled to a halt, there to greet them outside the Inn, also
about ten years younger, and, more importantly, alive, was
his grandfather. Max wrenched the door open, leapt out and
did something to his grandfather that he'd never done to anyone before, except to Rex. He hugged him.

"Come on Max," said his father opening the boot and taking out large over-stuffed carrier bags, "let's get all these presents under the tree."

Max stared even more now.

"Presents...?"

"Yes, presents," said his father. "Shopping trip, Christmas
tomorrow...?"

"But, we already did Christmas..."

"Now how could we have, Max?" said his mother. "It's only
January the fifth! Proper Christmas, *old* Christmas isn't till
tomorrow! I dunno Owen, what is he like?!"

"You been Travellin' again lad?" said his father with another smile.

Travelling? They know about the *Travelling?!* What...?! But
then Max just shrugged.

"You could say that, yes."

"Well, you can tell us all about it over a nice cup of hot
chocolate. Come on, let's get in out of this cold!" said his
mother, giving him a kiss on the forehead before following
his father and grandfather into the Inn.

Max just stood there for a moment, staring after them, and
then let out a laugh. If this was the new Time Path, then he
very much approved. But the best was yet to come. As he
followed his parents into the Inn, there was a huge cheer
and great applause from everyone inside. Max's gaze darted
around excitedly as everyone, the Brigadier, Nick behind the
bar, all the Tinkers Bubble people... and Joseph, and Myvi, all
raised their glasses, and all yelled "Wassail!"

"You did it, Max," said Myvi, throwing her arms around him. "You did it!" There was another cheer. But as Myvi let go of him, Max was only thinking of one thing.

"Myvi! You got out – out of..."

"Yes Max, thanks to you."

"And they all know, you know, about..."

"Yes, Max," said Joseph. "She told us."

Max turned to Joseph now. "You're Joseph of Arimathea. I never knew."

Joseph smiled. "You did once, Max."

"Does everyone know then?"

"Everyone here, yes."

"Huh."

"Happy Christmas Max!" said Myvi.

"Happy Chr - " Max stopped mid-word as his joy turned to panicked remembrance. He checked his pocket, and, no, it definitely wasn't there. "Myvi, I lost The Book – I had to give it to Bacon to get this Time Path back. He's free again Myvi!"

But Myvi didn't seem concerned – in fact, she was still smiling.

"I know Max, but it's OK – he's the young Roger Bacon now, before he turned."

"How do you know?"

Myvi gestured towards the bar. "Because he's over there..."

Max looked in the direction Myvi was pointing, but only saw a young man, mid-twenties probably, in modern-ish clothes and haircut. But then he looked again. Now he recognised him. It was the young Bacon he'd met in the tower in Oxford, with his older counterpart, the young Bacon he'd given The Book to, just before the older man disappeared into a lost dimension and everything went dark.

"Happy Christmas, master Tovey," said Bacon the younger with a smile.

Max just stared at Bacon, who now raised a glass to him. No, wait a minute...

"But if he's the younger Bacon, then the battle hasn't happened, and I haven't brought you back here."

Myvi looked confused for a moment, but then smiled again.

"No, it happened, and the older Bacon was imprisoned in Annwn. This is a *new* young Bacon, with no memory of any of that. It's like we've started again... again."

But Max wasn't convinced. "So why is he here?" Max went up to Bacon now and looked at him as menacingly as he knew how. "Why are you *here?!*"

But Bacon continued to smile.

"To help you get The Cross of course."

"And how are you going to do *that?*"

"Why, master Tovey, by showing you the way into Annwn."

"How?"

"With these," said Bacon, holding up his hand, The Ring on the third finger, and pulling back his coat to reveal The Brooch on his jacket lapel. And there they were – the Majyga, that Max and Bacon had made together, in Bacon's tower in Oxford. In all the excitement of the new Time Path, Max had almost forgotten about them.

But Max was still not to be distracted. He stared at the Majyga, thinking hard, and then looked forcefully at Bacon.

"Can we do Christmas first?"

Bacon gave a little laugh.

"Of course."

Max thought hard again, and then nodded.

"Alright then."

*

PART FOUR

CHAPTER TWENTY FOUR

"The castle is lost – save yourselves!"

Fireballs rained down on the defenders as they fled out of the giant gates of Caer Sidi and down the steep slopes of the hill it sat on to the woods below. The Plant Annwn, chief among the Tylwyth Teg, the Faeries of Annwn, were defeated, their fortress taken from them by the Demon armies of Rodrigo Borgia. For though his undead body had been destroyed, his spirit lived on in Annwn, as do those of all who have ever lived, and he was still fiercely determined to regain his rule over the Otherworld, before using its forces to retake his Earthly Empire. The first step towards this was Caer Sidi, the Castle of the Faeries, and home of Gwynn ap Llud, Lord of Annwn, ruler of the Tylwyth Teg, and master of the Cwn Annwn, the nine giant hounds that guarded the gates to the Underrealms. But even they had been routed in this battle, taken by surprise by the speed and ferocity of Borgia's attack, and now, with their master imprisoned in his own castle, his cross of power now around Borgia's neck, they commanded the flight of those that remained free.

The retreat secured, the forces of Caer Sidi regrouped on Bryn Cwrdun, from where they could view Caer Sidi in the distance, while safely out of range from the artillery of its new occupiers. The eternal sun shone down upon them, for no cloud shaded nor rain fell upon the lands of Annwn, but the beauty of the surroundings belied the gravity of their situation.

"How many are we, Menestyr?" King Locrin asked of the Commander of the Plant Annwn. The Lord of the Guardians remained in his Gurt Dog form, as did his fellow Guardians. The forces that had been repelled from Caer Sidi rested a way off, a great many tending to their wounds.

"Barely seven hundred my Lord," said Menestyr. He was taller than his fellow commanders, though he was still only at

eye level with the Cwn Annwn. His form-fitting battle tunic shone almost iridescent in the sun, soft as silk but as impenetrable as the hardest metal. Nonetheless, it showed the signs of desperate struggle. "We shall not retake the castle with this force."

"Indeed, Commander, indeed," said King Locrin, before staring out towards Caer Sidi in contemplation. "We must gather together the whole of the Tylwyth Teg, and the Ellyllon, and the Ellylldan, and even the Bwbachod, Gwyllon and Coblynnod, if we are to challenge the usurper Borgia."

"I doubt many of them will join us, my Lord," said Commander Garanwyn, one hand on the exquisite silver handle of his sword as if still expecting an attack. "They live in the rivers, and the woods, and the mountains – they care not for the fate of our castle."

"But they must, Garanwyn, if they wish to survive, for Borgia will not stop at Caer Sidi. He ruled in Annwn but recently, and he will rule again, unless we can stop him."

"But without the Lord Gwynn ap Llud to command them, they will not rise up - they will not follow orders from the Cwn Annwn. I mean no disrespect, my Lord."

King Locrin nodded his agreement.

"We *must* release the Lord Gwynn," said King Blaiddud.

"I agree my Lord," said King Locrin, "but none here will get within a mile of Caer Sidi before Borgia and his Demons sense them."

"Then we need someone he will not expect," said King Blaiddud.

The two giant dogs looked at each other, Locrin knowing exactly what Blaiddud meant.

"I do not think that is wise, my Lord," said King Locrin.

"We have no choice," said King Blaiddud. "Borgia has already declared his intentions to seek the boy out and possess him. He would be safer here, where the usurper would not expect him."

There was a long pause as King Locrin considered. Eventually he looked back at King Blaiddud and nodded again.

"You are right my Lord, as ever," said King Locrin.

"I shall leave immediately," said King Blaiddud.

"No my Lord, I need you here. Send the Gwragedd Annwn. Menestyr, I shall leave that to you. The Lord Blaiddud will give direction."

"Yes, my Lord," said Menestyr, and with that he and his fellow commanders followed as Blaiddud walked away, leaving King Locrin to contemplate this next perilous, but unavoidable move.

*

Max slept late, and it was almost eleven when he came down, fearing what he might find. He woke in a panic that the new path wouldn't be there, but as he arrived downstairs through the kitchen, his mother greeted him with a smile and a hug. Max instinctively recoiled, but then fought his instincts, and smiled at his new mother.

"Morning sleepyhead – happy Christmas!" said Sarah. "There's breakfast out there – tuck in. Thought you might be a bit hungry after all you've been through!"

Max surveyed the kitchen, awash with the ingredients for Christmas lunch. But this was not the Christmas lunch he was used to – every memory of this occasion was just the three of them, a shop-bought turkey crown, packet roast potatoes, and largely silence. But the scene he saw now was very different – a huge goose sat on one surface, alongside a side of beef, a leg of ham, and innumerable and unrecognisable beginnings of many other dishes. And in the middle was his mother, in control of what looked likely to be a huge feast. Except now she was looking everywhere for something that obviously wasn't there.

"Oh no – there's no onions!" she said, having checked every

drawer and cupboard. "Must've forgotten them, silly me! Oh well, back in a mo..."

As Max looked on, his mother flickered slightly, before suddenly having a bag of onions in her hands.

"There we are! What?" This last said looking at Max, who was staring, not quite believing what he'd just seen.

Max shook his head, and smiled at his mother.

"Sorry, but it's just that I've never seen you Travel before."

It was his mother's turn to stare now.

"Well of course you have – I do it all the time! When you're as forgetful as we are you'd be a bit stuck if you couldn't Travel!"

Max stifled a laugh, but then couldn't work out why he was stifling it, and instead just laughed.

"Sorry Mother, but..."

"Mother? My name's Mum! Less of that Mother stuff now boy! Oh, come here...!"

As his mother hugged him again, Max did one of the many double takes he would do this day.

"Sorry... Mum... but you didn't, you know, before...."

His mother looked curiously at him, and then realised.

"Oh my love, I'm sorry – it's a whole different Time Path for you isn't it?"

"Just a bit, yes."

"So, is it better?"

"Well, yes – no-one here thinks there's anything wrong with me."

Sarah looked askance at her son, not sure what he meant.

"How do you mean, wrong?"

"Well, you know, the psychiatrists, and the pills... No, you don't know, of course. No-one could understand why I could see the past all around me. They, you, thought there was something wrong. So I was put on the pills."

Sarah suddenly looked like she was about to burst.

"Oh love, really? We did that to you?" There were tears in

her eyes now.

Max also felt like he was about to burst now, and looked at his mother with love for the first time that he could remember.

"It's alright, Mum - they... you... didn't understand. But you do now. So, yes, it's better."

Sarah threw what she was doing onto the counter and rushed to her son and clutched him to her again.

"Oh love, I'm so sorry," she said, tears flooding down now. "But that wasn't me, not this me, nor your Dad neither. *We* understand, honest!"

"I know Mum," said Max, allowing himself to revel in the affection. "It's OK, really. It's not your fault. We can start again."

"Well, that's alright then," said Sarah, letting Max go, and wiping her eyes with the hem of her apron. "Now go on you, go and get yourself some breakfast while I get on with lunch, alright?"

She was pretending to be busy with her preparations again, and Max let her pretend.

"OK Mum," he said, smiling, to her and to himself, and headed out of the kitchen towards the bar, where there was indeed breakfast laid out, the whole works, kept warm in hotel-style covered dishes. The bar had been transformed into a dining room for the day, some of its tables put in line, while everywhere was decorated with holly, ivy and other greenery. At the table was sat his father, and Nick, and Roger Bacon.

"More bacon, Bacon?" said Owen, passing the mediaeval philosopher a tray, before bursting into laughter. "Never gets old that one!"

Bacon's look at Max suggested that it had got very old, but that he was putting up with it. Max smirked, and sat, and filled his plate with a breakfast the like of which he'd never seen his mother produce.

"So, how are you finding all this?" said Nick, polishing off

his last sausage. "Well," said Max, "I seem to be living in a pub with two parents I barely recognise, a bar manager who isn't actually here but asleep on a bed in another dimension and a thirteenth century alchemist who has tried to kill me at least half a dozen times in the last few days. So, I'm finding it a little strange to be honest..."

"You cannot condemn me for things I have not yet done, master Tovey," said Bacon.

"Yet..." said Max, giving Bacon a stare.

"They have told me the past actions of my older self," said Bacon. "And their consequences – I can assure you that you have nothing to fear from me."

Max just didn't know what to think, so he ate some breakfast instead.

"That's the trouble with Travellin' lad," said Owen, pouring himself some more coffee. "You don't know if you're comin' or goin'! Now eat up – your mother needs this clearin' for lunch asap."

Max looked at his father in amazement, and then at Nick, and Bacon, and the whole scene in general, before throwing his hands up in a yeah whatever kind of way and tucking into his breakfast. He was pretty sure it was the best he would ever taste.

The others cleared breakfast while Max went to get dressed, after looking through his new wardrobe with some confusion. There were no sensible shirts and trousers anywhere to be seen, just jeans, and T-shirts, and sweatshirts, and some things that looked scarily like hoodies. At least his duffle coat was still with him, but was this really the new him? Max dressed cautiously, feeling more and more uncomfortable with every moment, eventually coming up with a combination that was somewhere between the old him and what seemed to be the new him - jeans, yes, but a proper shirt, albeit one with logos and things on, and the only jumper he could find, even if it did have a hood. And... trainers... Max

had never worn trainers in his life, but it seemed he did now. Oh well, he thought, here goes...

Max got downstairs to a round of applause, from everyone. They were all here now – his parents, his grandfather, Nick, Bacon, the Brigadier, and Joseph, and of course Myvi. She was doing the most applauding.

"Oh, Max," said Myvi, giving him a hug that in equal measures made him feel extremely uncomfortable and extremely happy. "You're a real boy!"

Max just looked at Myvi as she started to laugh, and angered, but then, to his astonishment, let it go, and laughed possibly the loudest of all.

"It's a whole new world, Max," said Myvi, hugging him again, but this time kissing him lightly on the cheek. There was a very awkward pause, before they both pulled away, and looked at each other, suddenly this time neither being able to deal with the new reality. The awkward silence was broken by Max's mother coming in from the kitchen.

"Right you lot, off you go for a walk while I lay this up for lunch!"

Everyone looked around at Sarah, and all left the table immediately.

"Come on boy," said Max's grandfather as he rose. "You don't argue with your mother when she's in full flow!"

Everyone laughed, Max the most, as they headed for the door.

The Hill at least was the same, though the car park was almost empty.

"Everyone knows we close on old Christmas Day," said Owen, as if knowing what his son was thinking.

"Ah, right," said Max, as they went through the gate that led towards the war memorial.

"Quick once round then it's off to Church!"

"We go to *Church*...?!" said Max in alarm.

"On Christmas Day? Of course!" said Owen. "Where shall

we go today, Da?"

"I thought maybe Westminster Abbey, 1066?" said Percy. "See the Conqueror get crowned and that?"

"Ooh, yes," said Max's father, rubbing his hands together. "There was a right old punch up after that one wasn't there!"

"Which you started if I remember rightly," said the Brigadier, to much laughter.

"So Max," said Myvi, slipping her arm through Max's as they walked. "How's it going?"

"What, you mean the whole Travelling parents, Grandfather still alive, general happiness thing? Yes, I could give it a try, I suppose."

Myvi laughed, but then stopped still and stared at Max, a broad grin on her face.

"Max! That was almost sarcasm!"

Max thought about this for a moment, then smiled and shrugged. Myvi gave his arm a little squeeze, and they walked on to catch the others up.

*

By the time Christmas lunch was over it was dark outside, and the wind was beginning to rattle the windows a little. It had been an epic meal, a banquet indeed, with course after course after course, starting with mince pies – proper ones, with meat in them – and ending with a giant, flaming figgy pudding.

"Right then, who's for cheese?" said Sarah as she cleared up the last of the plates, none with a scrap of food left on them. There was a general groaning around the table, followed by laughter.

"That was simply marvellous, mother," said Owen, giving his wife an affectionate squeeze as she took his plate. "Best ever, I'd say!"

There was a general chorus of agreement, at which Sarah

blushed bright red.

"Oh, you lot – it was nothing, really. I cook more than that on a *normal* day!"

Max shook his head and gave a little laugh. His mother could cook now! Most of his life so far had been spent living on ready meals.

"Hold up, who's that?" said Percy looking at the window. There were three bright lights outside now, that seemed to be being carried, but their bearers were obscured by the glow. And now there was a knock on the door.

"Carol singers?" said Sarah as she disappeared into the kitchen.

"I'll go," said Owen, getting up with a slight over-fed groan. A moment later he returned, a look of part alarm and part amazement on his face. There was a gasp as the three light-bearers entered behind him, barely four feet tall, wearing long shimmering green cloaks that covered silvery white flowing dresses, tiny swords hanging from their belts in exquisitely wrought silver scabbards, and phosphorescent orbs encased in fine tracery atop their long staves.

"Erm..." said Owen, a little unsteadily. "Anyone here speak Faerie...?"

*

207

CHAPTER TWENTY FIVE

"She says they are the Gwragedd Annwn," said Bacon, "and they have been sent for Max. They..." Bacon struggled in translation for a moment, then got it. "...need his help!"

"Gwragedd who?" said Owen sitting down heavily, more from the shock of seeing his first Faeries than from the amount of Christmas lunch he'd just eaten. "And anyhow Bacon, when did you learn to speak Faerie?"

"They are the People of the Waters, Owen," said Bacon, trying not to sound condescending. "And it is not 'Faerie', it is the language of Annwn, the First Language, from which all others sprang. Percy and I have travelled extensively there recently: I have made their tongue my especial study."

Now all eyes were on Max, who was looking a little puzzled.

"Who sent them?" said Max, his mental blinkers not allowing the impossible presence of three Faeries in a Somerset Inn to distract him.

Bacon asked the question of them, and the answer came 'the High King Locrin'.

"Why couldn't he come himself?" said Max.

This too was answered, and now the assembly knew of the war raging for control of Annwn, and the imprisonment of its Lord Gwynn ap Llud. But Max was still not to be distracted.

"But we haven't done presents yet!"

Now everyone laughed, except for the Gwragedd Annwn, who looked at each other in puzzlement.

"Oh, love," said Sarah, giving her son's head a hug. He still wasn't used to the hugging, but he let it go. "It's Travellin', isn't it – we can go on adventures for years and still be back a second from now, and not a day older!"

"Yes, I never quite worked that out," said Max, trying to subtly extract himself from his mother's embrace. "Sometimes I feel like a thirty year old teenager. But anyway..." he

said, trying to stay on track, "...*we?* They said they were sent for *me*..."

"Well, you don't think we're going to let you go on an adventure like this on your own do you?" said Sarah, playfully cuffing Max around the head. "We can *all* go – just what we need, a nice adventure before the film starts on telly! What say you lot?"

All except the Brigadier gave a rousing chorus of approval.

"Love to," said Sir John, "but battle recreation to organise and all that. Only a day to go..."

"I'm in," said Nick.

"Can you *go* to Annwn, Nick?" said Max. "I mean, you're not even actually here..."

"Anywhere you go Max, I can go. And anyway, you need me – I'm your trail of breadcrumbs."

"That's settled then," said Sarah. "Mr Bacon, tell those Faeries that we'll come, but it's all of us or nothing."

Bacon tried not to smirk, and gave the Faeries the good news.

They conferred for a moment, and then turned back, the leader nodding at Bacon, although the nod looked a little reluctant.

"I'll get my adventurin' coat then!" said Sarah, heading back towards the kitchen. "Tell you what, Annwn ain't going to know what's hit it!"

*

The Gwragedd Annwn's lights illuminated the way through the winter darkness as the party followed them out from the Inn and into Norton Woods, before emerging in the valley that led to Pit Wood, a mile or so from Ham Hill. Max had been persuaded to change his trainers for sturdier boots before they left, and he was glad of them. Not that he had needed much persuading to discard the trainers of course. The

way through the woods was very muddy, and the path into the valley steep and slippery, and tricky footing, even with the Faeries' lights to guide them. But while the others were all in long, hooded, weather-proof waxed coats, Max had insisted on keeping with his trusty duffle coat.

"Where are they taking us, Bacon?" Max asked.

"Please Max, you must call me Roger," said Bacon. "We are on the same side now."

Max grumbled to himself, still unsure of this new turn of events, and instinctively still unable to trust the man. But he accepted it – this younger Bacon did seem genuinely to be one of them now.

"So where are they taking us, *Roger?*"

"To Pit Wood lake they say. Water is their portal to Annwn, and it is the nearest."

And so soon they reached Pit Wood, deep down in the valleys overshadowed by the great hill of Hamdun. The darkness was almost total, the mist enveloping the lake eerily illuminated by the Gwragedd Annwn's lamps.

The leader of them spoke to Bacon, and he relayed her words.

"We must walk out into the lake – they assure me we shall be safe."

As Max and the others watched with ever-increasing amazement, the three Gwragedd Annwn walked out into the lake, but their feet didn't even breach the surface. As they reached the middle, they turned, and beckoned the others to follow.

"Really?" said Max. "It's alright for them, they're magical or something, but we're human, and we *sink* in water."

"Trust them, Max," said Myvi. "They haven't come all the way from Annwn just to drown us."

With that, Myvi began to walk out into the lake, and just as with the Gwragedd Annwn, her feet also stayed above the waters.

"See - it's OK!" she said as she reached the three water Faeries. "Come on Max!"

Slowly, and carefully, Max put one foot onto the water, and felt it to be strangely solid. Trusting Myvi, he stepped onto the water's surface with one foot, and then the other, before walking towards her, cautiously at first, but then with more confidence, turning to the others as he got half way.

"Come on you lot – it's easy!"

And then they were all in the middle of the lake, and the three Gwragedd Annwn began to swirl their glowing staves around in the lake mist like children with sparklers, causing it to whirl, and eddy, and then swoop around them until it was a wild, rushing mass of flashing fog - and before they realised what was happening, suddenly everyone was hurtled down into the lake.

"Myvi...!" Max yelled as he was plunged into the waters.

"It's alright, Max!"

But then just as they were sure to be drowned, now in place of water there was solid ground, and in place of darkness there was light.

"Welcome back to Annwn, master Tovey," said Bacon, looking around at what were obviously familiar surroundings.

"Call me Max," said Max, looking around with slowly returning familiarity. He had been here... before... and it was every bit as beautiful as his now ever more rapidly returning memory recalled. As he looked up, he saw a great fortress, high up on the hill above them. Max quickly realised why the hill looked familiar.

"Is that Ham Hill up there?" Max asked Bacon.

"Yes and no," replied Bacon. "It is the same formation, as are all of the great hills, but instead it is in this dimension and not that."

"What is it called here?"

"That is Caer Fandwy, known to the ancient British as The Fortress of God's Peak."

"So where is the one we're going to, Caer Sidi, in our world?"

"Cadbury Castle. But Caer Fandwy is also one of the Gate Castles of Annwn that I mentioned before, and we shall return to it, if we are to find The Cross."

"The Cross is at Ham Hill?!" exclaimed Max in confusion. "Has it been there all along?! Why haven't we just gone and got it?!"

Bacon smiled a little.

"It is in many places Max, in Time, but as you know, that is its place of origin, and that is where we must look for it. But it has been hidden by Time - to find it again, we must first make a special journey, following in Joseph's ancient steps, as set out in The Book. Fortuitously, our present destination, Caer Sidi, is the first step on that journey. Joseph must reclaim the cross that is the key to the Castle, and close its gateway to our world."

"*Joseph* must?" said Max.

"It is one of our crosses," said Joseph. "When I first came to this country, I, and those that journeyed with me, visited the great castles, on our way from the coast to found our first chapel at Glastonbury, and gave to each castle one of the crosses that we brought from Judea."

"I know the story," said Max. "But how have they become the keys to the Gates of Annwn?"

"As they embraced the Gospels," said Joseph, "the people of the Castles believed the crosses had the power to keep darkness from the land, and so they were invested with this power. Belief was a much stronger force back then than in your time, Max."

In his head, Max was trying not to go 'this is the actual Joseph of Arimathea!', but he still had one more question.

"So why do these crosses lead us to *The* Cross?"

"Because in your past, it was my gravestone," said Joseph.

Max just looked at Joseph in amazement now, but any more questions he may have had, and he had a *lot*, were curtailed

by the Gwragedd Annwn.

"We must make haste," said their leader, at which everyone but Bacon and Percy stared at them.

"We can understand you now?" said Max.

"There is but one tongue in Annwn," she replied. "All are understood. My name is Gwynythyr." At this she held out her hand, and as Max took it, she gave a slight curtsey. "These are Gwaldredyr, and Annwddwyl." The other two now also curtseyed slightly.

"Why are you curtseying to me?" said Max.

"It is a mark of respect for The One who will save us," said Gwynythyr.

Max scowled at this. "How?! What can *I* do?!"

"The High King Locrin will explain all when we reach him."

"Where is he?"

"Near to Caer Sidi, preparing for battle, about a day's walk from here."

"Walk?" said Max in surprise. "Why can't we Travel there?"

"There is no Travelling in Annwn," said Gwynythyr. "We are outside Time here."

"Really?" said Max, a little confused. "So how am I going to help you then? Travelling is sort of what I do."

"That is for the Lord Locrin to say – we are merely to bring you to him, and to gather forces along the way."

And so they began to walk.

Though memory was returning of his previous visit to Annwn four years ago, Max was nonetheless still marvelling at its beauty as they walked, as were the others. It was as if someone had taken the gently rolling hills of England, removed all the roads and buildings made after the middle ages, and replaced every single tree, bush and flower with a stranger, more exotic and much more beautiful version. But as Max looked closer at a clump of bushes they were passing, though they looked like nothing on Earth, still he felt he recognised them. The bush was almost egg-shaped, with

alternating bright orange and green leaves, with a single blue and white flower growing from the top.

"They are in The Book," said Bacon, noticing Max's interest in the bushes. "All the flora in The Book was painted from life, here in Annwn. Or should I say they *will* be painted, for I have not yet begun The book, even though I carry it with me!"

"Ah, of course," said Max, before he and Bacon left the bushes and caught up with the others as they followed the diminutive Gwragedd Annwn. The grass felt soft and warm underfoot, cushioning their steps. There were no fields – no food needed to be cultivated in Annwn, for everything that was needed grew naturally – just lush, green undulating landscape occasionally interrupted by gatherings of stone and thatch cottages. But up above, clouds began to gather, and darken. Percy looked at the skies and frowned.

"The evil even affects the skies," he said to Max. "It has always been summer in Annwn, until now."

"Why would anyone want to spoil all this with war, Grandpa?"

"Human nature must survive even after death, I suppose," Percy replied. "As must evil."

"Grandpa..." said Max. He knew what he wanted to say but it kept coming out wrong in his head.

"I know, boy," said Percy, understanding the look on Max's face as the lad stared at him. "But I'm alive this time round, so let's try and keep it that way, eh?" With that, Percy patted Max on the shoulder and laughed. Max didn't want to join in, but he couldn't help it.

Presently they came upon a small collection of cottages, all arranged around a small pond, like something from the cover of a doctor's waiting room magazine. As they approached, Gwynythyr held up her hand for them to stop.

"We must be careful," she said, turning to her charges. "The influence of the Usurper spreads even to the most peaceful of

places. Wait here - we shall go ahead alone."

The three Gwragedd Annwn now drew their miniature swords, and crept towards the cottages. As they got nearer, a man emerged from the first cottage, dressed in linen shirt, leather trousers and sandals, and looked at the three strangers in alarm.

"Put away your swords, quickly!" said the man, rushing towards them. "I shall not hurt you, but Fymbldwn will if he sees you here. Get inside, quickly!"

"We have companions," said Gwynythyr, gesturing behind her to Max and the others.

"Then bring them all in, but hurry!"

Gwynythyr gestured urgently at the others to join her, and soon they were all crammed into the cottage's small kitchen. It was very country farmhouse, all time-worn wooden units, with a table and four chairs in the middle. A large pot of delicious-smelling soup was simmering on the stove, while above it hung a selection of copper pans and an assortment of utensils.

They quickly introduced themselves, and discovered that the man's name was Harald, a casualty of the first Saxon battles against King Arthur. The Travellers all looked at each other awkwardly on hearing this, but once they had established that none of them had killed him, things became a little more relaxed.

"That soup smells proper lush," said Sarah, peering into the pan. "Can I try a bit?"

Harald handed her a spoon, and Sarah took a slurp.

"Mmmm, lovely – what's in it?"

"It is mostly made from the fruit of the Cywiar tree."

Sarah took another spoonful and licked her lips.

"Fruit you say?" said Sarah, taking a little more. "Tastes like chicken..."

"So who is this Fymbldwn then?" asked Percy.

"The Giant who lives on the hill," replied Harald. "Up until

recently he has been very friendly, but now he has become aggressive, and demanding, and very distrustful of strangers."

"It is the Evil," said Gwaldredyr. "It spreads through Annwn with ever greater speed."

"Where are you headed?" asked Harald, stirring the soup.

"To Caer Sidi," said Annwddwyl, "to aid the Cwn Annwn in its recapture. We seek assistance from any that will join us."

Harald shook his head nervously. "I cannot go with you – I must tend to Fymbldwn. This soup is his lunch. If we do not feed him, he will eat *us* instead."

Max looked confused.

"Erm, I don't mean to be funny, but... aren't you already dead?"

Harald smiled – it was a common misconception among new arrivals.

"Our first lives are over, yes, but we are now in our second lives in Annwn. Those too can be ended, and then all is darkness."

Nick looked at Percy.

"A Giant might be useful in a fight..."

Harald shook his head.

"He will not join you, though formerly he would not have wasted a moment in doing so. I do not believe that he is evil now, but he is sufficiently tainted by it not to fight it."

Bacon came forwards now.

"Perhaps we could change his mind? There are plants that grow here that might improve his mood..."

Harald shook his head again.

"We have tried them – Anaxwl, Byrntwm, Gwlrwt and others, but to no avail."

"Have you tried *this* one?" said Bacon, taking out The Book and flicking through the pages before settling on one. "It is called Myrandwl, I believe. It is supposed to banish all feel-

ings of enmity."

Harald looked at the illustration, and nodded in recognition.

"Yes, I know of it – but we have been unable to harvest any."

"Why?" said Myvi.

"Because the only place it grows is upon Fymbldwn's hill."

*

CHAPTER TWENTY SIX

It was only a small hill, with a clump of maybe a dozen trees at the top. As Max and Myvi crept up, there was no sign of the Giant at first. But as they neared the crest of the hill they saw him, asleep against the trunk of one of the outer trees, and nearby him, a solitary Myrandwl bush. It was more of a small tree really, with a central trunk that bore the main head of large blue and green leaves, while other small clusters of leaf heads sprang from lower down. And projecting from each leaf head was a large solitary fruit of blue and white that looked like it had been cut in half, for the orange seeds were visible in the middle, while wispy fronds surrounded the whole fruit like a feathery halo.

But it was Fymbldwn that was taking most of Max's attention. It was his first Giant, at least that he remembered, and he didn't look anything like he had imagined a Giant would. No big beard and even bigger hair, no knobbly warty nose, just a very large version of a man, ten feet tall or more – it was difficult to tell when he was sitting down. His clothing was much the same as Harald's – plain open shirt and leather trousers, but in place of Harald's sandals were very big brown leather boots that reached up above his knees.

"He's asleep – this is going to be easy!" said Max rather too loudly, for now Fymbldwn grumbled under his breath, opened one eye slightly, before closing it again and going back to his snoring.

"Or maybe not," said Max, both he and Myvi having ducked out of sight. As they peered back up again, they breathed a sigh of relief. He was still asleep.

"OK, carefully now," whispered Myvi, "and *quietly.*"

Max nodded, and they both began to slowly crawl around the hill and then up the slope towards the sleeping Giant from behind the clump of trees. But as they got almost within reach of the bush, Max stepped on a twig, which snapped loudly.

At this Fymbldwn woke with a start and looked around, but saw no-one, largely because Max and Myvi were now hiding behind the trunks of two trees.

"Now what?" hissed Myvi.

Max peered out from behind his tree and surveyed the scene, and then looked like he had had an idea.

"See that branch there," whispered Max, pointing to a branch that overhung the Myrandwl bush.

"Are you serious?!" hissed Myvi, her eyebrows raised in derision. "He'll easily hear you coming!"

"It's worth a try," whispered Max, and began to climb the tree he was hiding behind. Like the rest of the plants in Annwn, it was like no tree he had ever seen, with a knobbly golden trunk, and branches that twisted and curled, intertwining with those of the neighbouring trees. It was relatively easy to climb across the lattice of branches, and soon Max was in the tree next to the one Fymbldwn was resting against, and so far without the branches creaking under his weight.

But now, as Max crept out along the branch that overhung the bush, its fruit tantalisingly close, the branch began to bend downwards slightly, and every move he made seemed to make, to Max, an ear-splitting sound. But he knew the volume was in his imagination, for the Giant hadn't stirred. But as Max's hand was inches away from the precious fruit, there was definitely a sound - a cracking sound. Max felt himself lurch downwards as Fymbldwn now looked around angrily.

"Max – look out!" came a yell from Myvi, and before Max could grab the fruit the branch gave way completely. Max, and the branch, fell right towards Fymbldwn, who looked up at the last moment; but it was too late, as the branch hit him on the head and Max fell to the ground. But though he was stunned, Fymbldwn wasn't knocked out by the blow, and now he was *really* angry, and gave out a ferocious roar.

"Run Max!"

Max was already doing exactly that, and was out of sight of

the Giant before he was spotted.

"Plan B!" yelled Myvi as they both hurtled down the slope towards the cottages. But Harald was already on his way up the slope, bearing the large pot of soup, a huge spoon sticking out of it.

"Fymbldwn!" yelled Harald. "I've brought you lunch!"

The Giant was already half way down the hill when he saw Harald and the soup, and went to swipe him off his feet with his massive club, but then he stopped, bent down and sniffed at the pan that Harald was very nervously holding out.

"Cywiar..?" said Fymbldwn.

Harald nodded furiously, smiling as widely as his nerves would allow. Fymbldwn reached down and took a spoonful of soup, and very noisily slurped it down in one. Harald flinched as Fymbldwn bent down again, but then relaxed, as the Giant smiled, and rubbed his belly.

"Mmmm, my favourite!" he said, taking the pan from Harald and stomping back up the hill, while shouting back over his shoulder.

"I'll bring the pot back!"

Max and Myvi were now safely back in Harald's cottage, and were puffing and panting heavily as they reported on their abortive attempt at getting some of the Myrandwl fruit.

"Well, we'll just have to try something else then, won't we?" said Sarah.

"Like what mother?" said Owen.

"Well I don't know – reason with him maybe?"

Harald shook his head. "Fymbldwn is like a child – there is no reasoning with him, only pacifying him with food. Most times he would sleep again after eating, but I suspect this time he won't, after what just happened. He will be on his guard."

"Then some of us will have to distract him while the others get the fruit," said Percy.

The Gwragedd Annwn conferred, and seemed in agreement.

"We shall lead the assault," said Gwynythyr, "whilst you – " but she was cut off by Harald.

"No!" he exclaimed nervously. "He doesn't like strangers much, and he *really* doesn't like Faeries. Besides, your swords would be useless against his thick hide. He would eat you as soon as look at you."

"Then *we* must do it," said Owen, pulling a sword out from under his long coat. Max did a double take at the sight of his father with a sword, but when his mother drew hers he failed to stifle a laugh.

"What's so funny boy?" said Owen, a little cross, but without venom. "You've seen your old man wield a sword many a time!"

But Max shook his head. "No, I haven't. I don't seem to have any memories of this Time Path. Not yet, anyway."

"Well, trust me love, we're pretty handy with them," said Sarah, wielding hers round in an attacking arc. "Granted we never took on no Giant before, but there's a first time for everything!"

And so a plan was formed. Percy, Owen, Sarah and Bacon would attack Fymbldwn, while Max, Myvi and Nick would grab the Myrandwl fruit.

"And what of me?" said Joseph.

"You stay here Grandda," said Myvi. "Your part has yet to come."

"Right then," said Sarah, sword still in hand. "Let's go and do us some Giant killing!"

"No!" exclaimed Harald again. "Don't kill him! He's not a *bad* Giant really..."

"Figure of speech, love," said Sarah with a smile, and with that they trooped out of the cottage and towards the hill.

This time they didn't need to sneak up on the Giant – they wanted him to know they were there, and as they climbed the hill, Owen, Sarah, Percy and Bacon made as much fighting noise as they could. But when they reached the top, to their

222

surprise, Fymbldwn didn't attack them, but just looked up from the soup pot nestled in his lap and growled at them, as a dog would protecting a bone from a rival. He did throw rocks though, and anything else he could reach while still sitting against the tree.

"Go away!" he growled, taking another mouthful of soup. "No fighting at lunchtime!"

His would-be attackers just looked at each other, not sure what to do next. They crept nearer, swords drawn, but then hastily retreated again as another rock hurtled towards them.

"Now what?" said Sarah. "We can't distract him if he won't fight now can we?"

"Wait till he's finished his lunch I s'pose," said Owen, shrugging.

An awkward silence fell on them now, as they just stood there, pumped up and ready for battle but unable to fight, as if they were on their way to a party but stuck in a lift.

On the other side of the trees, Max, Myvi and Nick were equally confused.

"What's going on?" said Myvi.

Nick peered out at the scene ahead from behind his tree, and grinned.

"Seems he's eating soup and throwing rocks."

"Well, maybe I could sneak up to the bush, if he's that focussed on his lunch," said Max.

The other two shrugged.

"Give it a go I suppose," said Myvi, shaking her head. "Giants – what can you do?"

Max took a deep breath, and started off around the trees, taking great care this time where he put his feet. He was only yards from the Myrandwl bush now, its melon-sized blue and white fruit almost out of the soup-obsessed Giant's peripheral vision. Maybe he *could* get it!

Step by step, Max crept ever nearer to the bush, and still Fymbldwn slurped unaware at his soup. Two more steps now

and he was there – one... two...

Max took hold of the fruit and pulled, but it didn't budge. He pulled again, but harder this time, but in doing so he made the bush rustle.

Slowly, very slowly, Fymbldwn turned his head towards Max and glared him.

"Leave – my – flower – *alone!*" he growled, deeply enough to shake the ground a little, before taking another mouthful of soup.

Max slowly withdrew his hand, looking around for the best escape route. He started backing away, very carefully, but now Fymbldwn slurped down the last drop of soup, put the soup down, and, with a loud belch, slowly got to his feet, picking up his huge club as he rose. For a moment both stood before each other motionless, waiting for the other to make the first move. And then Fymbldwn made it – more swiftly than his bulk would suggest he was able, he brought his club down on Max, but Max had seen it coming, and was already running back to Myvi.

"Run Myvi!" he yelled, but she and Nick were already doing so, and now all three were running from Fymbldwn around the clump of trees. However, though they were fast, Fymbldwn's stride was three times the size of theirs, for now he was on his feet they realised he was at least twelve feet tall. Round and round the trees they raced, as Fymbldwn got closer and closer to them. But as he was almost upon them, Max had an idea.

"Other way!" he yelled, and they instantly changed direction, running right at Fymbldwn, whose size prevented him from reacting quick enough.

"Mum, Dad, where are you?!" Max yelled as they ran round the trees as if they were being chased around a playground roundabout by the school bully.

"CHAAAARRRGE!" screamed Sarah, and suddenly the four of them were running full pelt at Fymbldwn. But he was

ready for them, his club swiping all of their swords out of their hands in one go.

"Oh-oh..." said Owen. "RUN!"

Ducking another murderous swipe, they ran for their swords and then turned to face Fymbldwn as he lumbered towards them. Now the fight began for real as they surrounded the Giant, dodging his club and aiming blow after blow at him, but none of them were doing any damage as they couldn't reach above the top of his boots, and their leather was so thick the only effect their swords were having was to make Fymbldwn angrier.

"The problem is," said Max as they watched all this from a safe distance, "they've got him distracted, but he's also right by the bush."

"You noticed that too?" said Myvi with a grin. Max just gave her a look, at which she grinned even wider.

"So what are we going to do?" said Nick.

"We'll have to distract him from being distracted," said Max. "Come on!"

And with that, Max ran towards the Giant, waving his hands and yelling furiously.

"Hey Giant, over here! Yes, that's right – it's me, the flower stealer!"

Fymbldwn stopped waving his club around for a moment, but then charged after Max, while his attackers charged after *him,* and all six of them raced round and round the trees again – but this time, as he passed it, Max leapt for the Myrandwl fruit and ripped it from the bush.

"What are you going to do with it?" said Myvi as Max passed her and Nick.

"No idea!" said Max as he went past her again, and then at the third pass, "I'm making this up as I go along!"

"Give me my pretty flower back!" yelled Fymbldwn, just missing Max with his club. But with a second swipe, the club caught Max's heel as he ran and he went flying to the ground,

landing face down in the grass. As he scrambled to get up he felt himself being lifted up into the air by the hood of his duffle coat, and now he was inches away from Fymbldwn's now heavily scowling face.

"Put him down!" shouted Sarah as she rushed to save her boy, but with one blow from his club he sent her flying off her feet to land by the others. They crouched down to her in concern, but she wasn't hurt, only dazed.

"Shan't!" said Fymbldwn. "All that running has made me *hungry!*" Fymbldwn held Max close enough now for Max to almost faint as the Giant belched soup fumes right into his face. "And *you'll* do nicely!"

Fymbldwn now opened his massive mouth, to reveal a set of blackened but obviously very sharp teeth, and though Max was struggling with everything he had, nothing could stop Fymbldwn from bringing him towards his waiting jaws.

"Nooo!" screamed everyone, but just at the last moment, Max remembered the Myrandwl fruit he held in his hand, and, as Fymbldwn's eyes closed, ready to eat Max head first, Max shoved the fruit into the Giant's mouth, which then crunched down sickeningly on it.

For a moment no-one moved, as Fymbldwn, eyes still closed, munched away on the fruit.

"Mmmm, human is *tasty!*" said the Giant, but then opened his eyes, to see the human still intact. Fymbldwn looked curiously at Max, who he was still holding up by his hood.

"I thought I was eating *you!*" he said, before pulling a stalk from his mouth, which still had enough of the fruit left on it to be recognisable.

"My flower!" he exclaimed in alarm, which soon turned to anger. "You made me eat my flower!"

But just as Fymbldwn was about to eat Max for real, a strange look came over his face. It looked like confusion at first, but then soon turned into what Max hoped was happiness, for the Giant began to smile, and lick his lips.

"Mmmm, my flower was *delicious!*" he said, putting Max down gently. "Thank you human – it's my new favourite thing to eat!"

Fymbldwn looked round at everyone now, as if he was seeing them for the first time.

"Hello..." he said uncertainly. "Who are you? My name is Fymbldwn!"

Hesitantly everyone introduced themselves.

"Well, it's nice to meet you," said the Giant with a smile. "What game shall we play next?"

Max couldn't help but laugh, and the others soon joined in, and soon even Fymbldwn was laughing, even though he obviously wasn't quite sure what it was that he was laughing about.

"That was funny!" said Fymbldwn. "Do it again!"

But now Max looked at Fymbldwn, and, reaching up, took his hand.

"Fymbldwn, we need your help," said Max gently, and then told him of Caer Sidi, and the Usurper Borgia, and the rout of the Cwn Annwn.

For a moment Fymbldwn looked puzzled, but then his expression turned to anger.

"But that's *wrong!*" he growled. "You can't take someone's castle! We must *do* something!"

"Yes Fymbldwn," said Max, smiling at the Giant, "we must. Will you help us?"

Fymbldwn thought about this for a moment, and then nodded like an excited child. "Yes," he said, smiling. "Can I bring some friends?"

*

CHAPTER TWENTY SEVEN

"So, I am dead...?"

"Indeed you are, Vellucci - welcome to your second life!"

The late Cardinal looked around at his surroundings in confusion, and did similarly at the young man before him.

"Where am I? And who are you, sir – you look a little familiar, but...?"

"I am Borgia - your Emperor, Cardinal, but made young again, as are all in the Otherworld. Including you."

Borgia gestured to his left; Vellucci turned, and caught sight of his reflection in one of the many mirrors that lined the walls of the huge ornate room he found himself in. He was indeed young again, but still in the scarlet robes of a Cardinal.

"But I *have* no Emperor..." said Vellucci, but then realised where he was. "*Had* no Emperor." But then he almost convulsed with strange, horrific memories that weren't his own. Except that he knew instinctively that they were. "I... have had *two* lives...?"

"You will become used to it in time," said Borgia. "The life you just left was one of simple service to your Church and to your Pope, but there was also a life of service to me, when I ruled the world!"

More awful recollection now flooded into Vellucci's head, of his other life, lived in a world ruled by an undead Emperor.

"And I shall rule again, Vellucci – the boy took it away from me, but I shall possess him, and with my new army restore my earthly Empire – and you shall help me!"

Vellucci looked at Borgia now, a powerful young man dressed in the Imperial finery of ancient Rome. Was he mad still, and evil, as in this other life he now fully and sickeningly recalled?

"But I am at peace now," said Vellucci. "If we are in heaven, then I have no need of earthly things."

Borgia brooded, glaring at his former Cardinal.

"Vellucci, I brought you here after your death in order that you lead my armies. We have conquered the Lord of Annwn and his castle already..." Borgia gestured around him. "If you do *not* do my will, I shall have you cast into oblivion!"

Borgia made another gesture, and two guards entered. Vellucci recoiled in shock at first, but then to his horror he recognised the guards. In his other life, they were the drooling, fork-tongued Demons that once stood beside the Emperor's portal to the other world – to *this* world.

Vellucci realised he had no choice.

"Very well," he said, with resignation.

"Very well, your *Majesty!*"

Vellucci stared at Borgia, and then sighed.

"Are we not all equal in death?"

"No."

Vellucci sighed again. "Then this is not the heaven we were promised. Your Majesty."

"It is neither heaven nor hell, Vellucci, but at the same time both. It is simply the next world."

"As the pagan Celts believed then?"

"It would seem so."

Vellucci sighed deepest of all now. "I feel... betrayed."

"No time for that, Vellucci," said Borgia, turning to leave the room, and gesturing for him to follow, which he did, followed by the two snuffling and growling Demon guards. "We have much planning to do!"

"So, your Majesty, how do we get to the boy?"

Borgia smiled. "We do not need to – once more, he is being brought to *us.*"

*

Harald had made good his promise to join them in their venture, but didn't walk with them, instead going in search

of his fellow fallen Saxon warriors, with a promise to meet them at Caer Sidi.

Fymbldwn had indeed brought some friends, seven of them in fact, all similar to him, in size and character. The Gwragedd Annwn were a little nervous at first, for they knew of Fymbldwn's dislike of Faeries, but it seemed the Myrandwl fruit had abated even this enmity, and now they ran alongside them without fear, and though they were less than a third the height of the Giants, they seemed to be able to run forever without tiring. The others were tiring quickly though.

"Honestly," said Sarah, "it's like taking a bunch of school kids on a walk! Oi you lot, slow *down!*"

Fymbldwn stopped at this and looked round, only for the Giant behind him to bump into him and knock him over. But far from being angry, they both giggled.

"We fell over!" they both said together, still giggling.

"Oh, good grief!" said Percy.

They reached Fymbldwn and his friend, Dwrandwn, as they were getting to their feet.

"You are going too fast for us Fymbldwn," said Bacon.

"Especially me!" said Joseph, puffing and panting as he brought up the rear.

"But we have to get to the nasty man!" said Fymbldwn.

Max shook his head. How much use these overgrown children were going to be in battle he had no idea.

"*I* know!" said Dwrandwn. "We could give them piggy backs!"

"Ooh yes!" said Fymbldwn, clapping.

Max and the others all looked at each other, all very unsure about this. But then they all shrugged – why not?

"Alright then," said Max to Fymbldwn, "but shoulders I think, not piggy backs."

"Even better!" said Dwrandwn, beckoning the rest of the Giants over. They all cheered when they heard the news, and then, as one, they knelt down and put their hands out to help

their new friends reach their shoulders.

"Right then," said Owen. "Pick a Giant I s'pose..."

And so the eight Travellers each climbed up onto the shoulders of their chosen Giant, and as the Gwragedd Annwn led the way, the Giants followed with only the odd complaint, mostly to do with their riders grabbing their hair to stop themselves falling off.

They were covering the ground at a great rate now. In the distance, a high hill was now just visible with a white fortress of many towers on its summit, gleaming against the almost black clouds that now filled the sky above it.

"Caer Sidi?" Max asked Gwynythyr, who ran beside Fymbldwn.

"Indeed," said Gwynythyr. "We shall be with the Cwn Annwn well before nightfall at this pace."

"Nightfall?" said Max curiously. "Do you sleep in Annwn then?"

"Of course," said Gwynythyr. "The mind must rest, even in the second life."

They came upon a small hill now, covered with a mass of what looked like small fruit trees, with seven point star-shaped leaves and almost iridescent blue and green furry fruit.

"Look Dwrandwn – Oddwrau!" exclaimed Fymbldwn, and, without warning, all the Giants bent over to pick a handful of the fruit, sending their passengers sprawling over their heads and into the fruit bushes with much alarm and complaint.

"Fymbldwn!" said Max, picking himself up.

"Ooh, sorry," said Fymbldwn, pausing from his feast. "I forgot you were there! Mmmm, yummy yummy!" he said, carrying on eating. "Try them – they're *really* tasty!"

Max picked one of the fruits and smelled it cautiously first. It smelled like bananas and custard. He took a small bite, and discovered that it tasted like bananas and custard too.

"Delicious!" said Max with a smile. "Try one, Myvi!"

Myvi ate one of the fruits and nodded in agreement. "Yes, they are," she said, gesturing at the Gwragedd Annwn, "but we must get on, Max."

Gwynythyr and her companions were standing and glaring at them impatiently.

"Yes, you're right," said Max. "Come on Fymbldwn, we have to go."

"Ohhh," said Fymbldwn, pouting. "But we want more fruit!"

"We have to get to the nasty man, remember?" said Max, at which the Giants looked at each other for a moment, then immediately stopped eating, stuffed their pockets with more fruit for later, scooped up their respective passengers and hurried across the top of the hill.

"Sorry," said Fymbldwn with a loud belch.

But as they reached the other side of the hill, the Giants suddenly stopped still, almost throwing their passengers off again, for before them was a wide lake, stretching for miles to left and right, although the opposite shore and the forest that led down to it was maybe only half a mile away.

"Now what?" said Max to Gwynythyr, still beside Fymbldwn. "Go round it?"

"There is neither time nor need," said Gwynythyr. "This is Llyn Tanddwr, our home."

Gwynythyr took out a tiny silver horn from under her cloak and put it to her lips.

"That's beautiful!" said Fymbldwn, as from the horn came an exquisite, ethereal sound, as if a whole Faerie choir were humming in perfect harmony.

Ahead of them the perfectly still waters of the lake now began to ripple slightly, and then churn. To everyone's amazement what looked like a huge swan's head now broke the surface, but it was soon obvious that it was the prow of the shimmering white boat that followed, made in the form of a giant swan, which now sailed silently towards the shore to

meet them.

"We'll never all fit in that," said Sarah from Dwrandwn's shoulders. "Not the Giants anyhow!"

"Don't worry about us," said Fymbldwn. "We can swim across!"

"Ooh, yes!" said Dwrandwn. "We *love* swimming!"

"Race you into the water!" said another, and suddenly the eight Giants quickly put down their passengers and ran towards the lake - but then Fymbldwn suddenly stopped at the water's edge, and the rest all piled into him and fell over. When they had stopped laughing, they all enquired noisily just why Fymbldwn had stopped. Fymbldwn pulled the fruit from his pocket.

"We can't swim with *these* in our pockets!" he said, and the others all exclaimed in realisation, then breathed a collective sigh of relief.

"That was close!" said Grwmbldyn. "That was very clever of you to remember, Fymbldwn!"

The others all agreed, and gave a polite round of applause, at which Fymbldwn blushed with pride.

"Why can't you take your fruit in the water?" said Max.

"Oddwrau berries don't like getting wet," said Fymbldwn.

"Why?" asked Myvi. "What happens to them?"

"They go bang!" said Dwrandwn, pulling out a large handkerchief and putting his fruit into it, as the others did in turn.

"Can you look after it for us please?" said Dwrandwn, lowering the parcel of fruit to Max.

"Of course," said Max, putting down what was to him a heavy sack.

"Thank you!" said Dwrandwn, and with that the Giants ran and leapt into the lake at once, laughing and yelling, and causing a huge wave that threatened to sink the Faerie vessel. As Fymbldwn and friends splashed about in the water, which also involved much splashing of each other, Gwynythyr led the Travellers onto the boat. There was just enough room,

and although their combined weight meant the water was almost up to the level of the sides of the boat, still it managed to set off for the other side, albeit with some wobbling.

"Keep very still," said Joseph. "The Giants may be enjoying themselves, but I shall not if I fall in, for I cannot swim."

In fact, the Giants were enjoying themselves so much they hadn't noticed that their new friends were heading away from them.

"Hey, wait for us!" yelled Fymbldwn as the Giants swam towards the boat, with what could only be described as a very inelegant doggy paddle.

But as they reached the Faerie boat, a mist suddenly came from nowhere and descended on the lake. Gwynythyr suddenly looked anxious.

"What is it, Gwynythyr?" said Max.

"I do not know – but I suspect..." said Gwynythyr.

But then they discovered exactly what it was, as half a dozen shapes rose slowly from the water and into the mist. They were tall, but still Faerie-like; however, their skin and clothing was not white, but grey. They didn't move, but just hung in the air, their feet not quite out of the water, and yet somehow gluing them to it.

"Return whence you came," said one of them, in a deeper voice than Max was expecting from a Faerie. "The Halls of Caer Tanddwr are fallen, your kin dispersed, or dead."

"Who *are* they?!" Max whispered to Bacon.

"They are the Fomori," Bacon whispered back. "Faeries of the Water, as the Gwragedd Annwn, but also shape-changers."

"What other shapes do they take?"

"Just hope you do not find out."

Gwynythyr clutched the hilt of her sword as, carefully, she stood up in the boat.

"Why have you done this to us, Lord Grymnwr? We have no quarrel with the Fomori."

"There is a new Lord in Annwn, and he has our allegiance. You seek to challenge him, this we know well, and thus you are our enemy."

Gwynythyr hung her head slightly, but then raised it again defiantly.

"We seek no fight my Lord, merely passage across our lake."

Max noticed that Gwynythyr's companions were now quietly loosening their swords in their scabbards, as were his parents and the others. A fight was obviously coming.

"It is *our* lake now, my lady Gwynythyr," said Lord Grymnwr, "and you shall have no passage."

"So be it!" yelled Gwynythyr, as all three drew their swords and dived headlong into the lake, to emerge near to the Fomori, and immediately gave battle. But as the Fomori engaged, they began to transform; their heads elongated, now with jaws full of razor-sharp teeth, their necks became snakelike, attached to new, bear-like bodies. Each of them was now almost as big as the Giants, but still they floated in and above the water.

But though the Gwragedd Annwn were now tiny in comparison, they fought the Fomori with renewed venom, their swords, small though they were, inflicting many wounds on their serpent attackers. But they were only three, and the Fomori were large and many.

"We have to do something!" said Max helplessly. They had swords, but they had no control over the boat as the battle raged away from it.

"Giants, up!" yelled Myvi. "We have the nasty man to deal with, and these monsters are in our way!"

At this, the Giants grabbed their previous passengers, put them upon their shoulders, and swam towards the battle. The Gwragedd Annwn were being beaten back, outnumbered and outsized, but now Fymbldwn and his friends launched themselves.

"Leave our friends *alone!*" yelled Fymbldwn, swiping at

the Lord Grymnwr with his club and knocking him almost back to the far shore. At the same time, Dwrandwn and the others swam towards the rest of the Fomori with one hand and lashed out at them with clubs in their other, while their passengers slashed at snapping jaws and stabbing spears with their own swords, a double edged attack, but still they were not winning the fight, for they were at a bad advantage, having to swim while the Fomori floated free of the water.

Trying not to be distracted by the strange sight of his parents' obviously well-honed sword-fighting skills, Max dealt the Fomori he himself was fighting a savage blow to the head with the flat of his sword, knocking it down into the water, before tugging on Fymbldwn's hair to get his attention.

"Ow!" said the Giant.

"Sorry Fymbldwn, but we have to get back to the boat!"

"Why? I'm having fun!" said Fymbldwn, swiping out at two Fomori who bore down on them, and knocking them both off their feet. But in moments, they reappeared, angrier yet.

"But we're not winning!" yelled Max. "Get me to the boat – I have an idea!"

With a little grumbling, Fymbldwn knocked the two Fomori over again, and swam back to the boat, depositing Max into it. Max opened up the sack of fruit, spilling its contents onto the floor of the boat.

"Pull the boat towards the fight Fymbldwn!" said Max.

"But..."

"Don't argue Fymbldwn – I know how to win this!"

Fymbldwn pouted, looking like a child that had been told off. Max looked at him and threw his arms up in despair.

"Fymbldwn, we don't have time for this – just pull the boat!"

And so Fymbldwn did, swimming with one hand and pulling the boat with the other, and now Max was within shouting distance of the rapidly advancing Fomori, and the rapidly retreating Gwragedd Annwn. The Giants were doing their

best, as were their sword-wielding riders, but they were no match for the now massive lake serpent Faeries.

"Get off him you gurt snake... thing..." said Sarah as she stabbed desperately at the Lord Grymnwr, who was bearing down on Max's father. The wound distracted him from the fight with Owen, but now he turned his attentions to Sarah.

"Oh-oh..."

Sarah fought valiantly, as did her Giant, but Grymnwr was too fast and too strong for them, and now lashed his fearsome tail around the Giant's neck, and began to squeeze the life out of Giant and rider alike.

"Get off my *mother!*" screamed Max, taking one of the Oddwrau berries and dipping it into the lake. Almost immediately it began to swell, and change colour to a very dangerous-looking red. Max threw it as hard as his tired arm would allow, and as the Lord Grymnwr's devilish jaws opened, and prepared to finish Max's terrified mother, suddenly he found himself swallowing a rapidly enlarging fruit. He only had a split second to register the fact that it tasted like bananas and custard before his body blew apart, his soul consigned to eternal darkness.

*

CHAPTER TWENTY EIGHT

The Fomori had fled under Max's barrage of exploding fruit, retreating into the depths of the lake, allowing the party to reach the safety of the opposite shore.

"That was good thinking, love," said Sarah with a proud smile. "Not sure how much longer we could have held those Fomori things off!"

"You were doing fine, Mum!" said Max, returning her smile.

"Well, you know, I do my best," said Sarah with a laugh, twirling her sword around.

They were making their way through the forest, the trees every bit as strange as the flowers they'd encountered before, with tall thin stems, each branch ending in one huge, green, spherical leaf, big enough for someone to sit inside, and all in all looking almost as if they had been drawn by a child. Fortunately the canopy was high enough up for the Giants to pass underneath without their passengers banging their heads on the branches.

The trees did however block out a lot of light, which slowed their progress, as the Giants kept tripping over unseen exposed roots.

"I think I'm feeling seasick," said Max as Fymbldwn stumbled again.

"I know what you mean," said Myvi with a half grin.

But then the Gwragedd Annwn suddenly stopped, and Gwynythyr held up her hand for the others to do the same. Max and Company pulled up their respective Giants just in time to avoid another pile-up.

Now Max saw the reason Gwynythyr had stopped – in the distance, shadowy figures were flitting through the forest gloom, appearing and then disappearing. The Gwragedd Annwn all drew their swords, before motioning the others to stay put, creeping forwards through the trees.

"You won't need those my Lady Gwynythyr," came a voice

from behind them, and then as if from nowhere they were surrounded, by more Faeries, dozens of them, these taller than the Gwragedd Annwn, with more elongated faces and hands. Gwynythyr and her companions turned, and relaxed.

"My Lord Emerydd, what brings the Tylwyth Teg to the Tall Forest?" said Gwynythyr, sheathing her sword.

"I could ask you the same question, my Lady," said Emerydd, as each clasped the other's wrist in greeting.

"We travel to Bryn Cwrdun, to deliver these," she gestured up at Max and his fellow Travellers, "to the Cwn Annwn, to aid in the relief of Caer Sidi."

Emerydd looked up at Max with an amused look.

"And how do the High Kings of the Hills see the Usurper being defeated by a handful of humans?"

"We are not mere humans, my Lord," said Bacon, making his Giant put him down in front of the Faerie leader. "We are The Travellers of the legends, The Teithwyr, and *he...*" Bacon gestured at Max. "...is The Gwaredwr."

"Is he indeed?" said Emerydd, but now there was less amusement in his face, and those of his companions. "He is a bit short for a saviour..."

"Maybe," growled Myvi, leaping from Dwrandwn's shoulders and landing, sword at the ready, right in front of the Fairie leader. "But he has defeated the Fomori already – imagine what he might do with an army behind him."

"No, *wait!*" said Max. "Fymbldwn, let me down." Max was now on the forest floor, looking wildly around. "Just stop a minute, *all* of you!"

It had all suddenly hit Max in a rush, and his head was whirling, days of improbable events welling up against his already shaky psychological dam, which was now threatening to burst.

"What?" said Myvi. "What is it Max?"

"It's just... I don't know – what's happening? We're heading for a battle, with Faeries, we're riding on Giants, and we're..."

Max crouched down now, his head in his hands.

Myvi touched him on the shoulder lightly.

"It's OK Max – you did well back there."

But then Max gave her a look that shook her to her bones.

"I'm fourteen, Myvi - I don't want to be *anyone's* saviour!"

But now Owen stepped up to the mark.

"It's alright boy, I understand – it was the same with me when I was your age, when your grandfather first took *me* Travellin'."

Max looked up at his father in a mixture of amazement and confusion, and then sighed deeply.

"Sorry... Dad. It's just that... look, a week ago I was in my room at home playing Warcraft, two days ago I was in a twenty-first century mediaeval Rome, and today an almost unrecognisable Christmas was interrupted by three Faeries. I mean, Christmas was nice, you know..."

"Oh, come here you," said Sarah, crouching down and giving him a big hug and Max managed not to automatically recoil.

"It's just a lot to take in, that's all."

As Max got shakily to his feet again, the Tylwyth Teg looked at each other almost in embarrassment, while the Giants shuffled awkwardly. But Emerydd looked at Max dubiously.

"Whether or not he is the Gwaredwr, he is of no use to us like this. The Gwyllon have come down from the mountains. Rumour has it that they now support the Usurper – they must be stopped before they can reach Caer Sidi."

But now Max angered, a red mist descending upon him as he spun to face Emerydd, pointing with his sword as he did.

"Look *you,* I'm just trying to get my bearings, *alright?!*"

But now everyone stared at Max, especially the Tylwyth Teg. For Max was no longer standing and pointing at the Lord Emerydd, he was behind him, his sword at the Faerie leader's back.

And now the Gwragedd Annwn, and the Tylwyth Teg, and

even the Giants, knelt down before Max.

"What?" said Max, not quite sure what had just happened. "What is it?"

"You just Travelled, Max," said Myvi. "You're not supposed to be able to do that in Annwn."

Max looked at the kneeling faeries and Giants, knowing now *what* had happened, but still not quite *how.*

"He *is* the Gwaredwr!" said Gwynythyr, as everyone bowed their heads.

*

"Why do we wait, your Majesty?" said Vellucci, looking out from the walls of Caer Sidi towards the enemy encampment on the hill in the distance. "They are being reinforced, and then they will come for their castle."

"Indeed, Vellucci," said Borgia, who stood next to him on the glistening white ramparts. "But I care not whether the castle stands or falls – all this was designed so that they would bring the boy, and they *are* bringing the boy – I have it on very good authority."

Vellucci nodded in understanding. "You have a spy in their midst, your Majesty?"

"Naturally, Cardinal, naturally."

*

The Tylwyth Teg took the lead through the forest, while the Gwragedd Annwn and the Giants now formed almost a guard around Max and the Travellers, their numbers now much reinforced as others of their fellow Faeries joined them.

"Nick," said Max. "Can the Major get us out of here if it all goes wrong?"

"Ah," said Nick. "I was rather hoping you weren't going to ask me that."

"Oh...?" said Max, looking intently at Nick now. "Why...?"

"Well, Annwn isn't just another dimension – it is at the beginning and the end of all dimensions."

"What's that mean then?" said Owen.

"It means," said Percy, "that we don't know – that it's never been done before. Doesn't it, Nick?"

"I'm afraid so, yes. Although it isn't impossible..."

Max turned to Bacon now. "But *you* know the way out, don't you." It wasn't a question. "You *told* me you did."

Bacon smiled. "In theory, yes."

Max looked nervously at Bacon now. "But you *have* got in and out, *haven't* you – you and Grandpa, you said so earlier! Grandpa...?"

Percy tried to look comforting, but didn't quite manage it. "Well, yes, we have, but only when it was just the two of us. With *this* many, it might be tricky."

"Don't worry, Max," said Myvi. "The Guardians will get us home, when the time comes."

Max nodded, reassured now. Yes, Rex would protect them, as he always had. So far. As long as they could get to him, of course.

Up ahead the Tylwyth Teg suddenly stopped, and Max could hear why. In the distance the sound of hundreds of feet crunching the forest floor was unmistakeable. The Tylwyth Teg and the Gwragedd Annwn walked almost silently, but whoever these were were obviously not concerned about being heard.

"It is the Gwyllon," said Gwynythyr." The Faeries of the Mountains."

"A mile or so away by the sound," said Gwaldredyr. "They come from the West."

Emerydd arrived now.

"It is indeed the Gwyllon, in greater numbers than I had feared. But we are ahead of them, and may yet spring a trap."

"What do you want us to do, my Lord?" asked Percy.

"Stay here, with the Giants – you will be safe."

"But we wants to help!" said Sarah, her sword drawn and twirling around. Emerydd smiled.

"And so you shall, my Lady, when we reach Caer Sidi."

Sarah blushed and giggled.

"Oh, no need for the my Lady bit, my Lord – just Sarah will do!"

"Very well – Sarah," said Emerydd, and gave a little bow. "I shall return once we have dealt with the Gwyllon."

Emerydd turned, and went back to his people, shortly disappearing from their sight.

"Well, what shall we do now then?" said Owen.

"I could go for a snack," said Sarah. "Oi, Fymbldwn, got any of them Oddwrau berries left?"

The Giants all felt in their pockets, but they were all empty.

"We used them all against the Fomori," said Myvi.

"I believe that large fruits grow at the very top of these trees," said Bacon.

Suddenly there was an almost thunderous noise, and the Travellers all looked around wildly.

"Sorry," said Grwmbldyn, rubbing his stomach. "It was my belly. It needs food too."

"I'd better get up a tree then," said Myvi with a grin. "Can't have *that* noise going on all day!"

Myvi quickly shinned up the tree trunk and through the canopy, where indeed large blue fruit the size of melons were sprouting.

"Catch!" she said, pulling one of the fruit from its stem and dropping it down to the others. But before she could pick another, she gasped as she saw something in the near distance. She looked over to the West, where the Tylwyth Teg were lying in wait, but the Gwyllon were no longer heading for their trap – they were heading right towards Max and the others below. Myvi quickly shinned back down the tree to the ground.

"What, no more fruit?" said Fymbldwn, pouting a little. "Grwmbldyn ate *all* of that one!"

"We've got bigger things to worry about than your stomachs," said Myvi. "The Tylwyth Teg have been deceived - we have to get out of here!"

But it was too late. They came out of nowhere, and all around them now were hundreds of grinning black Faeries, the tallest of all they'd seen so far, easily six feet tall, with thin but muscly black-armoured bodies, and oversized heads with wide jaws filled with jagged teeth.

"They're like those things in the Priory," said Max to Myvi.

"Yes," said Myvi, "but bigger, and *much* nastier-looking! *Now* what?"

"Now?" said a large Gwyll stepping forwards, "Now *he* comes with us, to Caer Sidi." He was pointing at Max.

"And the rest of us?" said Owen nervously.

"The rest of you die," said the Gwyll.

"I don't think so!" said Fymbldwn, and swiped at the Gwyllon leader, but his club swung through clear air as the Gwyll leapt out of the way and Fymbldwn overbalanced and toppled over, to be immediately swarmed over by Gwyllon like ants on an upturned beetle until they had him pinned to the ground and multiple swords at his throat. The other Giants tried to come to their friend's rescue, but they suffered the same fate.

Now the Gwyllon leader advanced on Max, two other Gwyllon by his side.

"Seize him!" yelled the leader.

But then Max's mother leapt in front of him.

"You'll have to go through me first!" she said, her sword waving between the three oncoming Gwyllon.

"And me!" said Owen, now side by side with his wife.

"And me!" said the others almost simultaneously, now surrounding Max.

"Oh, very well," said the Gwyllon leader, and launched at

245

them, twin swords flashing through the air to meet theirs. They held him back, just, but in the fury of his attack, he took his eyes off Max, who was now behind him, his sword blade on the Gwyll's throat. The other Gwyllon backed away on seeing this, both amazed and frightened by what they had just witnessed.

"What's your name, Gwyll?" hissed Max, pressing his sword harder on his captive's throat.

"I am Ashknau, Lord of the Gwyllon," the leader hissed, his windpipe now constricted by Max's sword.

"Well, Ashknau, put your swords down and you will be spared."

"You can't kill me – you're just a boy!" On that last word, Ashknau pushed Max's blade away sufficiently to free himself and spin round, both swords hacking down on Max. Except Max wasn't there, he was behind him again.

"I can do this all day, Ashknau," said Max, now Travelling to one side of the Gwyllon leader as he lunged, tripping him over and putting his sword to his throat.

"Who are you that you can do these things?!" said Ashknau in astonishment, the fight now gone out of him.

"He is the Gwaredwr," said Emerydd, as he and many hundreds of Tylwyth Teg now surrounded the Gwyllon.

"The Gwaredwr?! We had no idea!" said Ashknau, still flat on his back. "The Lord merely said a boy was coming, and to bring him to him."

Myvi loomed over the Gwyllon leader now.

"Is the Evil upon you then, Ashknau?" she hissed. "Do you truly serve the Usurper now?"

"Usurper?" said Ashknau, a little confused. "No, we serve the Lord Gwynn ap Llud. "There is no evil upon us!"

Now Myvi laid it all down for the Gwyllon leader, exactly who the Lord they were serving was, and what his evil intentions were. The Gwyllon were aghast.

"You know, looking at them," said Max to Myvi, "you'd sort

of assume they were bad guys."

"Nothing is what it seems in Annwn, Max," said Bacon, before turning to address the Gwyllon Lord again. "My Lord, we are journeying to join the Cwn Annwn, to aid them in retaking Caer Sidi and releasing the imprisoned Lord Gwynn ap Llud. Will you join us? The Gwyllon are many, and would aid our cause well."

Ashknau gestured at the tip of Max's sword, still at his throat.

"Let him up Max," said Myvi.

The Gwyllon leader now rose, and bowed to Max, at which all the Gwyllon did the same.

"My apologies, Gwaredwr," said Ashknau to Max. "Had I known, you would never have been in danger."

"I accept your apology Lord Ashknau," said Max, sheathing his sword. "Now, can you tell your men to release the Giants please? They're big, but they won't hurt you."

Ashknau gestured at his people, and the Gwyllon got off their struggling captives. The Giants rose now, but immediately raised their clubs at the Gwyllon and started to growl deeply and nastily.

"Fymbldwn.." said Max admonishingly. "I said you wouldn't hurt them – now put your clubs down..."

"Oh, all right," said Fymbldwn, and he and his fellow Giants all lowered their clubs, but not without much grumbling.

"The Guardians of the Hills will be pleased to have your support," said Gwynythyr as she approached Ashknau.

"The Gwyllon are no friends of the Cwn Annwn," said Ashknau with a little snarl. "But we shall support the Gwaredwr, and thus be their companions in battle."

"Right then!" said Sarah. "Better be off to this castle then I s'pose!"

*

CHAPTER TWENTY NINE

King Locrin looked out from Bryn Cwrdun towards Caer Sidi in the distance. As the other Kings, he remained as Gurt Dog. Their depleted forces seemed reassured by the sight of the Cwn Annwn in charge.

"What I do not understand," said Locrin, "is why the Usurper and his forces do not pursue us, but instead remain in the castle. It is as if they *want* us to attack."

"I suspect a trap, my Lord," said King Mynyr.

"More than likely," said King Blaiddud. "But we shall over-turn it, with Max's help."

"That is a lot of trust to put into one boy, my Lord," said King Mynyr.

"That trust has been rewarded many times in the past days," said Blaiddud. "It is well-placed – he will not let us down."

"I hope you are right, Blaiddud," said Locrin. "But surely he should have been here by now – the Gwragedd Annwn left nearly a day ago."

"Perhaps the Usurper has got wind of our plans, and has intercepted the boy?" said Mynyr.

"No," said Blaiddud, "he is well – I can sense his presence in Annwn still. Have patience, my Lord – he will be here."

At this moment the Plant Annwn Commander, Menestyr, came running towards them, a smile on his face.

"My Lords, look!" He was pointing down the slope of the hill. The three Guardians turned to look, and also smiled.

"The boy has come," said Locrin. "And he has brought a host with him!"

Sure enough, marching up the hill now were thousands of Faeries of all kinds, armour glinting and standards flying, as well as hundreds of Saxon warriors led by Harald, with Max, the Travellers and the Giants at the head of it all.

"Even the Gwyllon are joined!" said King Locrin in aston-ishment.

"Gather the Cwn Annwn, my Lord," said Blaiddud to My-nyr. "We must greet them as one." The other two smiled, and nodded their agreement.

As Max and his army reached the top of Bryn Cwrdun, there was a rapturous reception waiting for them, as Giant greeted Giant, and Faerie greeted Faerie. Not all the races were there – the solitary brown Bwbachod had had no inter-est in the fate of the Plant Annwn's castle, and the Coblynnod had stayed put in their mines – but many others had joined the Tylwyth Teg and the Gwragedd Annwn, from the Ellyl-lon, the tiny, almost transparent Faeries of the valleys and groves, to the equally small Ellylldan, Fire Faeries, resplen-dent in their glistening red armour.

Max and Myvi both beamed as they crested the hill and saw the Guardians, and ran towards Blaiddud, wrapping their arms around his huge neck.

"Rex!" said Max. "I thought I'd never see you again!"

"You have done well, Max," said Blaiddud. "But, you brought your parents...?"

Max and Myvi both laughed.

"They're not my parents," said Max. "Well, they are of course, but they're different. They're Travellers now, like me!"

"Not quite like you I suspect Max," said Blaiddud. "They could not have rallied an army such as this. *They...* are not the Gwaredwr."

At this, the Guardians of the Hills all bowed their heads.

"Oh, not you as well Rex!" said Max, blushing. "I didn't do much, really..."

Blaiddud smiled. "Max, I sense that you have overcome great danger to be here."

"But I am afraid there is more danger ahead young man," said King Locrin. "With the army you have brought, we shall strike at Caer Sidi this nightfall; but for you there is a very special, and very dangerous task. For under cover of battle, you must enter the castle in secret, and find and release the

Lord Gwynn ap Llud."

Max nodded. "Yes, I thought you might want me to do that. But I don't know where he is."

"He is imprisoned in the deep dungeons," said Locrin, "held there not just by chains, but also by some other, darker force of the Usurper's making."

"But I don't know how to *get* to the dungeons," said Max. "Not trying to be negative or anything..."

"I do," said Bacon, approaching the Cwn Annwn. Blaiddud looked with a little alarm at him.

"*You* are here?" said Blaiddud warily.

Max looked at Bacon, then at Blaiddud, and then realisation struck.

"Oh, right – no, he's different now too. He's the young Bacon, before he went, you know..."

But neither Locrin nor Blaiddud looked convinced.

"I can vouch for him," said Percy, also coming forwards.

"Percy!" said Blaiddud, a happier note in his voice this time. "You live!"

"As you can see," said Percy. "Time is a strange thing indeed. But Roger knows what happened before, and the consequences that his older self suffered. History will not repeat itself."

The Guardians still didn't look happy with the situation, but they accepted Percy's word.

"Very well, let it be so," said Locrin, looming over Bacon now. "But if you are deceiving us, Bacon, it will be your head. Do you understand?"

Bacon nodded quickly, his eyes wide and scared.

"Hmmm," said Mynyr, as Bacon backed away. "I think perhaps you two should go as well," he said, gesturing at Myvi and Nick. "Just in case." Blaiddud and Locrin agreed.

"Can't you just Travel us in?" said Max. "You Travelled me and Bacon to Oxford, surely you can get us into the castle?"

Blaiddud shook his head. "No, Max – it would reveal our

plans to the Usurper."

"Now you must all rest," said King Locrin. "King Blaiddud has command of this attack, and it begins in three hours."

"And I have much to do before then," said Blaiddud, before gesturing at Menestyr. "So if you will excuse me, Commander Menestyr will outline the plan for you."

Max and the other Travellers now all bowed to the High Kings, before following the Plant Annwn Commander to his quarters.

*

Under cover of darkness, the relief forces moved swiftly and unseen down the slopes of Bryn Cwrdun, taking cover among the woods at the foot of the hill that bore Caer Sidi.

The Giants, now numbering in their dozens, were the first part of the offensive, under Owen's command, throwing a barrage of huge rocks against the walls of Caer Sidi, prompting the Demons on the defending parapets to hurl fireballs in response. But the Cwn Annwn were expecting this; Blaiddud signalled to Sarah, and she sent in the Ellylldan, the Fire Faeries, who were expert at causing fires, but at the same time also expert at putting them out. They were also the only Faerie race apart from the Bwbachod who could fly. As each fireball was launched by the Demon defenders, so the miniature Ellylldan flew towards them and consumed their fire within them, before spewing it back at the walls of the castle, scorching the pristine white brickwork and anyone or anything within ten yards of it. The fireballs quickly stopped being thrown.

"This is but the beginning," said King Blaiddud to Max, who, with Myvi, Nick and Bacon, was with the Guardians, watching battle commence. Max was fascinated.

"It's my first battle," he said, watching as the Ellylldan flew counter attack after counter attack.

"No, it's not," said Myvi. "We have been in battle before."

Max and Myvi locked eyes, and then Max nodded, as he remembered the last time, when they almost didn't make it.

"Yes," said Max, remembering again. "But last time there were no Battle Faeries."

"And last time you were ten," said Myvi. "This time, you are the Gwaredwr, and we shall win."

Max gave Myvi an unconvincing smile, before going back to watching the attack being coordinated by the Guardians.

"What now, Rex?" said Max, excitement and anxiety welling up in equal measures. His part in the recapture of the castle would soon begin. "I mean, my Lord Blaiddud."

"You may call me Rex, Max," said Blaiddud. "Now, it is the turn of the Gwyllon." Blaiddud made a great roar, and, as the Giants continued to hurl rocks, uprooted trees and anything else they could find to keep the defenders away from the parapets, Percy held up his arm and then dropped it, and the Gwyllon launched their attack, racing and screaming out from the trees and up the slopes to the base of the castle. The walls seemed almost glassy smooth, but they were no defence against the Gwyllon, who swarmed up them like an army of spiders, before engaging the Demons on the parapet in fierce hand to hand battle. The Demons were larger, and more ferocious, but the Gwyllon had the strength of numbers, and knew no fear, and, though many fell, some hurled back over the ramparts, the Gwyllon were soon pushing the Demon defenders back from the parapets and down into the main body of the castle.

Now Blaiddud roared at Sarah, and the Ellylldan flew out once more in a cloud of flame, heading straight for the main gates, which were quickly alight. Owen's Giants now finished the job, hurling rock after rock at the burning gates until finally they exploded in a cloud of flaming splinters.

"Now their defence will begin in earnest," said Blaiddud.

"What do you think they will do?" said Max.

"I *know* what they will do – they will send out the Gythreuliaid."

"Who are the Gythreuliaid?" said Max, knowing the answer wouldn't be good. But then the Gwyllon came running out of the remains of the castle gates, as the most awful sound Max had ever heard split the air, a cross between the roar of a dozen lions and the squealing of a hundred angry pigs, but at a pitch that made fingernails down a blackboard sound almost pleasant.

"*Those* are the Gythreuliaid," said Blaiddud.

For now, from the shattered gates, came thousands of Demons the likes of which few there had ever seen, least of all Max. Some were short and fat with long spindly arms, others tall, with huge nobbly bodies; some breathed fire, while others threw it; some had many heads, others had many arms, while others crawled along the ground on all fours. But they all had two things in common – they were all terrifying, and they were all headed right towards them.

"Good," said Blaiddud, watching as the Gythreuliaid stomped ever closer.

"Good?!" said Max. "What's good about it?!"

"They have been drawn out of the castle," said Blaiddud, "allowing *you* to go into it." Blaiddud turned to Max and the others now. "Your part now begins, Max."

Max stared at the oncoming Demons and gulped.

"Do not worry," said Blaiddud. "They will not notice you – they will be far too busy defending themselves."

"Against what?!" said Max.

"Against this," said Blaiddud, rearing up on his hind legs and giving a great roar, at which the entire relief force streamed out of the woods towards the Gythreuliaid - Faeries, Giants, Saxon Warriors and all of the Cwn Annwn save Blaiddud, and at the head, Max's parents and grandfather, the whole host yelling out war cries so loud they drowned out even the Demons' unearthly screaming.

"Mum!" cried Max as he watched his mother charge into the thick of the Demons, a sword in each hand.

"Do not worry about your mother," said Blaiddud. "From what I see, it is the Gythreuliaid that should be worried. Show me your sword, Max..."

"My sword – why...?" said Max, pulling it out of its scabbard. Blaiddud now lowered his head, and gently breathed on the sword. As he did so, it went from its steely grey colour to a glowing silver.

"What have you done to it?" said Max, staring at the new beauty of his sword.

"It is now a Faerie sword," said Blaiddud. "It will light your way in darkness, and will cut through even the hardest of metals."

"Can *we* have one?" said Myvi, pulling out her own sword.

Blaiddud smiled, and nodded. "Of course," he said, transforming her sword, before doing the same to Nick's and Bacon's.

"And now you must go, to free the true Lord of Annwn," said Blaiddud. "Good luck, all of you. I know you will win the day."

Blaiddud now bowed to the four of them, which they returned, before giving a tremendous roar and racing out to join the battle.

"Right then," said Myvi. "Ready Max?"

"Not really," said Max, taking a deep breath. "Alright – let's go."

The battle raged hard below the castle slopes, with agonising death screams coming from all around, but all in all the Gythreuliaid were being held back. As they ran through the sea of unearthly warriors, ducking under sword after sword, dodging axe after axe, Max caught a glimpse of his mother, a grin on her now profusely sweating face as she slashed the heads off two Demons in one go. She saw Max as he ran past.

"Good luck love!" she shouted, waving. "Oh no you don't!"

she growled, whirling round and running through a two headed Demon charging straight for her back.

"Still weird," said Max, leaping aside as a smallish four armed Demon slashed at him, only for it to be felled by a Tylwyth Teg arrow.

"I know," said Myvi as three Saxon warriors took out a boar-headed Demon heading murderously towards her. The devastated gate was now only thirty or so yards ahead of them. "Come on," said Myvi. "We're nearly there!"

But as they raced past the battle into open space, the gate now just before them, the biggest Demon they'd ever seen stepped out into the gateway, its arms folded, huge battle axes hanging from both sides of its waist. Its head was massive, easily as wide as its shoulders. It opened its mouth in a savage grin, unfolding its bulging arms and taking up its gruesome-looking axes, as smoke wafted from between its jagged teeth. Max and the others screeched to a halt just yards away from it.

"It's a fire-breather!" yelled Bacon. "Duck!"

As they threw themselves to the ground, the Demon spat out a blast of fire that singed the air inches above their heads.

"Split up!" shouted Myvi. "It can't get all of us at once!"

"No, but it can get us one at a time!" Max shouted back as the gigantic Demon started to move closer. "What are we going to do?!"

But this question was answered for them, for just as the Demon was about to send another blast of fire their way, its head was taken clean off its shoulders by a huge flying boulder, and its massive body slumped to the ground.

Max and the others looked around, to see Fymbldwn smiling and giving the thumbs up. Despite the deadly circumstances, they all started laughing.

"Come on," said Max, getting up, and all four now ran for the gateway.

Inside, all was strangely quiet, the huge thick white walls

deadening to a certain extent the sound of battle outside.

"So, which way?" said Max to Bacon, who pointed to the head of a stone staircase going down into the depths of the castle.

"That way," said Bacon, heading for the staircase.

As they descended the long, winding stairs, two figures emerged from the shadows of the towering entrance hall they had just left.

"So, he is here," said Vellucci.

"Of course," said Borgia. "Everything is going nicely to plan."

And with that, they silently followed Max and the others down the stairs, accompanied by the Usurper Borgia's two faithful guard Demons.

*

CHAPTER THIRTY

"He's been under for hours," said Major Willoughby, looking at Nick's readouts on the control room monitor. "It's not safe - we must get him out!"

"We can't," said Gareth. "If we take him out, we lose the connection, and we lose contact with the boy. He'll be OK."

"Are you sure?" said Willoughby, rechecking the medication levels. They were on the limit.

"He has to be, Major," said Gareth. "He *has* to be."

*

Bacon held his hand up as they reached a corner, and Max and the others stopped. Bacon peered round, then signalled that the coast was clear.

As they crept down the dark, dank stone passage, their way lit only by the glow from their Faerie swords, they tried to step softly so as to make as little noise as possible. But Max was starting to feel something was very wrong.

"There should be guards or something, shouldn't there?" he whispered to Bacon.

"They must all be engaged in the battle," Bacon whispered back.

"I suppose so – it's just that... it just seems too *easy...*"

"So far Max," said Bacon, halting them again at another corner. "So far."

But as they rounded this corner, their way was barred by an iron gate. On the other side were steps, going steeply down, the way darker even than the depths they'd already been through.

"The deep dungeons lie down those steps," said Bacon. "We are nearly there."

"Just the matter of a solid iron gate to get through," said Nick.

"I could Travel us through it...?" said Max.

"No," said Myvi. "Remember what King Locrin said – the Usurper would sense us immediately."

Everyone stared at the gate in thought. But then Max looked at his sword and remembered what Blaiddud had said.

"We could cut it – Rex said these would cut through even the hardest metal!"

Max raised his sword above his head, preparing to strike at the gate, but Bacon grabbed his arm before he could.

"No Max! It will make too much noise!"

Max lowered his sword, resting it on the gate's lock, and sighed. "So what then...? Huh?!"

The gate had moved under the pressure from Max's sword. Bacon gave the gate a little push, and it swung open.

"It was open all along!" said Max. "I told you, this is too easy. Someone *wants* us to be down here!"

"Be on your highest guard," said Bacon as he started off carefully down the steps.

At the bottom of the steps was another gate, but this was open as well. Becoming increasingly nervous, they crept through the gate, to find themselves in another short passage.

"Sheath your swords," whispered Bacon.

"But we won't be able to see," said Max.

"Trust me," said Bacon, putting his sword away. The others followed suit, and now realised that at the end of the passage there was an opening, and beyond it, there was light.

"It is the final passage," Bacon whispered, as they crept along, step by step. "At the end of this is the great dungeon hall."

"How do you know?" said Max, still not entirely trustful of Bacon.

"Because I have been imprisoned there," said Bacon.

"And how did you get out?"

"I Travelled, of course."

"*You* can Travel in Annwn too?" said Max, feeling a little

less special.

"Of course," said Bacon. "I have the Majyga."

"Ah, right," said Max, secretly happier now.

As they reached the end of the passage, Bacon halted them again. "Now, all we have to do is identify which of the dozen cells holds the Lord Gwynn ap Llud."

Max peered cautiously into the dungeon hall and quickly pulled back into the passage.

"That's easy," said Max.

"Why?" said Bacon.

"It's the one with the Demon outside it," said Max. "*Big* Demon."

"We have to get it out of there," said Myvi. "Distract it somehow."

Myvi picked up a stone and threw it into the dungeon hall. Nothing happened for a moment, but then a fireball hit the stone where it fell.

"OK, maybe not," said Myvi. "Any ideas?"

"There are never any Giants around when you need them," said Nick.

"It has to be me," said Max.

"No Max – you'll fry!" said Myvi.

"I have a few tricks, remember?" said Max, and leapt out into the dungeon hall.

"Hey, Demon! Over here!" Max yelled as he leapt, and a fireball exploded where he wasn't standing any more.

"Missed me!" laughed Max, Travelling out of the way of another ball of flame from the Demon's fiery hand. It was indeed a big Demon, easily nine feet tall, like a bull standing on its back legs, and a horned head to match, fire constantly flickering around its hands.

Fireballs flew all around now as Max dodged around the hall just in time.

"It's getting angry," said Bacon as they listened and watched from the relative safety of the passageway.

"Really? You think?" said Myvi.

"We should be helping," said Nick.

Myvi peered out into the hall then ducked back in again as a fireball hurtled towards her.

"No, Max has got it covered – *duck!*"

They threw themselves to the floor as the fireball flew up the passage and exploded against the iron gate, ripping it from its hinges.

The Demon now looked wildly around the hall, but it couldn't see Max anywhere.

"You singed my *duffle coat!*" Max growled from behind the Demon.

The Demon whipped round but had no time to react, as Max drove his glowing sword up through its jaw and into its skull.

The others clamped their hands over their ears as an horrific piercing scream almost burned the air, as the Demon thrashed about, the sword still in its head, and Max still holding it, but then Max and his sword were thrown across the hall and into the dripping stone wall.

It took a step towards Max, and then another, and raised its arm, aiming right at him, but then exploded in a ball of flame that filled the hall. Max curled up tight as the fire licked around him, before it was sucked back to the centre of the explosion as if the film had gone into reverse and disappeared with another explosion, that while flame-less, still knocked everyone off their feet with its force.

A large set of keys fell clanking to the floor out of nowhere, and then it was over.

"What was that you said about it being too easy?" said Myvi as she and the others emerged into the fire-scarred dungeon hall. "You're alight," she said, patting at the back of Max's duffle coat to put out a small flame.

Eventually they found the right key, and opened the heavy wood and iron door to the cell, to find a man chained to the

rear wall, his expression motionless.

"My Lord Gwynn ap Llud, I presume," said Bacon. But the man didn't move, or even acknowledge them with a look.

"I know that look," said Max. "Rex said he was constrained by something dark of the Usurper's making. He has a Garcharwyr in his head!"

"It is a trap!" said the Lord Gwynn, before screaming and convulsing in pain.

"We figured that," said Myvi. "Don't worry, we'll get you out of here."

Max moved cautiously towards the Lord Gwynn, and saw the Garcharwyr's eyes in his. But he knew exactly what to do this time.

"Listen to me, Garcharwyr," said Max in as deadly a voice as he could manage. "You know who I am - I am the Gwaredwr."

The Lord Gwynn's head flickered as its captor shifted its grip on his mind.

"You possess the Lord Gwynn ap Llud, Garcharwyr, but I know that you now sense a bigger prize. Your master would be *very* grateful if you possessed *my* mind. So, what are you waiting for?"

Suddenly the Lord Gwynn convulsed again as, in a split second, the Garcharwyr leapt from inside his head and flew straight for Max. But it wasn't quick enough, as Max's Faerie blade cut it in two in mid-air.

"There are more!" said the Lord Gwynn weakly, clutching his head. "I told you it was a trap!"

And then a flood of Garcharwyrod flew screaming out of the dungeon walls, but they instantly met the same fate as their fellow Demon at the hands of Max and the others.

But still they came, and still they died, until there were no more, and the dungeon floor was littered with Demon bodies.

"That was very impressive."

They all spun round at the voice, and saw Borgia and Vellucci standing at the door, jagged black swords in hand, and a whole troop of slavering Demons at their back. And around Borgia's neck, was a wooden cross – the cross of power of Caer Sidi, the key to the gateway to the First World.

"So, you are free my Lord," said Borgia. "Well, enjoy it while it lasts, which will not be long. You have at least been useful in luring the boy to me."

But now the door slammed behind them, shutting Vellucci and the Demons out.

"Your Demons can't help you now, Usurper," said Max, now behind Borgia at the door, but almost quicker than Max had Travelled, Borgia now appeared behind Myvi with a dagger at her throat.

"I do not need their help," said Borgia. "Now lay down your sword, boy – I know this girl means something to you. If you value her life, you will give me yours."

But Borgia's dagger suddenly disappeared, to reappear in Max's hand.

"Get down Myvi!"

As Myvi bit Borgia's hand, forcing him to release her, Max threw the dagger at him, but Borgia ducked at the last second, and it caught him in the arm.

"You will pay for that, boy," said the Usurper, wincing as he pulled out the dagger and launched himself at Max, giving him no time to react other than to draw his sword and parry Borgia's furious attack.

"Pah! Call that a sword?" said Borgia, hacking at Max as his much smaller weapon just managed to deflect the blow.

"No, I call *this* a sword," said Max, bringing what had been Borgia's sword down upon its former owner. Borgia dived and rolled at the last second as the evil blade crashed into the dungeon floor. But now Borgia simply lunged at Max, grabbing him from behind and pinning his arms to his side.

"I *will* possess you, boy," snarled Borgia, as his spirit began

to waft out of his body and towards Max's mouth, now open in horror.

"NOOOO!" yelled Max, and with a strength no-one knew he possessed, least of all him, threw Borgia off him, his spirit still leaking from his body.

"You will do no such thing – now stay STILL!!" said Max pointing at Borgia, in a voice so deep and resonating he didn't recognise it as his, even though he knew it must be. At this, Borgia and his spirit, still trying to find its new home, both froze to the spot, before a sword ran through him from behind. Bacon's sword.

"Many thanks, Max," said Bacon, ripping the cross from Borgia's neck and hanging it around his own. "I could not have done it without you."

As he spoke, Bacon began to change, to age, his beard growing, his hair greying, until he was no longer the young Bacon, but Bacon the elder.

As Max and the others stood transfixed, Bacon smiled, and casually unlocked the dungeon door again, revealing the dozen drooling and snarling Demons outside. On seeing his dead master lying on the floor, Vellucci fled, almost in relief.

"The power of Caer Sidi is mine now," said Bacon. "And soon the others will fall to me too."

"Bacon, you promised...!" yelled Myvi, launching herself sword-first at the now older Alchemist. But the tail of one of the Demons at the door whipped out and grabbed her in mid charge, lifting her off the ground and towards his waiting claws.

As one, Nick and Max leapt for Myvi and grabbed a hand each, before all three cried out simultaneously.

"Major, get us out of here!" yelled Nick.

"Max, get us out of here!" yelled Myvi.

"Rex, get us out of here!" yelled Max.

*

The preparations for the Battle of Badon Hill Recreation were going very well, and Sir John was very pleased. The local Territorial Army regiment, as well as schoolchildren from a wide area, were all now dressed either as Britons or Saxons, with very authentic tunics and armour, and even proper metal swords the kids had forged themselves as part of their DT coursework. Both 'armies' were resting on either side of the first of the three fields in front of rows of tents, which housed their 'battle support' - blacksmiths, medical teams, and of course refreshments - all waiting for the signal for battle to begin, and all as wonderfully authentic as only Sir John could organise.

The Brigadier was a little surprised when Max, Myvi and Nick appeared out of nowhere, but he recovered – it wasn't the first time he'd seen this happen.

"Ah, there you are," said Sir John. "Wondered what had happened to you lot."

Max, Myvi and Nick looked around, a little disorientated at first.

"Battle Recreation..." said Sir John, in response to their quizzical looks.

"Ah, right," said Max, and then all three began to laugh. They were safe. But then they stopped laughing, as both armies, Britons and Saxons alike, started screaming. Max wheeled round, to see two entirely different armies had also arrived on Ham Hill – armies of thousands of real Saxons, Faeries, Giants and Demons.

*

CHAPTER THIRTY ONE

The Demons were as confused as anyone initially, and in the middle of the field, for a moment, no-one and nothing moved. But then they did.

"What happened?!" said Max, staring at the scene.

"I'm guessing the power with which we were Travelled here cracked things open and brought that lot here too," said Nick.

"Get the kids out of here!" Myvi yelled at the Brigadier, but they needed no encouragement, for several hundred teenage warriors were now running screaming out of the field and towards the safety of the coaches that had brought them there.

But still, no-one knew what to do – Demons, Faeries, Giants and Saxons alike had in an instant been transported from the slopes of Caer Sidi to an unknown hill, by unknown forces, and, though they had been in battle but moments earlier, still they held off from fighting each other on this strange ground.

But then Harald and his Saxons took the initiative.

"Charge!!"

Now the Demons were on familiar territory, and soon the middle of the field was full of flashing swords, and flame, and screaming, and blood.

"What do we do, Sir?!" said Captain Norton, the commanding officer of the Territorials, as his men, dressed as fifth century Saxon warriors, watched as the otherworldly battle raged a hundred yards from the tents where they had regrouped.

"We engage, Captain!" said Sir John, himself done out in the uniform of an ancient British warrior chief.

"But... there are... Demons... and... things...?"

"Nothing a good bit of hard steel can't dispatch Captain!" said Sir John, watching the proceedings with ever-increasing excitement. It had been a good while since he had had a decent Demon scrap. "Form the men up Captain – we're going in!"

"Er, yes Sir," said the T.A. Captain, entirely unconvinced. "But shouldn't we call for reinforcements – you know, the police, or the army or something...?"

"By all means Captain," said Sir John, peering at the battle scene through a pair of very un-fifth century binoculars. "But be quick about it – we have Demons to slay!"

"And what do *we* do?" said Max. "We should be helping, shouldn't we? I mean, apart from anything else, my parents are out there."

Sir John refocused his binoculars on Owen and Sarah, who were in the thick of the fighting, back to back, dispatching Demon after Demon and loving every moment.

"You don't have to worry about your parents," said Sir John with a hint of a grin, which now faded as quickly as it had arrived. "But you do have to worry about *him*."

Sir John was pointing towards a figure who had just materialised behind the battle. Max didn't need binoculars to know it was Bacon, and the Brigadier didn't need to be told that he had deceived them – it was obvious from his Demon guards, and from the cross that hung from his neck.

"Your mission is simple now, Max," said Nick. "Get to Bacon, take The Cross, The Book and the Majyga from him. If you don't, the whole of the Demon horde of Annwn will flood into this world, which will then be under Bacon's control. Just like before."

Just like before. Max stared at the scene ahead of him as if for the first time, and suddenly his head was full of pain.

Just like before. Last time it was Romans and Demons, but Bacon was in the middle then and now, directing the fiery assault on the world of men. This was where it had all begun. The therapy, the pills, and the fear.

"Come on Max, let's go get him!" said Myvi, drawing her sword.

"Max...?"

Max was in a huddle now, crouched on the ground, his

head between his hands.

"Max, come *on!*"

But Max wasn't moving, instead gently rocking back and forth, and moaning. Everything had come crashing down on him at once, the memories, the insecurities, and the terror, everything he had rebuilt over these last days vanishing into a fog of helplessness.

"It's all my fault." He kept repeating it.

Myvi tried pulling him to his feet, but he wasn't budging.

"Max, come on," she said, trying again, "or Bacon will win this time!"

But still, Max just rocked back and forth, moaning his defeated mantra. "It's all my fault."

But now Myvi finally understood, and crouched down alongside Max, putting her arms around him.

"Max, it's alright. You've been through a lot, I know, but you can't stop now. Look at what you've done – you restored Time. You killed the Usurper Emperor – twice!"

However, no matter what Myvi did, Max still wasn't responding. But he just *had* to.

"Max, you're not the frightened kid anymore," she said, pulling him tight to her. "You *are* the Gwaredwr – you've proved it over and over, to everyone. And to me."

Now, finally, Max stopped rocking, and, slowly, looked up at Myvi with a look that sent a tear rolling down her cheek. For a moment they just looked at each other, not speaking, just looking, both remembering the same shared memories as they played themselves out at the same time.

"You can do it, Max," said Myvi, just not knowing what else she could do. "Come on, one more push, yeah?"

Max dropped his head, and said, quietly, "but I'm just a kid Myvi."

Myvi threw back her head and uttered a sigh that would have brought the angels down.

"No, you're not Max – you are the Gwaredwr." But this

wasn't Myvi. This was a much deeper voice.

Max looked up again, to see that he was now in the middle of a circle of Giant hounds, their heads bowed towards him, and in their middle, the Lord Gwynn ap Llud, now in gleaming battle armour.

"Our forces are holding Max," said the Lord Gwynn, "but they await a leader."

Max sighed. Not again. He was too tired for this. "But *you* are their leader – *you* are the Lord of Annwn."

"No, Max," said the Lord Gwynn, taking Max's hand and trying to help him to stand. But Max wasn't ready to stand, not yet. "Annwn is lost, unless we win this battle, and defeat the new Usurper. We need you, Max – we need your powers."

Max shook his head in an attempt to get some kind of reality back into it. He just didn't care about the cause of Annwn anymore. He just wanted to sleep. But now he noticed Myvi looking very worried as she stared out over the battle.

"What is it Myvi?" said Max, trying to see where she was looking, but all he could see was the dead and the mythical locked in a combat that would never end.

"It's Percy, Max," said Myvi, a choke in her throat. "Your grandfather."

"What's wrong?" said Max, already knowing the answer. And as he looked out on the battle, the answer was confirmed. His grandfather was in the midst of it all, fighting furiously, one on one, with Bacon. Just like before.

"No," said Max, finally standing. "No!" More firmly this time. "I have seen him die too many times at the hands of that man. It *will* not happen again."

"Erm, Brigadier, Sir..."

Sir John in turn dragged himself back into some sort of reality and looked around at Captain Norton, who had returned.

"What is it, Captain?" said Sir John, slightly annoyed that the momentum had been halted by a part-time soldier whose

life mostly revolved around wholesale electrical supplies.

"The, erm, police aren't, erm, coming," said the Captain. "Nor the army."

Sir John knew the answer but asked the question anyway. "Why not?"

"Well, Sir..." said Captain Norton, as if he was trying to believe their take on the situation but knowing he couldn't. "I told them what was happening, and..."

"And they didn't believe you...?" said Sir John impatiently.

"No Sir," said the Captain.

"Hardly surprising," said Sir John. "They probably heard 'Prince of Wales Inn' and came to the wrong conclusions. Well, looks like it's just us and them then. Are your men ready?"

The Captain looked very alarmed, and shifted on his feet like a schoolboy selected for the school team of a game he'd never played.

"What, to fight those... Demons... Sir?"

"Yes, Captain."

The poor man was obviously trying to think of any reason why not, and then finally settled on one that made sense.

"But we're not trained in swords, Sir..."

"Captain," said Sir John, in a manner that made Captain Norton realise that not only was the world that was now confronting him real, but it was one that he had to deal with. "You are either with us, or you're all dead, and the world is at an end. Understand?"

"Yes *Sir!*" said the Captain, with a gulp, but with the best salute he'd ever done.

"Right!" said Max, drawing his sword. "Let's do it!"

"Alright!" said Myvi, drawing her own.

The Lord Gwynn came a little closer to Max, and bowed. "The Cwn Annwn are at your disposal."

"OK then," said Max with a slight shrug. "Erm, cover me...?"

Myvi grinned, and thrust her sword towards the enemy.

"Let's GO!!"

Max ran as fast as he could towards the battle, all around him the Cwn Annwn, the Guardians of the Hills and of Time, ripping into any Demon that dared even to think of attacking Max, while the Territorials brought up the rear, nervously at first, but growing in confidence after their first kills, until they were side by side with the Faeries and the real Saxons, hacking off Demonic limbs and heads, left, right and centre.

But Max wasn't giving any of this any attention – he had but one goal, to get through the Demon ranks and get to his grandfather, and with Rex to his left and the Lord Gwynn to his right, and with Myvi and the rest of the Guardians covering his rear, Max burst through the circle of Demon guards that protected the very personal fight that was going on between Percy and Bacon.

As Myvi and the Cwn Annwn ploughed into Bacon's personal Demons, and as the Plant Annwn formed a new defensive ring, Max threw himself in between Bacon and his bruised, scarred and exhausted grandfather.

"Max, no!" said Percy, but he knew he hadn't the energy to resist. He had kept Bacon at bay, but rescue had come with only minutes to spare before even Percy's Travelling skills were overcome by Bacon's newly enhanced powers.

"Ah, Max," said Bacon, without seeming the slightest bit fatigued by what had obviously been a hard fought battle with Percy. "At last, the main event. Shall we...?"

At this   a dozen daggers flew towards Max from nowhere, and thudded into a conjured wooden shield now on Max's arm, before Max dropped a hay cart out of the air on top of Bacon, who Travelled out of its way at the last second.

"Very good," said Bacon, just managing to conceal his shock.

"Max, leave it!" yelled Myvi. "We can take him!"

But Max held up his hand.

"No Myvi, *I* have to do it - for *me*."

272

Max was suddenly surrounded by fire as Bacon brought a flaming pyre underneath the teenage Traveller's feet. Max leapt off and rolled over and over to put out the flames that had caught his coat, in doing so bowling Bacon off his feet and leaping on top of him, dagger pointed right at Bacon's head. Bacon shifted a few feet to the right, but to his alarm Max was still on top of him, and now everywhere Bacon tried to Travel, Max was there with him, second guessing his every move, until their respective powers were nullified, only physical power now remaining.

"I am older and stronger than you Max," said Bacon as he grasped Max's wrist, trying to stop the dagger from reaching its target, but realising to his horror that it was still getting nearer. At the last moment Bacon stopped struggling and allowed the dagger through, rolling his head so that the dagger plunged into the ground instead. In the split second that Max pulled the dagger out, Bacon was above him, bringing a huge axe down and sending Max's head rolling across the ground, blood spilling from his neck into an ever-growing stain on the ground.

"Well, I must be going," said Bacon, reaching The Coin up to The Brooch.

"NO!!" yelled Myvi, leaping towards Bacon, but before she could get to him, a sword was thrust through him from behind, and he fell to the ground, vanishing in a cloud of whirling smoke.

"Good luck in oblivion Bacon," said Max, now revealed as the smoke of Bacon's departed spirit cleared.

"Max...?" said Myvi, a choke in her throat, staring unbelieving at him.

"Oh, love...!" said Sarah, doing the same.

"But..." said Blaiddud, equally confused.

"It was a projection," said Max, sagging from the effort. "Wasn't sure if I could do it without Bacon realising, but I suppose it worked out."

"It would have been useful to know, Max," said Myvi, trying to hide her tears by looking cross.

But now neither could keep a straight face, and both began
to laugh and cry at the same time, before Myvi gave Max a
huge hug, and this time, not only did he not resist, he actually
hugged her back.

Percy picked up the fallen Majyga and put them in his
pocket.

"What are we going to do with them, Grandpa?" asked
Max.

"Put them somewhere very, *very* safe, my lad," said Percy.

"And The Cross?"

"That is for me to deal with, Max," said Joseph, bending
down and picking it up. As he did so, it glowed in his hands,
and the glow began to spread from him, embracing the whole
of Ham Hill. Now everything began to swirl, and buckle, and
blur, as the remaining inhabitants of Annwn, dead and alive,
were picked up into the air like dust, now hurtling around in
a giant vortex until individuals were no longer identifiable,
only an otherworldly cloud that whirled high in the sky before plummeting to Earth, and disappearing into it.

"The Gate of Caer Sidi is closed," said King Locrin solemn-
ly, as the Travellers of Hamdun and the Guardians of the
Hills all now bowed their heads towards Max.

"You did it, Max," said Myvi, kissing him lightly on the
cheek.

Max just blushed.

*

Outside the Inn, in the crisp sunny January day, hundreds
of schoolchildren and part time soldiers dressed as Saxons
and Britons drank their drinks and chatted excitedly about
the events of the day and their parts in it. But inside, the
Travellers were largely silent. Joseph stood at the bar with the

Brigadier, while Percy stood behind it, and Sarah and Owen distributed endless rounds of sandwiches. Nick had disappeared the moment Joseph clutched the Cross, whipped back to the safety of the TRD, while the Guardians had left for their respective hills.

Max and Myvi, meanwhile, sat the other side of the bar, by the other fireplace, neither having said a word for a good while, just trying to take it all in. But then Max found the question he was looking for.

"So, when are you going back?"

Myvi looked at Max curiously.

"How do you mean, back?"

"You know, back home – to your proper home, in the first century." Now Max looked at Myvi very intently.

Myvi sighed for her friend, and then smiled right into his eyes. "This *is* my home, Max – I couldn't go back there now."

But Max returned her intense look. "So you weren't just with us, with me, until we made it safe to return?" This was his main worry. "It wasn't all a lie...?" His look said that he really couldn't stand it if it had been, and Myvi knew it.

"You really thought that, Max? After what we've been through?!"

"It was a possibility..."

"No Max, it wasn't," said Myvi softly. "It was all real."

And now they just looked at each other again, deeply, and silence returned between them. Owen finally broke the tension.

"Well, one Cross down, eight to go!"

Max smiled wearily, and nodded.

"Yes Dad. All we have to do is work out where and when they are. Easy, eh Grandpa...?"

Percy smiled.

"We'll get there Max, don't worry. We're not safe yet – but we *are* a little safer than we were."

"Jolly good, more adventures!" said Sarah as she came back

into the bar from the kitchen.

Max smiled at his mother. "Yes Mum, more adventures."

Myvi squeezed Max's arm.

"This isn't going away, Max - *really.*"

Max looked around the bar at this strange new life that he seemed to have, then looked back at Myvi, and smiled, and nodded.

"Yes, I know. But there's still one more thing we need to do."

"What's that, love?" said his mother.

"Presents, of course!"

Everyone was exhausted, mentally and physically, but it didn't mean they couldn't laugh.

*

In a narrow, anonymous Westminster side street, a door flickered slightly before opening. Two men stepped out and breathed in the air deeply.

"Good to be back, Major."

"Yes, Sergeant, it is. Not for long though, I suspect..."

Unseen by the two TRD men, at a second floor window in the building opposite, a curtain opened a little, and a man looked out on the scene below.

"So, the boy *is* The One then," he said to someone out of view behind him.

"It would seem so, yes."

"Hmm. Well, good. We must take a little more interest in him now, I feel..."

"Yes, we must."

*

ACKNOWLEDGMENTS

My parents, of course, Iain and Angela Swinnerton, for their constant love and support.

My sister Jo, for her always expert advice and support.

Mike and Nicki, landlords of the Prince of Wales Inn, Ham Hill, for their hospitality, and of course their beer. The view from their pub garden would inspire any writer!

Michael Zair, founder of Tinkers Bubble, for his inspiration and knowledge.

Serena Mackesy and Alex Marwood, for their never-stinting help and support.

Dave Loxton, for listening to me moan and buying me beer.

Tom and Lynn Dunbar, for the same reasons.

In no particular order, for their love and encouragement, Kirsty Swinnerton, Tim Bell, Jill Brett, my cousin Suzi Sadecki (yes, you can finally read it now!), Tom Ashton, Nick Martinelli, Mike Fallows, and of course Chris Panzner, without whom I'd be a lot less sane. Or is that more sane...?

And finally, Elisha Neubauer, my wonderful publisher. Let's hope this takes us both a long way.

ABOUT ALASTAIR SWINNERTON

Alastair has been writing for children's television for over twenty five years. Among his many credits are 'The Wombles', 'Sabrina, Secrets of a Teenage Witch', and the Bafta-nominated CBBC Christmas Special 'The Tale of Jack Frost', which he wrote, co-produced and co-directed. He was also one the co-creators of Lego® Bionicle®. 'The Multiverse of Max Tovey' is his first Young Adult novel.

Alastair lives in Somerset with his family, and spends much of his spare time walking the dog, more often than not at his beloved Ham Hill.

CPSIA information can be obtained
at www.ICGtesting.com
Printed in the USA
BVHW080150240119
538478BV00010BA/176/P

9 781943 755127